NEVER
PLEAD
GUILTY

Cover Design by Linda Siegel
Cover Photograph by Jason Shaw

ISBN
978-1-952612-22-0 E-Book
978-1-952612-23-7 Paperback
978-1-952612-24-4 Hardcover

NEVER PLEAD GUILTY

A MIKE DALEY/ROSIE FERNANDEZ THRILLER

SHELDON SIEGEL

Novels By Sheldon Siegel

In loving memory of our beloved cats who were wonderful company for many years.

Wilma (2004-2017)

Betty (2004-2024)

1

"I'VE HEARD A LOT ABOUT YOU"

The Honorable Jonathan Stern tapped the microphone in his stuffy courtroom on the second floor of San Francisco's crumbling Hall of Justice. "Good morning, Mr. Daley."

I responded in an upbeat tone. "Good morning, Your Honor. Congratulations on your appointment to the bench."

"Uh, thank you."

The dour rookie judge seemed surprised by my cheerful voice. *You will learn soon enough that not every moment in court involves hand-to-hand combat. Everybody who works here knows everybody else. It's better for everyone's mental health to remain civil until we need to start lobbing grenades.*

He hunched his narrow shoulders, squinted at me through his John Lennon spectacles, and spoke in a nasal rasp. "I've heard a lot about you."

Uh-oh. "Good things, I hope."

"Mostly. I didn't expect to see the head of the Felony Division of the Public Defender's Office at an arraignment on misdemeanor charges."

"Co-head," I corrected him gently. "My colleague assigned to this case is in trial this morning, so I'm pinch-hitting."

His thin lips turned down. "Suit yourself."

I will.

It was ten AM on Tuesday, October fifteenth, 2024. A week ago, Jon Stern was a partner in the Tax Department of Story, Short, and Thompson, a megafirm housed on the top five floors of the prestigious Four Embarcadero Center high-rise. The Marin County native was a graduate of the elite and very private Branson School in Ross, Yale, and Stanford Law. After a clerkship with a federal judge in New York, he returned to the Bay Area and spent fifteen years poring over the Internal Revenue Code to help conglomerates, tech startups, crypto companies, venture capitalists, and sovereign wealth funds of oil-rich countries engage in what is colloquially referred to as "sophisticated tax planning." For those of us who operate in the real world, it's more accurately described as "tax avoidance."

Time for one more quick suck-up. "I hope your transition is going smoothly."

"So far, so good."

"Excellent." *I love appearing before rookie judges.*

The freshly-minted jurist scanned his windowless new domain, which was a far cry from his cushy corner office with a view stretching from the Golden Gate to the Bay Bridge. When it opened in 1961, the Hall of Justice was considered state-of-the-art. It replaced its not-so-beloved 1900-era predecessor across the street from Portsmouth Square in Chinatown. Six decades later, our aging relic was condemned because of earthquake safety issues, asbestos-laden walls, faulty plumbing, and an overwhelmed electrical system. The courts and SFPD's Homicide Detail are still here, but the District Attorney, the Public Defender, the Southern Police Station, and the Medical Examiner have fled to buildings with functional bathrooms and working elevators. The chaotic old jail on the sixth and seventh floors was mothballed and replaced by a newer building next door. The old cafeteria in the basement where I cut countless plea-bargain deals over boiled hot dogs, overcooked hamburgers, and surprisingly tasty grilled cheese sandwiches is now used for storage.

Judge Stern glanced at the gallery, which was filled with ADAs, Deputy PDs, and a few private defense lawyers who were staring at their phones while waiting for a few moments of assembly-line justice. They were joined by our regular contingent of homeless people, law students, courtroom junkies, retirees, and other hangers-on who passed the time watching the wheels of justice grind ever-so-slowly in San

Francisco's crumbling bazaar of criminal law. A homeless guy known only by his first name, Mel, was sleeping soundly in his usual spot in the back row next to the chipped gray wall.

Judge Stern scrunched his narrow face. Although he had just turned forty, his pale complexion, pronounced widow's peak, and thick crow's feet reflected the fact that he had spent more time reading the Internal Revenue Code than hanging out on the patio next to the pool of his hilltop McMansion in Tiburon. "What's that smell?"

"Mildew," I said. "You get used to it." *Not really.*

He pointed at the water dripping from a rusted spot in the asbestos-laden ceiling tiles and into a bucket next to his bailiff. "How long has that been leaking?"

"About six months. They think it's coming from the old jail upstairs, but they can't tell for sure unless they rip out the walls."

"I see."

Still glad that you gave up a seven-figure draw to preside over misdemeanor cases in an airless courtroom in a condemned building? I bet your pals at the Pacific Union Club were impressed when you told them that you were becoming a judge.

"How is your father?" I asked.

"Fine, thank you."

"Good to hear. Please give him my regards."

"I will."

Actually, you probably won't. Two decades ago, I left the PD's Office after my then-supervisor and current boss, Rosita Fernandez, and I got divorced. Rosie is now the Public Defender. I spent five years as a junior partner at a big law firm at the top of the Bank of America Building until I was unceremoniously fired because I didn't bring in enough high-paying clients. Rosie rented me an office at the solo practice that she was running at the time, and we've been working together ever since—first at our two-person law firm and, for the last decade, back at the PD's Office. Judge Stern's father, Charles Stern, is another terminally morose tax attorney who was a partner at the firm where I used to work. He led the charge to get me fired. In a moment of whimsy and less-than-stellar judgment, I had dubbed him with the nickname of "Chuckles," which stuck. When I heard about Jonathan's appointment to the bench, I anointed him as "Baby Chuckles." You know that you've been around the block a few times when you're appearing before a judge whose father used to be your law partner.

Judge Stern turned to the prosecution table. "Good morning, Mr. Paolini."

The earnest young ADA sprang to his feet, tugged at the lapels of his baggy Men's Wearhouse suit, and invoked an ingratiating tone. "Good morning, Your Honor."

Ernie Paolini is a third-generation native of the City. His great-grandfather, Luigi, immigrated from Palermo and opened a deli in North Beach. Seven of Luigi's eight sons became police officers. The black sheep was a firefighter. The next generation included a judge, two ADAs, a union organizer, and a member of the Board of Supervisors. Ernie's parents moved to the foggy Sunset District, a few blocks from the house where I grew up, after my family moved from an apartment in the Mission. He graduated from St. Ignatius High School (also my alma mater), USF, and USF Law School. He's a nice young man who has been a baby ADA for about a year and a half. He's starting to get the hang of it.

Judge Stern nodded at his bailiff. "Please call our case."

"The People versus Sean Murphy, et al. Arraignment."

"Et al.?"

"There are twelve defendants, Your Honor. They're waiting in the holding tank down the hall."

A smart-aleck reporter at the *Chronicle* had dubbed them the "Dirty Dozen."

"Bring them inside," the judge said.

The bailiff motioned to a burly sheriff's deputy, who headed out the door and returned a moment later leading a motley procession of a dozen people clad in ill-fitting orange jumpsuits. They ranged in age from early twenties to mid-eighties. While they came in various shapes, sizes, and genders, the family resemblance was evident. Sean Murphy led the parade. He was a sixty-year-old retired Muni bus driver with an erect bearing, a confident manner, and anger management issues. His younger sister, Katie Murphy O'Brien, followed him. She worked at PGE and was also a hothead. Her husband, Tim O'Brien, a decorated firefighter prone to emotional outbursts, trailed Katie. Various children, grandchildren, nieces, nephews, and cousins tagged along behind them, expressions somber, eyes down. Bringing up the rear was eighty-five-year-old Jacob "Jake" Flynn, a combative retired cop whose pronounced limp required him to walk with a cane. Sean, Katie, Tim, and Jake joined me at the defense table. The rest of the Murphy clan lined up in front of the jury box. Per my instructions, they stood with their arms at their sides, eyes forward, mouths shut.

Judge Stern surveyed the conga line and spoke to Paolini. "Charge?"

"The defendants violated California Penal Code Section 415."

The judge's quizzical expression indicated that this wasn't in the Tax Code. "Which is?"

"Disturbing the peace."

That's my cue. "It was a misunderstanding, Your Honor. Mr. Paolini is blowing this matter out of proportion."

"It was a brawl," Paolini said. "It took a dozen police officers to stop what Mr. Daley has mischaracterized as a 'misunderstanding.'"

Baby Chuckles was intrigued. "Where did this alleged misunderstanding happen?"

"At a funeral."

"Seriously?"

"Seriously."

Seriously.

Judge Stern rested his chin in his hand. "What happened, Mr. Paolini?"

"The defendants attended the funeral of Ms. Fiona Flynn Murphy, who passed away last Friday at the age of eighty-seven. Ms. Murphy was the mother of defendant Sean Murphy and defendant Kate O'Brien. She was also the sister of defendant Jacob Flynn. The funeral took place at St. Peter's Catholic Church in the Mission where Ms. Murphy was baptized and where she married her late husband."

The judge exhaled heavily.

Paolini was still talking. "During the funeral mass, defendant Sean Murphy and defendant Kate O'Brien exchanged heated words about their respective inheritances. As the mourners were filing out of the church, Sean said something to his sister to which she objected. Defendant Timothy O'Brien interceded and shoved Mr. Murphy, who responded by hitting Mr. O'Brien. Other family members joined the melee, and things got out of hand. Defendant Jacob Flynn struck defendant Sean Murphy in the forehead with his walking stick which resulted in a bloody bruise."

I'll bet that Thanksgiving dinners at the Murphy house are a riot.

Jake spoke from his seat at the defense table. "They were being disrespectful to my sister."

Yes, they were.

The judge turned my way. "Mr. Daley, please instruct your client not to address the court unless I invite him to do so."

"Yes, Your Honor." I turned to Jake. "Please."

"Fine."

Paolini spoke up again. "The fight escalated on the steps of St. Peter's as the casket was being taken to the hearse. Defendant Timothy O'Brien shoved defendant Sean Murphy into the casket and almost knocked it over."

All true. "For the record," I said, "they did not knock it over, and the decedent's body remained inside."

The judge nodded. "Good to hear, Mr. Daley."

Paolini was on a roll. "A dozen current and retired police officers attended the service out of respect to their former colleague, defendant Jacob Flynn. They interceded and broke up the fight. Fortunately, other than a bloody bump on Sean Murphy's head and a few bruises, nobody was seriously injured."

"How fortunate," the judge said.

"All in all," Paolini continued, "it was a very sad and undignified way to end a beautiful memorial service for a beloved member of our community."

Amen.

The judge took off his glasses and pointed them at me. "Do your clients dispute any of what Mr. Paolini just described?"

Not really. "Emotions sometimes run high at funerals."

"True. You were once a priest, weren't you, Mr. Daley?"

"Yes, Your Honor. It was a long time ago."

I decided to become a priest after my older brother, Tommy, died in Vietnam. I always loved the spirituality of the Church. After three long years at St. Anne's in the Sunset, I concluded that I wasn't adept at saving souls, and I was terrible at Church politics. I turned in my collar and went to law school, much to the chagrin of my late father, a San Francisco cop who knew Jake Flynn. Pop was even more upset when I decided to become a Public Defender.

The judge eyed me. "Did you ever officiate at a funeral where emotions led to a brawl?"

"No, Your Honor."

"I didn't think so. How do your clients wish to plead?"

"I would appreciate it if you would give me a few minutes to provide a little context."

"This is an arraignment, Mr. Daley. The sole purpose is for your clients to enter their pleas. Guilty or not?"

"Just a moment of your time, Your Honor. Please?"

He made a big display of rolling his beady eyes. "I'll give you one minute."

"Thank you. I would like to call a witness who saw everything."

Paolini was on his feet. "You can't call a witness at an arraignment."

"Yes, you can," I said.

Judge Stern put his hand over his microphone, turned to the bailiff, and spoke in a whisper. "Can he call a witness at an arraignment?"

"If you let him."

The judge turned back to me. "Who do you wish to call, Mr. Daley?"

"Father Guillermo Lopez, the priest at St. Peter's Catholic Church."

The new judge took a moment to get his bearings. The question of whether I could call a priest as a witness at an arraignment in a case involving a brawl at a funeral probably wasn't addressed during his one-day judicial orientation program. It *definitely* wasn't covered in the Internal Revenue Code.

Paolini pivoted to his go-to move—whining. "Your Honor, this is highly irregular."

Yes, it is. "Your Honor has discretion to allow Father Lopez to testify. He is waiting in the hall, and he welcomes the opportunity to do so." *And if you don't let him, you're going straight to hell.*

Paolini tried again. "But, Your Honor—,"

The judge stopped him with an upraised hand. "I will hear Father Lopez's testimony."

So far, so good.

The deputy summoned Father Lopez from the corridor. The charismatic priest bore a striking resemblance to Pedro Pascal. He strode down the aisle, was sworn in, and took his place in the box.

He smiled at the judge. "Congratulations on your appointment, Your Honor."

"Thank you, Father Lopez."

I was standing at the lectern. "May I approach the witness, Your Honor?"

"You may."

I walked to the front of the courtroom and stopped a respectful distance from the box. "You are the priest at St. Peter's Catholic Church in the Mission?"

"Yes, Mr. Daley. For twelve years."

"You enjoy doing God's work?"

He adjusted his traditional collar. "Very much."

I've known Gil for years. Now pushing forty, he is one of the younger priests at the church where Rosie and I were baptized and later married. So were my parents. And our daughter. Gil had attended St. Peter's Elementary School, St. Ignatius High, and USF before heading to the seminary. Smart, savvy, charismatic, and intensely political, he is primed to lead the historic church deep into the twenty-first century.

I moved closer to the box. "You officiated at the funeral mass for Ms. Fiona Murphy?"

"I did. She was a member of our parish for her entire life. She was a lovely woman and a warm and generous soul."

"Was there a misunderstanding at the conclusion of the service?"

"Yes. There has been tension among Fiona's children for many years. Some of those feelings came out during and after the funeral. It was unfortunate."

I'll say. "I understand that they got into a fight on the front steps of St. Peter's."

"I would call it a conversation."

Just the way we rehearsed it. "Several other relatives joined the conversation?"

"They did. Unfortunately, when emotions run high, people sometimes say and do things that they regret."

Like shoving someone into his mother's casket. "How long did this misunderstanding last?"

"Just a few minutes. As you know, Jake Flynn is a retired police officer. Several of his former colleagues attended the funeral. They were able to de-escalate the situation, and cooler heads prevailed. Thankfully, nobody was seriously injured. They instructed each of the participants to come to Mission Police Station to sort things out. At my request, they let the family attend the burial at Holy Cross Cemetery and turn themselves in afterward."

I pointed at the Murphy family members sitting at the defense table and lined up in front of the jury box. "My clients conducted themselves appropriately at the cemetery?"

"They did."

"And they apologized to you and each other after the burial was concluded?"

"Yes."

"You found their apologies to be sincere?"

"I did."

"You forgave them?"

"Of course." Another tug at the collar. "The Bible encourages us to forgive those who acknowledge their mistakes, offer sincere apologies, and show contrition."

That's the way it worked when I was a priest. "Do you believe that any useful purpose would be served by proceeding with criminal charges against the defendants?"

"Objection," Paolini said. "Father Lopez isn't a lawyer. With respect, he is not qualified to opine on legal matters."

Give me a break. "I am not asking Father Lopez for a legal opinion. I'm asking him to comment about a moral issue."

"Overruled."

Gil sat up taller. "Secular law isn't my area of expertise, but I believe that I have some understanding of a higher law. Given the sincerity of your clients' apologies, I believe that no useful purpose would be served by bringing criminal charges."

"Thank you, Father Lopez. No further questions." I retreated to the defense table.

"Cross-exam, Mr. Paolini?"

Do you really want to cross-examine a priest, Ernie?

"No questions, Your Honor."

Good call. "Your Honor, in light of Father Lopez's testimony, we respectfully request that the charges be dismissed."

Paolini bounced to his feet. "This is a more serious situation than Mr. Daley has led you to believe. Substantial police resources were expended to stop a fight that almost turned into a riot."

Oh please. "Mr. Paolini is exaggerating."

"No, I'm not. We seriously considered bringing felony assault and battery charges against defendants Murphy, O'Brien, and Flynn. We are giving them a very lenient deal by charging them with misdemeanor disturbing the peace."

"That's ridiculous," I said. "This case isn't even a wobbler."

"A wobbler?" the judge asked.

It's your first day on the job. "A case that could be charged either as a felony or a misdemeanor in the DA's discretion."

"I see."

Paolini's tone became adamant. "We can't just let this go. It would be disrespectful to the police officers who broke up the brawl. And it would set a bad precedent."

Happens all the time.

The judge looked my way. "Mr. Paolini has a point. I am not inclined to simply dismiss the charges."

In a few weeks, you'll be dismissing the charges on cases like this in a hot minute. I turned to Sean Murphy. "Would you please tell the judge how you and your family feel about your behavior?"

Sean did his best to feign contrition. "We are very sorry, Your Honor. We behaved badly, and we are embarrassed. We apologize to the court, the police, and Father Lopez."

And now for a little old-fashioned Catholic guilt. "How do you think your mother would have felt about your behavior?"

"She would have been embarrassed, too."

Yes, she would have.

The judge spoke to me. "Do you have a suggestion as to how we might resolve this matter?"

I was hoping you would ask. "I do. Disturbing the peace can be charged as an infraction instead of a misdemeanor. There would be no jail time, and the maximum fine is two hundred and fifty dollars." *Here goes.* "Each of my clients will plead guilty to an infraction and pay a fine of fifty dollars. They will proceed to St. Peter's, where they will go to confession with Father Lopez and do whatever penance he requires. Finally, everybody will do ten hours of community service at St. Peter's. The social hall needs a new paint job. After everybody fulfills those conditions, the infractions will be expunged from their records." I invoked my best priest-voice. "There would be an acknowledgment of responsibility, an expression of contrition, and a concrete act to rectify their mistake through community service."

Judge Stern spoke to Gil. "Does that work for you, Father Lopez?"

"Yes, Your Honor."

He turned to Paolini. "What about you?"

"I suppose so."

"Good." The judge contorted his face into a pained expression suggesting that he was trying to smile. "We have a resolution." He turned my way. "You and Mr. Paolini will prepare the necessary paperwork?"

"Yes, Your Honor. Congratulations on resolving your first case." *Welcome to your first day on the bench, Baby Chuckles.*

"Thank you, Mr. Daley." His tone was less than convincing when he added, "I will look forward to seeing you again in my courtroom in the near future."

My suit jacket was drenched in perspiration as I walked down the sauna-like corridor of the PD's Office at eleven-ten that same morning. Twenty years ago, we moved into a repurposed auto repair shop on Seventh Street, a half block south of the Hall of Justice. At the time, it was a substantial upgrade from our ratty old digs where the heater worked sporadically, there was no air conditioning, the walls were covered in lead-based paint, and the plumbing operated on its own schedule. Two decades of deferred maintenance later, our "new" office is in better shape than Judge Stern's courtroom, but it needs a tune-up.

I inhaled the stale air and stopped at the workstation outside my office. "Good morning, Terrence."

My onetime client, longtime assistant, recovering alcoholic, and former small-time professional boxer and shoplifter,

Terrence "The Terminator" Love, looked up from his computer and spoke in a high-pitched voice that seemed out of place for a guy who was six-six and weighed three hundred pounds. "Good morning, Mike. I heard you got the 'Dirty Dozen' off with an infraction and community service. Nice work."

"Thanks, T."

Terrence had planned to retire at the end of last year, but I was able to persuade him to stick around and work two days a week and every other Friday.

"How's your granddaughter?" I asked.

He smiled broadly, flashing his signature gold front tooth. "She's starting to walk."

"That's great. She'll be running soon."

"I won't be able to keep up with her."

"You're still pretty light on your feet. Anything I need to know?"

He pointed at the open door to the office next to mine where the nameplate read, "Rosita Fernandez, Public Defender." "The boss needs to see you right away."

I headed into Rosie's workmanlike office, where I found her sitting behind the oak desk that she had bought on her own dime. Thirty years after we met and twenty-six years after we got divorced, she's still the most beautiful woman on Planet Earth. I took a seat in the chair on the opposite side of her desk.

She flashed a radiant smile. "I trust that the members of the Murphy family expressed their gratitude?"

"Everybody except Uncle Jake. He's still pissed off."

"He'll calm down. What was it like appearing before Baby Chuckles?"

"He's as sour as his father."

"The lemon didn't fall far from the tree." Her expression turned serious. "How's your time?"

As co-head of the Felony Division, I spend most of my days dealing with staffing, budgets, and other administrative tasks. Once or twice a year, I handle a trial.

"Not too busy," I said. "I'm working on our budget."
"I need you to step in and take the lead on a murder trial."
Excellent. "When does it start?"
"A week from Monday."

2

"HE RETIRED"

"Which client?" I asked.

"Freddie Alvarez," Rosie said.

Alvarez was a homeless man accused of bludgeoning a hotshot lawyer to death in front of his multimillion-dollar house across the street from the Palace of Fine Arts in the upscale Marina District. I had assigned his case to Jeff Henderson, a twenty-year veteran of the PD's Office.

"Jeff's handling it," I said.

"Not anymore. He retired."

Huh? "He was here an hour ago."

"He gave his notice while you were in court."

Uh-oh. "Is he drinking again?"

"Unfortunately, yes."

Crap. "Maybe we should give him one last chance."

"We've given him ten last chances, Mike. He's eligible for his pension. I told him that if he retired immediately, we would characterize his departure as voluntary."

"Too bad." *The burnout rate of Public Defenders is high.* "He's a good lawyer and a decent guy."

"Yes, he is. It's also been excruciatingly hard on his ex-wife and kids."

"I need to talk to him about the Alvarez case."

"He isn't available. He's angry at me and frustrated with himself. I encouraged him to check into another treatment program. He said that he would."

I hope so. "I'm flying solo on the Alvarez case?"

"Yes."

"I'll request a continuance."

"You can ask Freddie about it, but he's been in jail for more than a year. I don't think he'll want to wait another year for a new trial date. Jeff had everything ready." She grinned. "You just need to read the record, show up in court, present the case, and get an acquittal."

It may not be quite that simple. "It's a tight time frame."

"It won't take you long to get up to speed." She reminded me of several cases where I had stepped in on short notice. "The facts aren't complicated. Freddie passed out in the decedent's driveway in the middle of the night after drinking a bottle of vodka and smoking heroin. When he woke up the next morning, there was a dead body next to him. Freddie swears that he didn't kill him. You just need to show that he couldn't have acted with the requisite premeditation for the prosecution to make first-degree murder."

"The jury can also convict for second-degree. The judge may also give them the option to convict for manslaughter."

"I would acknowledge that the degree of difficulty is high."

No kidding. "We can argue self-defense. And if he was high, we can argue diminished capacity."

"That would suggest that Freddie did it. He says that he didn't. The DA doesn't have any witnesses." Her grin broadened. "Just like old times, Mike. You'll get the jury to reasonable doubt. You've done it before."

It seems that I don't have any choice this time.

I met Rosie three decades ago in the file room of the old PD's Office. I was a new Deputy PD fresh out of law school. She had just been promoted to the Felony Division after spinning out of an unhappy marriage to one of her law school classmates. She was intrigued by the possibility of dating an ex-priest. I was intrigued by the possibility of dating somebody who seemed to like me. We got married after a quick and acrobatic romance. Our daughter, Grace, was born a year later. She just turned twenty-seven and works at Pixar along with her husband, Chuck. Rosie and I divorced two years after we got married when the pressures of a baby, our jobs, and our egos overwhelmed us. Our son, Tommy, came along ten years later. Old habits. He's a senior at Cal.

First things first. "Kids okay?"

"Fine."

Good. "Your mother?"

"Status quo, although her knee is bothering her."

"Did you ask her again about moving into independent living?"

"Yes. The answer is still no."

No surprise. Sylvia Fernandez is eighty-seven. My ex-mother-in-law is as sharp and opinionated as ever, but she steadfastly refuses to acknowledge that two artificial hips and an artificial knee have slowed her down. She still lives in the two-bedroom bungalow in the Mission that she and her late husband, Eduardo, bought almost sixty years ago. She can handle living on her own, but the twelve steps from the garage to the front door are becoming more challenging—especially since she refuses to use the cane that her doctor recommended when she got her first hip replacement. During Covid, she grudgingly hired somebody to come in a couple of mornings a week to help her clean the house and do her laundry.

"You okay?" I asked.

"Fine."

As if you would ever admit that you're anything but "fine." "Your opponent took another gratuitous potshot at you last night."

"Comes with the territory, Mike. San Francisco politics isn't like a friendly game of pickleball."

Rosie is running for her third and (she swears) final term as Public Defender. Her first challenger dropped out after Rosie outraised her ten-to-one. We thought that she would glide to re-election unopposed until a tech billionaire bankrolled the son of one of his venture capital pals to run against her. Rosie's new opponent is an earnest young criminal defense attorney who also graduated from my alma mater, Berkeley Law. He is quickly getting the hang of the dark art of San

Francisco politics. Rosie has a healthy lead in the polls, but her once-overwhelming advantage in fundraising has vaporized.

"I don't know how you deal with politics," I said. *Actually, I do—you love it.*

She grinned. "It's fun."

"You're going to win."

"Yes, I am."

"Does Rolanda have time to sit second chair in the Alvarez case?"

"Afraid not. She's starting a trial on Thursday."

That's unfortunate. Rolanda Fernandez is the co-head of the Felony Division. She's also Rosie's niece and, I suppose, my ex-niece. Like Rosie, Rolanda graduated from Mercy High, San Francisco State, and what was then known as Hastings Law School, and is now called UC Law San Francisco. She and her husband, Zach, yet another lawyer, are the proud parents of a three-year-old daughter and a six-month-old son. In the latest version of Rosie's master plan for the PD's Office and the universe, Rolanda will succeed her as PD in four years.

Rosie's tone remained even. "Nady handled Freddie's intake interview. She's familiar with the facts, and she's met him."

"She's in trial."

"Not anymore. She settled her case while you were in court. She has time."

Excellent. Nadezhda "Nady" Nikonova is one of our best young trial lawyers.

"Tom Eisenmann was the investigator on Freddie's case," I said. "Obviously, he isn't available."

Eisenmann was one of our longest-tenured and most effective investigators. Unfortunately, he died of complications from long Covid six months ago.

Rosie gave me a knowing smile. "Go ahead and call your brother."

My younger brother, Pete, is a former SFPD cop who now works as a private investigator. Almost thirty years ago, he and his partner broke up a gang fight in the Mission with a little too much enthusiasm. One of the brawlers suffered a concussion and a dislocated shoulder. It turned out that the kid was the nephew of a member of the Board of Supervisors. When the family filed the inevitable lawsuit, the City threw Pete and his partner under the bus. Pete became a PI. His partner became an alcoholic.

"Do we have money to pay him?" I asked.

Her eyes twinkled. "You just said that you were working on the budget."

Got it. I stood up and headed toward the door. "I'm going to see Nady."

"Great." Her expression turned thoughtful. "Mike?"

"Yes?"

"Thanks."

3

"HOW SOON CAN YOU START?"

I knocked on the open door of the windowless office across the hall from mine. "Got a sec?"

Nadezhda "Nady" Nikonova took off her reading glasses, tugged at her shoulder-length blonde hair, and smiled. "For you, always."

Nady is a brilliant, creative, and driven woman of thirty-nine. When she was a kid, she accompanied her single mother to the U.S. from Uzbekistan. They moved in with cousins in L.A. where Nady learned English on the fly. She graduated at the top of her class at UCLA and then Berkeley Law. She spent three years at a big firm downtown poring over mind-numbing loan documents for commercial real estate deals. I recruited her to the PD's Office where she quickly became one of our go-to lawyers. Her husband, Max, is a partner in the antitrust group of the same firm where Baby Chuckles used to work. Rosie's succession strategy contemplates that Nady will move up into my slot as head of the Felony Division when Rolanda becomes PD. Rosie likes to plan ahead.

I walked into her closet-sized office which had just enough room for a metal desk, a file cabinet, a credenza, and a bookcase, none of which matched. She was one of our few lawyers who didn't have to share an office. I took a seat in one of her creaky swivel chairs.

"Rosie told me about Jeff Henderson," she said. "My case settled, so I can help you with the Alvarez trial." She pointed at her laptop. "I've started looking at the files."

"Great." I looked around her office. "Where's the Chief?"

She pointed at the Keeshond sleeping in the corner. "Luna has been waiting for you."

I crossed the room, took out a treat, and held it under the dog's nose. Her left eye opened halfway. The forty-pound ball of silver and black fur wagged her tail, licked her chops, gave me her best smile, and pulled herself up into the sitting position. Without prompting, she went through her full repertoire: she extended a paw, lowered herself to the floor and then raised herself back up, picked up her teddy bear and offered it to me, and then extended her other paw.

I held the treat in my fist. "Have you been good today?"

Her ears perked up. I handed her the treat, which she devoured. Her huge brown eyes opened hopefully as she waited for seconds.

"That's the last one," I said.

Her expression transformed into one of profound disappointment. She slunk down to the linoleum floor, curled up, and resumed her nap.

Nady grinned. "You'll make it up to her tomorrow."

When Nady came to work for us, I declared that the PD's Office would be dog-friendly, much to the chagrin of my bureaucratic masters at City Hall. In fairness to the pencil pushers, City policy legitimately prohibits bringing pets (other than service animals) to work in the interest of "public and employee safety." After a couple of weeks of back-and-forth, I wore down the City Attorney, who grudgingly approved the "Mike Daley Exception," and Luna became the most beloved member of our office.

"What do you know about Freddie Alvarez?" I asked.

Her expression turned serious. "I did his intake interview before you assigned the case to Jeff. Freddie isn't a bad guy. Thirty. Grew up in the Mission. His father left when he was a baby. His mother had addiction issues. He spent time in foster care. He graduated from Sacred Heart, then spent three years in the Army. He did a tour in Afghanistan and hurt his knee when his unit was ambushed. He came back with PTSD. He worked security and drove for Uber. He developed a drinking problem, got addicted to heroin, lost his job, and ended up on the street. He lived in the Tenderloin for a couple of years, then he moved around from North Beach to the Presidio to the Marina."

"Pretty upscale," I observed.

"He was robbed in the TL, so he tried to stay in safer neighborhoods. A few days before he was arrested, he had set up his tent in some bushes next to the lagoon at the Palace of Fine Arts."

I asked about prior arrests.

"A couple of shoplifting hits. He was a heroin user, but he never got nicked for possession. He swore to me that he never sold."

"He's charged with murder."

"The DA claims that he bludgeoned a lawyer to death in the driveway in front of his house across the street from the Palace of Fine Arts. The driveway was being repaved. The alleged murder weapon was a rusty steel rod that would have been used as rebar. A neighbor discovered the body the following morning. Freddie was passed out nearby. The bloody rod was on the ground between Freddie and the decedent. Blood on the rod matched the decedent's. Rust on Freddie's gloves matched rust on the rod. They charged him with murder the following day."

I asked if they found any fingerprints on the rod.

"No. They didn't find any of the decedent's blood on Freddie's hands or clothing, either."

"Seems odd if he hit the decedent at close quarters. What do you know about him?"

She glanced at her laptop. "A personal injury lawyer named Frank Moriarty. Sixty-six. San Francisco native. Grew up in the Sunset and was an all-City offensive lineman at Archbishop Riordan High. Spent two years in the Marines, then he graduated from USF and USF Law. He worked for a big firm for a few years, then he went out on his own."

I recognized the name. "He had a reputation for theatrics."

"He made a ton of money and bought a big house in the Marina. He had a Maserati and a Tesla Cybertruck. He was a member of the Olympic Club."

Not bad. "Criminal record?"

"No. He was arrested once for assault after a bar fight, but the charges were dropped. A client accused him of withholding money from his trust account, but the claims were resolved without disciplinary action."

"Personal life?"

"Ugly. Married and divorced three times. Two grown kids from the first marriage stopped talking to him. The first ex-wife is deceased. The second lives in Portugal. The third was in New York on the night that he died. He had a drinking problem and a temper. The third ex-wife called the cops twice to report domestic violence, but she didn't file charges. There is no evidence that she was involved in his death."

"When was he last seen?"

"He left the Horseshoe Tavern on Chestnut Street at twelve-twenty AM. According to the bartender, Moriarty was a regular. It's about a twenty-minute walk to his house."

"Witnesses?" I asked.

"None. No security or other video from Moriarty's driveway, either." She said that the security camera above Moriarty's garage had been disconnected during construction. "There is security video from a neighbor around the corner showing our client walking by her house at twelve-thirty AM. Moriarty walked by about ten minutes later." She said that the security cameras from the Palace of Fine Arts didn't show Moriarty's house.

"Time of death?"

"According to the Medical Examiner, it was between twelve-forty and four AM."

"Why was Freddie walking down a quiet street in the Marina at twelve-thirty AM?"

"He was heading to his tent. He bought a bottle of vodka at Walgreens on Lombard. He walked past Moriarty's house on his way. He said that his knee hurt, so he stopped in the construction area on the driveway, drank his vodka, smoked a little heroin, and passed out. The next thing he remembers is the cops waking him up in the morning next to Moriarty's body."

"Did he know Moriarty?"

"He told me that he didn't."

"How did he explain the fact that the rust on his gloves matched the rust on the rod?"

"He said that he must have touched it when he sat down on the driveway or after he passed out. He was adamant that he didn't kill Moriarty."

"Did Moriarty try to attack him?"

"Freddie said that he didn't. There was no evidence of defensive wounds or a struggle. That would seem to rule out self-defense."

There appear to be some holes in our client's story. "Has the DA suggested a motive?"

"She thinks it was a botched robbery, but the police didn't find any of Moriarty's money or belongings on Freddie."

There appear to be some holes in the DA's case, too. "Let me see if I have this straight. The DA claims that Freddie ran into Moriarty in the construction zone in his driveway, tried to rob him, and then whacked him with a steel rod at close range without getting any blood on his hands or clothing—all with premeditation? And then he passed out a few feet away from the body?"

"That seems to be the DA's theory."

"We'll have to poke enough holes in the evidence to convince the jury that the DA hasn't proved her case beyond a reasonable doubt."

"That was Jeff's plan. It would help if we could find some evidence that would credibly point at some other potential suspects."

"Rosie authorized me to hire my brother to investigate."

She smiled. "Pete is very good. He'll find something."

There was a knock on her door. Our part-time paralegal, Debra "Dazzle" Diamond, flashed the smile that she displayed five nights a week at the Gold Club, a high-end strip club that caters to the tech bros in the office buildings surrounding Moscone Center. "Rosie asked me to help with the Alvarez case. I've started going through the files and looking at video."

"Thanks, Dazz," I said.

Dazzle is a Daly City native, a single mother, and a San Francisco State alum. After she was laid off from her job as a paralegal at a corporate law firm during the Great Recession, she started performing at the Gold Club. I represented her several times after she pilfered cash from her customers while they were entranced by her dancing skills. She wasn't a very good thief, but she's an outstanding dancer and an excellent paralegal. I hired her last year when she wanted to make additional money after her daughter went off to college. She works three days a week. So far, she's been a model employee.

"Trial starts a week from Monday," I told her.

"I'm not dancing tonight. I'll work late."

"Thanks." I looked at Nady. "What was Jeff's narrative?"

On my first day at work, Rosie taught me that trial work is theater, and the best courtroom lawyers develop a simple narrative that's compelling to the jury. It's a bit of an oversimplification, but Rosie believes that the side that tells the better story wins.

Nady looked at her laptop. "Freddie was high on heroin and drunk on vodka. He didn't have the capacity to bludgeon a bigger man, and there was no blood on his hands or clothing. He couldn't have formulated premeditation to be guilty of first-degree murder."

That gets us only partway. "It may get us an acquittal or a hung jury for first-degree, but the judge will instruct the jury that they can convict for second-degree." I reminded her that the judge also has the authority, but not the legal obligation, to instruct the jury that it can convict for voluntary or involuntary manslaughter.

"Then we'll need to find one or more alternate suspects to give the jury a reason to doubt that Freddie killed Moriarty."

"Nobody else was around."

"That's why we have your brother." Her voice turned somber. "If he can't find a viable alternate suspect, we may need to put Freddie on the stand to issue a strong denial."

"Only if we're desperate," I said. "The DA will eat him alive on cross-exam."

"Unless we can find some other potential suspects, we *will* be desperate."

True.

"Any chance that we can negotiate this down to second-degree murder or even manslaughter?" Nady asked.

"Doubtful," I said. "The ADA is Catherine O'Neal."

Nady scowled. "She's very good."

Catherine "No Deal" O'Neal is a tenacious ADA who takes pride in *not* settling cases.

I added, "Melinda Wong is the Homicide Inspector."

Nady's frown became more pronounced. "She's good, too."

Wong is a native of the Sunset and a graduate of Lowell High School and UC Davis. Her father was a captain at Taraval Station. The twenty-year SFPD veteran doesn't arrest people without substantial evidence.

Nady drummed her fingers on her desk. "The DA is up for re-election in three weeks. It will enhance her chances if she convicts a homeless guy of murder before election day. From a political standpoint, it's understandable that she assigned O'Neal to this case. We might get a better deal if we ask for a continuance and go to trial after the election."

"We'll ask Freddie about it, but I don't think he's going to be receptive to a delay."

We strategized for a few more minutes. Dazzle promised to summarize the evidence, organize the files, look at video, and work on our trial exhibits. Nady and I would also go through the files in detail. At trial, it's always critical to know the record.

I spoke to Nady. "I'm going to see Freddie this afternoon. Can you join me?"

"Yes."

I stood up and grabbed my laptop. "I'm going to call Pete."

I took a seat at my desk and punched the second number on my speed dial.

My brother answered on the first ring. "You calling about Freddie Alvarez?"

"Yes, Pete. How did you know?"

He spoke in a raspy voice. "Rosie texted me."

Figures. "Trial starts a week from Monday. Do you have time to help? I don't want you to get in trouble with Donna and Margaret."

Pete's wife, Donna Andrews, is the CFO of a big law firm downtown. Their daughter, Margaret, is a sophomore at UC Santa Barbara.

"I'll make time, Mick," he said. "Is this a paying gig?"

"Yes."

"Good."

Most of the time, I found a way to pay him. On occasion, we had to work out an extended payment plan. In a few instances, he worked pro bono, and I bought him dinner.

"How soon can you start?" I asked.

"Now."

4

"NEVER PLEAD GUILTY"

Freddie Alvarez fidgeted with the sleeve of his baggy orange jumpsuit. "You're my lawyers now?"

"Yes," I said.

"What happened to Jeff?"

"He retired."

His jet-black eyes locked onto mine. "He's drinking again, isn't he?"

"I can't talk about it."

His raspy voice softened. "I'm sorry."

At one-fifteen that same afternoon, Freddie, Nady, Pete, and I were sitting in plastic chairs around a gray table in a cramped consultation room in the bowels of San Francisco County Jail #3, the Costco-like edifice on San Bruno Mountain about ten miles south of the Hall of Justice. The boxy structure seemed out of place in a quiet suburban community. It opened to great fanfare in 2005 and was a substantial upgrade over the Depression-era jail a couple of miles away. A few dozen guards in high-tech pods monitor about eight hundred prisoners. It is the nicest facility in the San Francisco jail system.

Freddie's eyes darted from me to Nady, to Pete, and then back to me. "Do I have any choice about lawyers?"

"Not if you want to go to trial a week from Monday," I said. "If you want a different attorney, I can ask the judge for an extension."

"Can you get up to speed in time for trial?"

"Yes."

"What would you do if you were in my shoes?"

I answered him honestly. "Ask for a delay."

"How soon can I get a new trial date?"

"At least six months. More likely a year."

"I'm not going to rot in here for another year."

"Then you get Nady and me."

Freddie was thirty, but he looked older. He was five-ten with a wiry frame and muscular tattooed arms. His intense eyes sat below a shaved head. His pockmarked face was covered with gray stubble. His olive skin had a yellow cast.

"Are you any good?" he asked.

"I've been a defense lawyer for three decades. I've handled two dozen murder trials."

"Just because you've done this for a long time doesn't mean you're good."

True. "The State Bar once said that I was one of the best PDs in California."

"I don't care what the State Bar thinks."

Fair enough. "Ask around."

"I will." He looked at Pete, who was sitting with arms folded, unblinking eyes staring at Freddie. "What's your story?"

My brother adjusted the collar of the bomber jacket that he always wears even though it was eighty-five degrees in the room. At fifty-eight, he's two years younger and a little stockier than I am. His full head of hair was once darker brown than mine, but it's now a distinguished shade of silver matching his trim mustache.

"I've been a PI for twenty-five years," he said. "Before that, I was a cop."

"Why aren't you still a cop?"

"I got into trouble for hitting somebody who resisted arrest. Are you eating?"

"Some. My stomach feels like it's been through a meat grinder. The good news, I suppose, is that I haven't had a drink or any heroin in a year."

"Helluva way to get clean. You sleeping?"

"Not much."

"Working out?"

"A little."

"We need you to be strong for trial. You got a cellmate?"

"Yes. He sleeps most of the time."

"Good. Be careful what you say to him. And don't talk to the guards or anybody else about anything other than the weather. Nobody here is your friend." Pete looked my way.

"I trust that Jeff explained to you that we have only one rule: you have to tell us the absolute unvarnished truth, and you can't leave out anything important."

Freddie's eyes locked onto mine. "He did."

"Everything you told him was true?"

"Yes."

"Anything you'd like to reconsider?"

"No."

So far, so good. "Nady and I have been through your file, but we'd like to know more about you." *And I want to get you talking so that maybe you'll start to trust us. More importantly, I want to know if I can trust you.* "Tell us a little more about yourself."

"I didn't kill Frank Moriarty."

"We'll get to that shortly."

"We'll get to it now. I didn't kill him. I didn't even know him."

Good to hear, but it's a mixed bag from a legal standpoint. The California Rules of Professional Conduct prohibit attorneys from letting our clients lie on the stand. If I find out that you killed Moriarty, I can't let you testify to the contrary. Defense lawyers engage in all sorts of intellectual contortions to dance around this rule, but I prefer to avoid it altogether.

"We'll talk about what happened in a minute," I said. "I understand that you grew up in the Mission. St. Peter's Parish?"

"Yes. I was baptized there."

"Me, too. So were my parents. We moved to the Sunset when I was a kid."

His scowl softened a bit.

"St. Peter's School?" I asked.

"Yes. I went to high school at Sacred Heart."

"St. Ignatius," I said. I pointed at Pete. "Him, too."

"We didn't like kids from S.I."

"We didn't have any hard feelings toward Sacred Heart." *Except when we played them in football.* "Are your parents around?"

"My mom still lives in the Mission and works at a dry cleaner when she's clean. She was in and out of rehab when I was a kid, so I spent time in foster homes. My dad left when I was a baby. I think he's living in Arizona, but I haven't heard from him in years." He said that he had an older half-brother who lives in L.A. "I haven't talked to him in a long time. It isn't easy being related to a homeless addict."

"Recovering addict," I said. "We'll get you help to stay clean after the trial. In the meantime, we'd like to talk to your mother."

"Fine with me, but I don't know if she'll talk to you." He gave us a phone number. "She started drinking again. She hasn't come to see me in a few months." His voice softened. "Tell her that I'm sorry for the trouble that I've caused."

"We will." I glanced at Nady, who picked up the cue.

"How long were you living on the street?" she asked.

"About five years. After high school, I went into the Army for three years. I did two tours in Afghanistan, and I wrecked my knee in an ambush outside of Kabul. I came home with a bad leg and PTSD. After I was discharged, I worked as a security guard and drove for Uber. Some of my friends drank a lot. A few of them did crack and heroin, and they offered it to me. It's hard to stop once you get started. I got hooked on heroin, lost my job, and couldn't make my rent, so I got tossed out of my apartment. My mom was drinking, so I couldn't live with her. I stayed with friends for a few months, then I started sleeping in my car. When it got towed, I ended up on the street."

He said that he lived in the Mission, Potrero Hill, South of Market, and, eventually, the Tenderloin. "I was robbed a couple of times in the TL, so I moved to North Beach and then the Presidio. Eventually, I found a spot in the bushes next to the lagoon in front of the Palace of Fine Arts. The Marina is quiet. It's pretty easy to disappear if you're careful."

"You were able to find heroin in the Marina?"

"You can find it anywhere if you know where to look."

"The Medical Examiner believes that Moriarty died between twelve-forty and four AM on September fifth of last year. The police reports said that you were found unconscious in the driveway in front of Moriarty's house at six AM. How did you get there?"

"I bought a bottle of vodka at the Walgreens on Lombard around twelve-fifteen AM. I was walking back to my tent when I stopped at Moriarty's house around twelve-thirty. The driveway was being replaced, and there was a dumpster in front of it, so I didn't think anybody would see me. My leg was bothering me, so I took a break for a drink and a smoke."

Nady kept her voice even. "What happened next?"

We defense lawyers rarely ask our clients flat-out if they killed somebody. It's better to ask open-ended questions and let them tell their story.

Freddie took a deep breath. "I passed out on the driveway. The next thing I remember is that Moriarty's neighbor and the cops woke me up at six AM. Moriarty's dead body was a few feet away from me."

"You don't remember anything between the time that you stopped at Moriarty's driveway and when the cops woke you up?"

"I didn't kill him."

"You just said that you don't remember what happened."

"I would have remembered if I killed him."

"Did you see Moriarty?"

"Not until I woke up. He was already dead." His voice filled with desperation. "I didn't kill him," he repeated. "I swear to God."

"Freddie," I said, "the police found a rusty steel rod next to your right hand. It was covered with Moriarty's blood."

"I didn't hit him. And if I did, I wouldn't have used my right hand. I'm left-handed."

Good to know. "They also found rust on your gloves matching the rust on the rod. How did it get there?"

His eyes darted around the room. "I must have touched it when I sat down on the driveway or while I was sleeping. Or maybe somebody put it next to me. Either way, I didn't hit him."

I asked if he saw anybody else.

"No."

"But you're saying that somebody else hit Moriarty?"

"Yes."

"Did you know Moriarty?"

"No."

"Had you ever seen him or talked to him?"

"No."

"Did he say anything to you that morning?"

"No."

"Is it possible that he came after you, and you hit him in self-defense?"

"No."

"Is there anyone who can corroborate your story?"

"No." He flashed the first hint of anger. "Do you really think I would have stayed there if I had killed him?"

"Probably not." *Then again, if you were drunk on vodka and high on heroin, you would have had trouble walking.*

We sat in silence for a moment. Freddie stared down at the table. Nady pretended to look at her notes. Pete's eyes remained locked on Freddie.

Freddie's voice filled with resolve. "I didn't kill him, Mike. I swear that it's the truth. I need you to believe me."

I'm going to try. "Good to know."

He changed the subject. "How are you planning to play this?"

"You're charged with first-degree murder. The DA has to prove beyond a reasonable doubt not only that you killed Moriarty, but that you did so with premeditation. We'll challenge everything, but the circumstantial evidence is damning."

"Somebody else hit him."

"We'll make that argument, but it will be a heavy lift unless we can find a plausible alternate suspect. We will also argue that you didn't know Moriarty, and that you therefore couldn't have acted with premeditation. At the very least, it gives us a decent argument that you shouldn't be convicted of first-degree murder."

"Jeff said that I could still be convicted of second-degree, which has a minimum sentence of fifteen years."

"That's true. The judge will instruct the jury that even if they don't find you guilty of first-degree, they can still convict you of second-degree. She also has the option to instruct the jury that they can find you guilty of voluntary or involuntary manslaughter. A manslaughter conviction isn't ideal, of course, but the sentence would be shorter. If we're going to consider talking to the DA about a potential deal, now is the time."

He pushed out a frustrated sigh. "Maybe I should just cut a deal and plead guilty to second-degree. At the very least, it will limit the sentence."

"You sure you want to do that?"

"No, but it might be my best option."

"You said you didn't kill Moriarty. Are you prepared to plead guilty to a crime that you didn't commit and do the time?"

"Maybe. What do you think?"

I don't have time to play games. "Did you do it?"

He didn't hesitate. "No."

"Never plead guilty if you're innocent, Freddie. We can win this case. I can't make any promises, but we have a decent chance of getting at least one juror to reasonable doubt. If we do, the jury will hang, and the prosecutors will need to decide whether they want to go through the time and expense of another trial."

His expression indicated that he wasn't convinced. "What would you do?"

"We still have a week and a half until trial. Let's see how it plays out. If things aren't looking good, we can try to cut a deal."

He took a moment to consider his options. "Fine."

Pete spoke up again. "Did you see anybody after you left Walgreens?"

"There were a few people on Chestnut Street." He said that he didn't see anybody near Moriarty's house.

"Do you know anybody who lives in the Marina?"

"Are you serious? The cheapest houses start at two million dollars. Moriarty's was probably worth three times that. Do you really think I had friends there?"

"I was referring to other unhoused people."

Freddie's tone softened. "A few lived in Moscone Park. Some had tents by the Palace of Fine Arts. A lot of people lived in the Presidio. Nobody stayed in one place for long. Most of the people who were there a year ago have probably moved on by now."

"Any chance you have any names?"

"Afraid not."

"What did you think of Freddie?" I asked Pete.

"Hard to say." He pulled up the collar of his bomber jacket as the afternoon wind whipped through the parking lot of San Bruno Jail. "He stuck to his story. He didn't make excuses. That's usually a sign that somebody is telling the truth." The corner of his mouth turned up. "Then again, you know that my motto is 'trust but verify.'"

Your instincts are second only to Rosie's. "I need you to find at least one other plausible suspect. Preferably more."

"Working on it."

Nady was skeptical. "How do you explain the rust on his gloves?"

The unyielding voice of reality. "I don't know—yet." I opened the door to my Prius. "I'll drop you off at the office. I want you to track down Freddie's mother and Moriarty's third ex-wife. Maybe they'll tell us something we can use."

"I will. Where are you going?"

"To talk to the DA." I turned to Pete. "What about you?"

"I'm going down to the Marina to talk to some homeless people."

5

"PROFESSIONAL COURTESY"

"Thank you for seeing me," I said.

Assistant District Attorney Catherine "No Deal" O'Neal spoke in a measured voice. "We always try to cooperate with the PD's Office."

Of course you do.

At three-fifteen on Tuesday afternoon, O'Neal sat behind a modular desk in her utilitarian office on the third floor of a refurbished industrial building at the base of Potrero Hill, about a mile south of the Hall. Unlike the old DA's Office, the plumbing and air conditioning worked, and her desk, two chairs, credenza, and file cabinet matched. Her window looked into another refurbished building across the alley. Her "ego wall" was modest: her Stanford Law diploma, a few bar association citations, and a photo with her boss. The only personal item was a picture of her husband, a staff attorney for the California Supreme Court.

Her voice softened. "Sorry to hear about Jeff Henderson. We had our moments in court, but he's a decent guy."

"Thank you."

Her sentiment was genuine. Most of us who operate in the trenches of the justice system understand that people must deal with medical issues, family emergencies, cranky spouses, young kids, and elderly parents.

She moved straight to business. "I heard you picked up the Freddie Alvarez case. I presume that you're going to ask for a continuance?"

"No."

At thirty-five, O'Neal's brown eyes sat above high cheekbones. The native of Palo Alto is the daughter of a tech executive and a law professor. She began her career at the Contra Costa County DA's Office, moved into a supervisory position in Alameda County, and was hired by her friend, former colleague, and law-and-order zealot, Vanessa Turner, when she was appointed as San Francisco DA after her predecessor was unceremoniously recalled when voters decided that he was soft on crime. Turner cleaned house and brought in a half-dozen aggressive prosecutors, including O'Neal, with a mandate to take drug dealers, car thieves, and shoplifters off the streets. The new regime's tactics have been heavy-handed, but effective. Turner is running for re-election in a few weeks, so a conviction would look good on her campaign materials.

O'Neal played with her hoop-style earrings. "Are you really going to take this case to trial a week from Monday?"

"Yes."

"Do you think that's wise?"

No. "It's what our client wants us to do."

"Then I'll see you in court."

"I was hoping that we could take a few minutes to talk about Freddie's case."

"I'm under no obligation to talk to you."

"Professional courtesy."

She feigned impatience. "The charge is first-degree murder. Judge Elizabeth McDaniel is presiding. You know her better than I do. She's very smart, she's been around the block, and she doesn't take any crap."

All true. Betsy McDaniel is a Superior Court veteran who went on senior status a few years ago. She was an ADA for twenty years before she was appointed to the bench. She's meticulous, thoughtful, and prepared. I like her, and she seems to like me. She *really* likes Rosie, with whom she attends Pilates classes. She's always given me a fair shake.

O'Neal folded her hands. "We sent our preliminary witness list to Jeff. I don't anticipate any additions. We have a meeting with Judge McDaniel on Friday to discuss pretrial motions. We exchanged draft jury questionnaires. Everything else should be in Jeff's files. That's all that I can tell you at this time."

You can tell me more. "You have a legal obligation to turn over evidence that would tend to exonerate my client. You are also required to identify witnesses who can corroborate our client's story, as well as potential alternate suspects."

"There is none, and there are none. There are no eyewitnesses and no relevant security or other videos from the scene."

"There is a security video from a neighbor who lived around the corner from Moriarty's house. It shows Moriarty walking home at twelve-thirty-nine AM."

"The same video shows your client walking by that house at twelve-thirty AM. Obviously, your client ambushed him when he got home. A different neighbor found him the following morning. Your client was passed out near Moriarty's body. A bloody steel rod was next to his hand. The blood on the rod matched the decedent's. Rust on the rod matched rust on your client's gloves. We aren't going to need a jury of PhDs from MIT to connect the dots."

"The rod was next to Freddie's right hand. Freddie is left-handed."

"The rod was also within inches of his left hand."

"Our client says that he didn't kill Moriarty."

"Then you can put him on the stand and let him try to sell it to the jury."

"You have no corroborating witnesses."

"We don't need any."

"You don't know what happened."

"Yes, I do. Frank Moriarty walked home after having a couple of beers at the Horseshoe Tavern on Chestnut. Your client was smoking heroin in the construction zone in his driveway. Your client tried to rob him. He whacked Moriarty in the back of the head with a rusty steel rod. Moriarty died instantaneously."

"Freddie didn't steal anything. Moriarty's wallet was still inside his pocket."

"Your client wasn't a competent thief."

"Freddie would have run away if he had killed Moriarty."

"He passed out after he drank vodka and smoked heroin. You can argue diminished capacity if your client is willing to tell the truth and admit that he killed Frank Moriarty."

"He's a little guy with a bad leg. There's no way that he could have killed Moriarty."

"Moriarty never saw it coming."

"You'll never prove premeditation."

"The jury will be able to put the pieces together."

"Motive?"

"We don't have to prove one."

"A jury won't convict for first-degree murder unless you can show that there was a reason." *Well, maybe.*

"Robbery. And your client had history with the decedent. They exchanged angry words a few days before your client killed him."

What? "Freddie told me that he had never met Moriarty."

"He lied to you."

"Who's the witness?"

"I'm under no obligation to tell you. That wouldn't constitute exculpatory evidence."

That's technically correct. "You'll never make first-degree murder, Catherine."

"I disagree. We aren't going to let homeless people roam our streets and kill people. We are sending a message that we are going to put the criminals away."

"Nobody is questioning your toughness, Catherine."

"They question it every day, Mike. We've been getting an insane amount of heat because of the homeless situation."

"You inherited it."

"We own it now."

True. "You're over-charging. You'll never prove first-degree or even second-degree murder. You're going to have a hard time proving manslaughter."

"I disagree."

"Are you prepared to discuss any sort of reasonable resolution?"

"If you're suggesting a deal, the answer is no." Her voice evened. "Vanessa isn't going to authorize a plea bargain. My orders are to take this case to trial and get a conviction. You need to talk to your client and insist that he tell you the truth. When he does, you should call me, and I will try to persuade Vanessa to work something out."

Nady was standing in the hallway when I returned to the office. "Did you get anything useful out of O'Neal?" she asked.

"No." I described my conversation. "She claims that she has a witness who saw Freddie arguing with Moriarty a few days before Moriarty died."

"I'll check the file again. Did you explore the possibility of a deal?"

"O'Neal and her boss aren't in a dealing mood."

"Have you heard from Pete?"

"He's looking for witnesses in the Marina."

"Are you going to join him?"

"I'm going to talk to the lead homicide inspector first."

6

"READ MY REPORT"

Inspector Melinda Wong sat down behind her gunmetal-gray desk, checked the messages on her phone, and feigned impatience. "I promised you five minutes. You're down to four and a half. Talk fast."

I was sitting in a wobbly card chair jammed between her desk and the wall. I had tracked her down outside the courtroom of my longtime friend and occasional drinking buddy, Judge Peter Busch. Wong was the prosecution's star witness in an assault trial in which Rolanda was handling the defense. I like Wong. More importantly, I respect her. She's a straight shooter who doesn't screw around. She's a formidable witness in court.

"How did trial go today?" I asked.

"Same as always."

Good answer. Says nothing. "Rolanda told me that there are some holes in the prosecution's case."

"You defense attorneys always say that."

Yes, we do.

At four-forty-five on Tuesday afternoon, we were sitting in the drab bullpen housing San Francisco's two dozen homicide inspectors. Wong's colleagues were out of the office tracking down witnesses. The only noise came from the standing fan pushing the heavy air from one side of the room to the other. The circulation would have been better if the windows opened, but they were painted shut in the Eighties.

"Is Pam okay?" I asked. Wong's wife is a Superior Court judge.

"Fine, thanks."

Wong is in her mid-forties with expressive features and an empathetic manner that makes her especially effective at drawing out information from suspects and witnesses. The twenty-year veteran comes from an SFPD family and is one of the first lesbians in Homicide. She has worked alone since her last partner, Inspector Ken Lee, took early retirement. Coincidentally, Lee was trained by the legendary Roosevelt Johnson, San Francisco's most decorated homicide inspector. A half-century earlier, Roosevelt walked the beat in the Tenderloin with my father.

She pointed at her watch. "Four minutes."

"I'm taking over the Freddie Alvarez case from Jeff Henderson."

"I heard. I am under no obligation to talk to you. Catherine O'Neal will be unhappy if she finds out that I did."

"This stays between us."

"There's no such thing as attorney-homicide inspector privilege."

True. "You must be very confident in your evidence. Mind sharing a few highlights with me?"

"Read my report."

"You homicide inspectors always say that."

"You ought to cut a deal. If you grovel, you might be able to persuade Catherine to go down to second-degree murder."

"Catherine isn't in a dealing mood. Neither is her boss. Freddie says that he didn't kill Frank Moriarty."

"Let me spell it out for you. The murder weapon was a steel rod sitting next to your client's right hand, a couple of feet from Moriarty's body."

"Freddie is left-handed."

"The rod was within a few feet of his left hand. Rust on the rod matched rust on your client's glove. Moriarty's blood was on the rod."

"Freddie stopped in front of Moriarty's house to drink vodka and smoke heroin. He sat down and passed out on the driveway before Moriarty showed up."

"Says your client. You can argue diminished capacity, but your client would have to admit that he killed Moriarty."

"He won't."

She smirked. "Then I guess that won't work."

"Catherine told me that she thinks it was a botched robbery, but there's no evidence. Moriarty's wallet was still in his pocket."

"Your client wasn't a very good robber."

"Freddie has no history of violence."

"He does now."

"Did you consider the possibility that somebody else hit Moriarty?"

"We found no evidence, Mike."

"You didn't list any witnesses who saw Freddie hit Moriarty."

"There aren't any."

"I didn't see any mention of video from Moriarty's house."

"There is none."

"There's video from one of Moriarty's neighbors."

"Your client was spotted in a security video taken at twelve-thirty AM by a neighbor's camera around the corner from Moriarty's house. Moriarty was filmed by the same camera at twelve-thirty-nine."

"Was anybody else in the video?"

"Two homeless people walked by about ten minutes after Moriarty. They went by the names 'Jack' and 'Jill.' We tracked them down in the Presidio and questioned them. They didn't see anything. We found no evidence that they were involved."

"You believe that Moriarty found Freddie in his driveway?"

"Yes. That's when your client killed him."

"There's no mention of Moriarty's blood on Freddie's hands or clothing."

"The rod was four feet long. The Medical Examiner said that your client hit Moriarty from behind. Moriarty fell forward onto his chest. That's why there was no blood on your client's hands or clothing."

"You believe that Freddie whacked Moriarty and passed out near his body?"

"Yes."

"That's convenient."

"That's what happened."

"Freddie had no history with Moriarty."

"He does now."

"O'Neal told me that you have a witness who said that Moriarty and Freddie argued a few days before Moriarty died."

"We do."

"Got a name?"

"Ask Catherine."

"I did. She wouldn't tell me."

"Neither will I. It isn't exculpatory evidence."

True. "The fact that Moriarty and Freddie may have argued at some point doesn't prove that Freddie hit him."

"I'd rather try to sell our story to the jury than yours."

So would I. "According to the file, a neighbor named Henry Keller found the body."

"He did. He lived next door to Moriarty. He's a billionaire real estate investor. He found the body when he took out his garbage at six AM. He's been fully cooperative."

"Any history between Keller and Moriarty?"

"They were neighbors for twenty years."

That doesn't exactly answer my question. "Any evidence that Keller may have had any animosity toward Moriarty?"

"You'll have to ask Keller."

I will. "I understand that David Dito was the first officer at the scene."

"He was."

Sergeant Dito is a solid young cop who works out of Northern Station. He's a member of a distinguished multigenerational SFPD family scattered in the bungalows in St. Anne's Parish. David, his wife, five-year-old daughter, and infant son still live in the Sunset.

"I trust that you have no objection if I talk to him?"

"I can't stop you. He's under no obligation to talk to you."

I probed for a few more minutes, but the default response of an experienced homicide inspector was to refer to her report.

She looked at her watch. "Your five minutes are up."

A gust of wind hit me as I walked down the steps of the Hall toward Bryant. I stopped next to the smokers' area, pulled out my phone, and punched in Pete's number.

He answered on the first ring. "What is it, Mick?"

"I talked to Catherine O'Neal and Melinda Wong." I summarized my conversations.

He listened intently and offered his always-practical summary. "Doesn't sound like you got anything that will help us, Mick."

"Any luck finding witnesses?"

"Working on it."

"David Dito was the first officer at the scene."

"I know. I'll track him down."

"There's security video from a neighbor showing Freddie and Moriarty walking toward Moriarty's house within minutes of each other. A couple of homeless people walked by a few minutes later. They went by Jack and Jill, but I don't know if those are their real names. I will try to track down their last names. O'Neal and Wong also claim they have a witness who saw Moriarty and Freddie arguing on at least one occasion prior to the night that Moriarty died."

"Got a name?"

"Not yet. At the very least, we'll want to talk to Moriarty's next-door neighbor, Henry Keller. He found Moriarty's body."

"He won't be hard to find. Are you going back to the office?"

"No, I'm going to see the Medical Examiner."

7

"THE DECEDENT WAS WALKING AWAY"

The Chief Medical Examiner of the City and County of San Francisco fingered the top button of her white lab coat. "Nice to see you again, Mr. Daley."

"Nice to see you, too, Dr. Siu."

I have asked Dr. Joy Siu to call me by my first name many times, but she isn't a first-name person. She was sitting on the opposite side of a glass-topped table in a windowless conference room next to her spacious office on the second floor of the new Medical Examiner's facility in a warehouse-like building halfway between the ballpark and Candlestick Point. The furnishings are sparse, the ambiance sterile. The state-of-the-art examination rooms and expanded morgue are a substantial upgrade from her old quarters behind the Hall of Justice.

"I understand that you were in Rio," I said. "Vacation?"

"Autopsy."

No surprise. Dr. Siu is one of San Francisco's hardest working public servants. From her pressed lab coat to her meticulously-applied makeup to her precisely-cut black hair, she embodies exactness. At fifty, the Princeton and Johns Hopkins Medical School alum and former researcher at UCSF is a world-class academic and an internationally recognized expert in anatomic pathology. The one-time Olympic figure-skating hopeful spends about a quarter of her time consulting on complex autopsies around the world.

I tried to engage her. "How was the food in Rio?"

"Nothing special." Her intense expression didn't change. "Two days in a Brazilian morgue is about the same as two days in ours."

"Any truth to the rumor that you may be going back to academia?"

"No comment."

My moles in the ME's Office have told me that Dr. Siu may be returning to UCSF.

"I wish you well if you decide to make the move," I said.

"Thank you."

That's it for the chitchat. "I trust that you've heard that I am stepping in for Jeff Henderson on the Freddie Alvarez trial. Your name is on the DA's witness list."

"Catherine O'Neal asked me to be available to testify."

"You performed the autopsy on Frank Moriarty?"

"I did. I am sure that my report is in your file. Cause of death was a blow to the back of the head from a rusty steel rod found next to your client's right hand. Mr. Moriarty had a fractured skull." She confirmed that Moriarty was seen leaving the Horseshoe Tavern at twelve-twenty AM. "He was later seen in a neighbor's security video at twelve-thirty-nine AM. I therefore placed time of death between twelve-forty and four AM."

"Can you tighten the window a little?"

"I'm afraid not."

Medical Examiners are loath to lock themselves into narrow time frames. It gives pesky defense attorneys something to nitpick.

"Any chance that Mr. Moriarty fell down on his own and fractured his skull?"

"No."

"Did you find any evidence that my client struck Mr. Moriarty?"

"The steel rod was covered in rust. We found traces of matching rust on your client's gloves."

"My client told us that he sat down in the construction zone in the driveway where Mr. Moriarty's body was found. Did you consider the possibility that he got rust on his gloves when he did so?"

"Anything is possible, Mr. Daley."

"Defensive wounds or evidence of a struggle?"

"None."

"Is it possible that my client may have acted in self-defense?"

"He hit Mr. Moriarty in the back of the head. It indicates that the decedent was walking away from him."

"Maybe he turned away just before he was hit."

"I didn't find any evidence."

"Any evidence that somebody else struck Mr. Moriarty?"

"Not from my examination of the body, Mr. Daley."

It's about what I expected. "Did you perform toxicology tests on Mr. Moriarty?"

"Of course. He had consumed enough alcohol to be over the legal limit, but he was able to walk home. A credit card receipt indicated that he had consumed three beers. Even if he was impaired, it doesn't change my analysis."

"Drugs?"

"Traces of cocaine."

"Coke is a stimulant. Maybe he was agitated and attacked my client."

"I found no evidence, and it doesn't change my conclusions."

"Did you find evidence of other medical issues for Mr. Moriarty?"

"He was overweight and had liver issues possibly related to alcohol consumption. Otherwise, he appeared to be a reasonably healthy sixty-six-year-old."

"Anger issues?"

She shrugged. "That's outside my knowledge."

"Other injuries?"

"None." She said that I would find autopsy photos in her report.

"Did you find any blood on the steel rod other than the decedent's?"

"No."

"Did you find any evidence connecting anyone other than my client to the body?"

"No."

"Did the evidence techs find any blood on my client's hands or clothing?"

"Not that I'm aware of."

"Does it strike you as odd that you believe my client managed to hit Mr. Moriarty in the head at close range without getting any blood on his hands?"

"That's a question for SFPD's blood spatter expert."

Our blood spatter expert will undoubtedly have a different take.

She looked at her watch. "I'm late for another meeting. Nice chatting with you."

I was driving to the office when Pete's name appeared on my phone. I answered using the hands-free. "Give me something that I can use."

"How soon can you get down to the Marina, Mick?"

"Twenty minutes."

"I persuaded the first officer at the scene to show us where Moriarty was killed."

8

"HE WAS DISORIENTED"

At seven-thirty PM, the evening fog hit my face as I waited in the driveway of Frank Moriarty's three-story mansion on the corner of Baker and North Point, across the street from the lagoon and park on the east side of the Palace of Fine Arts. Moriarty's century-old stucco house was painted a creamy white with gold trim. It had a green terracotta roof, red brick stairs, and decorative ironwork. The rooftop deck had an unobstructed view of the Golden Gate Bridge. While most of the Marina consisted of tightly packed two-flats and three-story apartment buildings, Baker Street was lined with detached houses. Teslas, BMWs, and Mercedes were parked in the driveways. Several houses were being renovated.

Pete parked his ancient black Crown Vic in the short driveway. He exited the car, checked his phone, and pointed at Moriarty's house. "Nice, eh?"

"Not bad."

He looked across the street at the illuminated dome of the Palace of Fine Arts, the crown jewel of the 1915 Panama Exposition World's Fair, which celebrated the opening of the Panama Canal. "I wouldn't mind waking up to that view every morning."

Neither would I. Inspired by a Piranesi engraving of a Roman ruin, renowned architect Bernard Maybeck designed the magnificent structure that he said embodied "the mortality of grandeur and the vanity of human wishes." With Corinthian columns topped by female figures draped in stolas, intricate sculptures, majestic arches, and a Greco-Roman rotunda, the exhibition hall is the only remaining building from the fair.

After World War II, it fell into disrepair and was used as a military storage depot, a warehouse for the Parks Department, a telephone book distribution center, and a temporary Fire Department headquarters. It was renovated in the Sixties. For many years, it was the home to the popular Exploratorium science museum, which moved to Pier 15 in 2013.

I turned and admired the row of stunning houses on Baker Street. When I was a kid, the Marina was still home to working-class people, and the business district on Chestnut Street had a hardware store, two movie theaters, several neighborhood restaurants, a donut shop, a pharmacy, a five-and-dime, and a dry cleaner. Nowadays, it's lined with upscale boutiques, designer coffee shops, Pilates studios, and the obligatory Apple Store.

Pete was getting impatient. "Did you get the order for David?"

"Yes." I held up a plastic bag. "Potstickers, hot-and-sour soup, Mongolian beef, mu shu pork, and sesame chicken. And, of course, a double order of General Tso's."

"Good work, Mick."

On my way here, I picked up takeout from Tai Chi, a hole-in-the-wall on Polk Street that's been serving hearty food for almost a half-century. The house specialty is General Tso's chicken, a heart attack on a plate made of deep-fried chicken nuggets sauteed in a flaming hot sauce made from a secret combination of ginger, garlic, soy sauce, vinegar, sherry, sesame oil, and hot chili peppers. When Rosie and I lived in the City and our constitutions were sturdier, we used to head over to Tai Chi on Friday nights to eat copious amounts of General Tso's and drink gallons of ice water until our stomachs surrendered.

A police unit pulled up in front of Moriarty's house and parked in front of the driveway, blocking Pete's car. Sergeant David Dito emerged, uniform pressed, star polished, shoulders broad, bearing erect. He put his nightstick into its holder and walked over to join us. His face was still boyish, but there were worry lines on his forehead, and his black hair was now sprinkled with gray. He walked with a slight limp—a souvenir from breaking up a domestic disturbance in the Mission when he was a rookie cop.

David, Pete, and I exchanged handshakes and greetings.

"Is your uncle okay?" I asked.

David grinned. "Which one?"

"Phil."

Phil Dito was my classmate at St. Ignatius and a fellow backup on the football team who had worked with Pete at Mission Station.

"He's enjoying retirement," David said.

"Good to hear. Please give him my best."

Pete handed him the bag of food. "Among other things, we brought you a double order of General Tso's from Tai Chi. That should tide you over for a few days."

"Thank you. Is your family okay?"

"All good. Margaret is a sophomore at UC Santa Barbara. Yours?"

"My daughter is starting kindergarten in the fall."

"Time flies. You going to stay in the City?"

"We're thinking about Novato. The schools are better."

Many San Francisco cops and firefighters move up to Novato when they have kids. The houses are more affordable, the weather is warmer, and the public schools are good. The law enforcement presence also makes it one of the safest communities in the Bay Area.

Pete turned to business. "Mike is going to handle the Freddie Alvarez trial."

"I've been told." David looked my way. "I heard that you aren't going to ask for a continuance. I take it that your client overruled your advice?"

"Possibly. Would you mind telling us what happened?"

"Catherine O'Neal doesn't want me to talk to you."

Pete answered him. "You showed up anyway."

"We've known each other for a long time."

"We're off the record, David."

"No such thing, but I'll give you a few minutes."

I always enjoy watching Pete work. More important, I like to have a non-lawyer with me when I interview witnesses. If necessary, Pete will corroborate (or rebut) David's account of our conversation in court. It's also nice to have an ex-cop present when I talk to law enforcement.

Pete pointed at Moriarty's house. "Is anybody living there now?"

"Not at the moment. The decedent's children sold it six months ago. All cash. Seven million. The new owner is from Hong Kong. She wanted a place to stay when she's in town."

Not bad for a little pied-à-terre.

"Where did Moriarty die?" Pete asked.

"Here in the driveway. Your client was passed out near the body when I arrived." He confirmed that the driveway was under construction. "There was a dumpster over where my car is parked. Your client was lying down next to it. Moriarty's body was near your client."

"Who found the body?"

"The next-door neighbor. He's a real estate billionaire named Henry Keller. He's lived here for years." David spoke in clipped cop dialect as he confirmed that Keller found the body at six AM when he took his garbage cans to the curb. "Keller phoned 9-1-1. I picked up the call and came right over. I arrived at six-twelve." He said that he called for backup and attempted to administer first aid to Moriarty. "The EMTs arrived at six-fifteen. Backup arrived at six-nineteen. Moriarty was pronounced dead at six-thirty-five by the lead EMT who was on the phone with an emergency room doctor at S.F. General."

Pete surveyed the driveway. "Was Freddie awake when you got here?"

"Barely. He was disoriented. I made sure that he was unarmed and attempted to administer first aid. He was not cooperative, but he wasn't violent."

"Did he try to run?"

"He couldn't. I helped him sit up and turned him over to the EMTs. He looked like he had taken drugs or alcohol or both. The EMTs got him onto a gurney and gave him an IV."

"Did you question him?"

"To the extent that I could. He told me that he didn't kill Moriarty, but he didn't know what happened. He was mostly incoherent. The EMTs took him to San Francisco General with a police guard. The doctors confirmed that he was coming down from a heroin high."

"Did you arrest him?"

"No. Inspector Wong questioned him at San Francisco General. She placed him under arrest later that same day."

I asked if there was evidence of a struggle.

David shrugged. "Not as far as I could tell. It looked like Moriarty had suffered a blow to the back of the head from a rusty steel rod that I found between the body and your client's right hand. There was blood on the rod. Your client's gloves were covered in rust."

"Did you see any blood on Freddie's gloves, person, or clothes?"

"Not that I recall."

"Did you notice anything else in the immediate vicinity?"

"An empty vodka bottle and drug paraphernalia. It's in the police photos."

Pete re-entered the conversation. "You talked to the neighbor who found the body?"

"Yes. Mr. Keller was a little shaken up, but he was cooperative. He gave a statement to Inspector Wong, and he answered all of my questions."

"Any hard feelings between Mr. Keller and Mr. Moriarty?"

"Not that I'm aware of."

"Any prints on the rod?"

"No."

"Was anybody else around?"

"No. Obviously, after several police cars and an ambulance arrived, the neighbors came outside to see what was going on." David confirmed that he and his colleagues secured the scene.

"We interviewed the neighbors. Other than the fact that Keller found the body, nobody saw or heard anything."

Pete's expression turned skeptical. "Security video?"

"The security camera on Moriarty's garage was turned off. A neighbor named Shreya Patel provided security video from her house around the corner. It showed your client walking by her house at twelve-thirty. Moriarty followed at twelve-thirty-nine."

"Anybody else?"

"A homeless couple walked by at twelve-forty-five. We found them the following day at their tent at the Presidio. Their names are Jack Allen and Jill Harris. They didn't see or hear anything."

"Did you consider the possibility that they may have been involved in Moriarty's death?"

"Of course. We found no evidence that they were."

I pointed at the lagoon across the street. "Did you consider the possibility that somebody might have come over from the Palace of Fine Arts?"

"Yes. We canvassed the park. We didn't find anybody."

"Was anybody at Moriarty's house that night?"

"No. He lived by himself. He was estranged from his ex-wives and children."

"Girlfriend?"

"No." David eyed me. "His phone records suggested that he engaged the services of escorts from time to time, but we found no evidence that he met with somebody from one of those businesses on the night that he died."

That's juicy gossip, but not a fact that would tend to exonerate Freddie.

"Melinda Wong told me that she found a witness who said that Moriarty and Freddie got into an argument a few nights before Moriarty died."

"I have no reason to doubt her, but I don't know who it is."

"Who else should we talk to?" Pete asked.

David pointed at the house next door. "Keller lives there. Patel lives around the corner. I don't know if they'll talk to you."

"David," I said, "do you see a lot of homeless people around here?"

"Some. It isn't as bad as the Tenderloin or Sixth Street. They tend to stay out of sight during the day. We know that they're around at night, but they're harder to find."

"Any chance another homeless person may have had something against Moriarty?"

"We found no evidence, Mike."

We talked for a few more minutes, but David had nothing more to offer. We thanked him for his time, and he thanked us for the General Tso's. He returned to his car.

"We need to talk to the neighbors," I said to Pete. "Start with Keller and Patel."

"Keller is in Palm Springs until later tonight. Patel is in L.A. until tomorrow morning."

"I take it this means that you have people watching them?"

"That's why you're paying me the big bucks, Mick."

"Are you going to look for witnesses in the neighborhood?"

"Later. Let's go back to your office. Nady has been trying to reach Freddie's mother and Moriarty's third ex-wife. Dazzle is looking at the security videos from Patel's house."

9

"THERE ISN'T MUCH"

Nady looked up from her laptop. "Freddie's mother is in rehab and won't talk to us. Looks like he isn't going to have anybody in his rooting section at trial."

Unfortunate but not surprising. "Were you able to reach Moriarty's third ex-wife?"

"I left voice and email messages for her. She's a real estate lawyer with an office in Jackson Square. I haven't heard back. Hopefully, she'll talk to us."

Hopefully.

The PD's Office was quiet at eight-thirty on Tuesday night. The aroma of Nady's kale salad, Dazzle's chicken Caesar, Pete's pepperoni pizza, and my turkey sandwich wafted through our conference room. When I first became a PD, trial war rooms were filled with file folders, charts, exhibits, whiteboards, three-ring binders, and mountains of paper. Nowadays, the only items on the table were takeout containers, Uber Eats bags, laptops, and cell phones. We're probably more efficient and our food choices are more nutritious, but I miss the old-fashioned clutter.

I summarized our conversations with O'Neal, Wong, Siu, and Dito. "As you might expect, they're playing their cards close to the vest."

Nady turned to Pete. "What are the chances that your people will find a new witness or two who will help us?"

"Hard to say."

That's Pete-speak for "It's doubtful."

I asked Nady if she had found anything useful in the police reports.

"There isn't much. We haven't received any new evidence from the DA or additions to her witness list. It may take us longer to pick a jury than for the DA to present her case. They're planning to call the neighbor who found the body, the first officer at the scene, the Medical Examiner, a couple of evidence techs, and Inspector Wong."

I turned to Dazzle. "What about video?"

"I watched the security video taken by a camera mounted on the garage of a neighbor who lived around the corner from Moriarty. Her name is Shreya Patel. Forty-two. Divorced. A twelve-year-old daughter. She's a venture capitalist."

Pete spoke up again. "Dito mentioned her. She's out of town at the moment, but I'll track her down when she gets back tomorrow. Let's see the video."

Dazzle's fingers flew over her laptop. The flat-screen TV came to life. A color video appeared on the screen. The caption read, "SFPD. Security video. 2370 North Point, San Francisco, CA. Tuesday, September 5, 2023. 12:20 AM."

We sat in silence as Dazzle ran the video. Unlike old-time grainy security videos from convenience stores, Patel's Ring system had a high-def color picture. Through the fog, the camera showed Patel's driveway, North Point Street, and a two-flat across the street. A Mercedes coupe was parked in the driveway of the two-flat.

Dazzle narrated. "There was no auto or pedestrian traffic for ten minutes." She paused the video at twelve-thirty AM when a slender man limped past Patel's house. He wore a Giants cap pulled down over his eyes, a black hoodie, and jeans. She stopped the video. "That's Freddie."

"He could barely walk," Pete observed. "It would have been hard for him to keep his balance if he attacked Moriarty."

"We'll bring it up at trial," I said.

Dazzle hit the "Play" button again, and the video resumed. There were no pedestrians or vehicles between twelve-thirty and twelve-thirty-nine AM. The wind whipped through the trees, and a few birds flew by.

Dazzle stopped the video again at twelve-thirty-nine and pointed at the screen. "There's Moriarty."

He was built like an offensive lineman. Moriarty wasn't as big as Terrence "The Terminator," but he was still imposing at six-four and at least two-sixty. He trudged past Patel's driveway wearing a Patagonia windbreaker, khaki pants, and a black beret. It was difficult to see his face in profile, but his expression appeared grim.

Pete pointed at the screen. "Let's see the rest of it."

Dazzle started the video again. There was no activity for the next five minutes. Finally, at twelve-forty-five AM, a tall man and a petite woman walked by Patel's house. He wore an overcoat and carried a shopping bag. She wore a Warriors sweatshirt and a baseball cap. They were in and out of the frame in two seconds. The video ended a minute later.

Dazzle pointed at the screen. "His name is Jack Allen, fifty-five. Hers is Jill Harris, thirty-two. They weren't married, but they were a couple. He was on heroin. She was on crack. They lived in the Presidio. Inspector Wong talked to them the following day. They said that they were on their way back to their tent after they collected bottles and cans on Chestnut Street to turn in for cash at the recycling center. They didn't see or hear anything at Moriarty's house."

Pete's voice was skeptical. "Did Wong consider the possibility that they were involved in Moriarty's death?"

"Yes. She didn't find any evidence."

"Maybe she didn't try very hard."

I interjected. "We may be able to use this to our advantage." I turned to Pete. "I need you to find Jack and Jill."

"I'll get right on it, Mick." Pete pointed at the TV. "Play it again in slow motion."

Dazzle played the video twice at regular speed and three times in slow motion.

On the final run-through, Pete asked Dazzle to stop the video at twelve-thirty-five AM. He pointed at a shadow on the garage across the street. "There's somebody behind the Mercedes."

I squinted at the screen. "I don't see it."

He asked Dazzle to enhance the video. Pete got out of his chair and moved in front of the TV. He pointed at a black spot on the garage door. "There's somebody there."

It reminded me of the times when I accompanied Rosie for her sonograms when she was pregnant with Grace and later Tommy. The OB would point out heads, arms, legs, fingers, and other anatomy. I always nodded and smiled, but it looked like a test pattern.

Dazzle spoke up again. "I'll try to enhance it."

Her fingers sprinted across her keyboard as she manipulated the frozen video. She zoomed in and made the picture a little crisper.

"There may be somebody there," I said.

Nady moved next to Pete. "There's definitely somebody there."

Pete pointed at the screen. "He's behind the car." He squinted. "He's wearing an Oakland A's cap."

I remained skeptical. "It doesn't mean that this guy—if he's really there—had anything to do with Moriarty's death."

"Doesn't matter. He's a potential suspect. We don't have to prove that he's the killer. We just need to make a plausible case to suggest it."

Nady wasn't buying it. "It's a stretch."

Also true.

"At the moment," Pete said, "it's all that we have."

"We should ask Freddie about it," I said.

Pete glanced at his watch. "We won't be able to talk to him until tomorrow morning." He turned to Nady. "Is there anything in the police file about this?"

"No." Her eyes were still locked on the TV. "We should ask the DA or the cops to help us identify the guy in the video."

"Not yet," Pete said. "They may not have seen him. If we can identify him first, we may be able to use it to our advantage." He chuckled. "If you're trying to find somebody, you never start with the cops or the DA if they have a vested interest in your *not* finding him."

The voice of practicality. "Who should we talk to?" I asked.
He responded with a sideways grin. "The neighborhood
bartenders."

10

"YOU WON'T HAVE ANY TROUBLE FINDING HIM"

The stocky bartender with spiked blond hair, tattooed arms, and smoker's voice leaned across the bar. "Haven't seen you in a while, Pete."

"Been busy, Brian. How's business?"

"Great. We're finally back to pre-Covid numbers."

"That's terrific." Pete pointed at me. "This is my brother, Mike."

"Brian Holton." His handshake was firm. "What can I get you?"

He didn't have Guinness on tap, so I ordered Drake's. Pete asked for coffee.

"Coming up."

The Horseshoe Tavern was quiet at ten-fifteen on Tuesday night. Opened in 1934, the neighborhood watering hole is one of the few remaining old-time businesses on the otherwise gentrified commercial strip on Chestnut Street. You can still get a shot and a beer at seven AM, but if you're hungry, you have to go to Los Hermanos next door. The top shelf behind the carved wooden bar is filled with trophies from softball and soccer teams sponsored by the "Shoe." The paneled walls are filled with TVs; Giants, Niners, and Warriors memorabilia; and neon beer signs. The light fixtures above the pool tables are adorned with Budweiser logos. The selections in the jukebox range from the Rolling Stones to Taylor Swift.

Holton returned with our drinks. The bar wasn't crowded, so he stuck around to chat.

As always, Pete took the lead. "The place looks good. How are things in the neighborhood?"

"Same as always. The trendy shops come and go. The Shoe is still here."

"You got issues with the homeless?"

"It's a lot worse in the Tenderloin." Holton shrugged. "San Francisco has never been an easy place to run a business. The geniuses at City Hall aren't doing enough about the homeless or keeping the streets clean, and people are pissed off. Maybe we'll have a new mayor in a few weeks and things will change."

"Maybe *you* should run for mayor."

"Maybe I should."

I nursed my beer and kept my mouth shut as the chatty bartender and the stoic PI shot the breeze about sports, business, politics, kids, and life. Even though Pete had met Holton only a couple of times, he made him feel like they were old pals.

Pete deftly slipped into detective mode. "Mike is with the PD's Office. He's representing Freddie Alvarez, the guy accused of killing Frank Moriarty."

Holton tensed. "Oh, yes."

"Freddie's trial starts a week from Monday. Mike had to step in at the last minute to handle it, and I'm helping him. Mind if we ask you a few questions?"

"Uh, sure."

"Did you ever meet Freddie?"

"No."

"But you knew Moriarty?"

"Yes. He used to come in once or twice a week."

Pete feigned surprise. "I've been patronizing the Shoe since before you started working here, Brian. I appreciate the fact that you take care of working guys like me. I'm a little surprised a big shot lawyer like Moriarty used to hang out here."

"We don't check our customers' portfolios before we pour them a beer."

"Good policy."

"Good business. Frank Moriarty was a successful lawyer, but he was never condescending or snooty. He had a stressful job, so he came here to unwind. He'd have a couple of beers and watch the Giants on TV."

"Good customer?"

"Yes. He was respectful to our staff and left a nice tip."

"Good guy?"

Holton paused. "Most of the time. He got a little aggressive when he chatted up younger women. And he had a temper after he had a couple of beers. One time he went off on a customer who accidentally jostled him."

"Did he hit him?"

"No, he just yelled. Frank was a big guy who was used to getting his way. I was able to calm him down pretty quickly. I've had a lot of practice."

I'll bet.

Pete took a sip of coffee. "Did anything really piss him off?"

"Frank loved his cars. He parked his Maserati around the corner one night. When he went back outside, somebody had smashed his windshield. Frank blamed a homeless guy who used to hang out on Chestnut, but the cops couldn't prove it. After that, Frank had a big problem with the homeless."

"Did he ever do anything about it?"

"He called the cops. They didn't do much. It was very frustrating for him." Holton shrugged. "I can't say that I blame him."

"The police reports said that Moriarty was here right before he died."

"He was. I gave my statement to the police and provided a copy of his tab." Holton said that Moriarty came in by himself. "I served him a few beers."

Pete asked about Moriarty's mood that night.

"Nothing out of the ordinary. We talked about the usual stuff: sports, news, politics."

"Did you ask him about the homeless?"

"Nope." Holton grinned. "Don't poke the bear." He confirmed that Moriarty left at twelve-twenty AM. "He said that he was going to walk home." Holton said that he didn't remember anything else about Moriarty's visit. "Just another night at the Shoe."

Pete put his phone on the bar and showed Holton the video of Freddie walking past Shreya Patel's house at twelve-thirty AM. "That's our client."

"I'll take your word for it. I never met him."

Pete then showed him the video of Moriarty walking past the same house a few minutes later.

"That's Frank," Holton said.

Pete pulled up a screenshot of the man and woman who walked by Patel's house at twelve-forty-five. "The police said that they're homeless people who go by the names 'Jack' and 'Jill.'"

"Sorry. I've never seen them."

Pete showed Holton a screenshot of the man crouched behind the Mercedes. "Ever seen this guy with the A's cap?"

Holton studied the picture. "It might be Eddie Reynolds."

"Is he a customer?"

"No."

"Does he work here in the Marina?"

"You might say that." Holton grinned. "He steals cars for a living."

"Do you have any idea where we can find him?"

"425 7th Street."

It was the address of County Jail #2, the Plexiglas-covered facility that was shoehorned between the Hall of Justice and the I-80 Freeway in the Nineties. The cops dubbed it "The Glamour Slammer."

He added, with a grin, "You won't have any trouble finding him."

"How long has he been there?" Pete asked.

"About six months. He got picked up for grand theft auto and breaking into garages."

11

"AFRAID NOT"

The self-assured young man with the buzz cut and a scar running from his left ear to his chin leaned forward, looked at me through the Plexiglas divider, and pressed the closed-circuit phone to his ear. "My lawyer told me not to talk to you."

"You came anyway," I said.

"I have nothing to hide." He added, with a smirk, "I have nothing else to do."

I showed him a photo of the man in the A's cap in front of the house across the street from Moriarty's neighbor. "It looks like you, Eddie."

He grinned. "Afraid not."

At nine-fifteen the following morning, a Wednesday, Pete and I were sitting on one side of the divider, and Eddie Reynolds was on the other side in the airless visitor center in the basement of the Glamour Slammer. Reynolds was a cocky twenty-five-year-old who grew up in the projects near Candlestick Park. He joined a gang when he was in high school and was recruited by a car-theft ring in Hunters Point. His superiors had the wherewithal to pay for a private defense attorney who specializes in representing gang members. His rap sheet included car thefts, breaking and entering, and a DUI. His luck ran out six months ago when an off-duty cop caught him breaking into a car on Potrero Hill. We defense lawyers like to say that there's no such thing as an open-and-shut case, but this was about as close as it gets. Eddie's lawyer cut a quick deal with the DA.

Pete took the handpiece from me and showed him a photo of the man and woman known as "Jack and Jill." "They walked by the same house while you were hiding across the street. Do you recognize them?"

"I wasn't across the street. And I don't recognize them."

"A few minutes later, a man named Frank Moriarty was murdered around the corner. These people may be your alibi."

"I wasn't there. I don't know who they are. And I sure as hell didn't kill anybody." He fingered the sleeve of his orange jumpsuit. "If that's all you have, I think we're done."

"Did you ever meet Moriarty?"

"No."

"You sure?"

"Yes."

"Did you ever try to break into his garage?"

"No."

Pete leaned forward and lowered his voice. "How much longer are you here?"

"Nine hundred and twenty days. Less with good behavior."

"I take it this means that you took a deal?"

"Yes."

"Where did you get picked up?" Pete asked, already knowing the answer.

"Potrero Hill."

"Bad luck."

"Bad timing."

"Yeah." Pete's tone remained nonconfrontational. "You got plans after you get out?"

"I have a job waiting for me."

"Good for you." Pete showed him the video again. "Sure looks like you."

"You're still mistaken."

"I talked to one of my friends at Northern Station. He showed me the inventory of clothing that you were wearing when you were arrested. It included an A's cap."

"Coincidence."

"You were seen a block from the spot where Frank Moriarty was killed."

"Another coincidence. I wasn't there."

"Moriarty walked by the same spot four minutes after this video was taken."

"Yet another coincidence. And I still wasn't there."

"You saw a rich guy walk down the street and turn the corner, didn't you?"

"No."

"You followed him, didn't you?"

"No."

"And you tried to rob him. When he resisted, you whacked him with a piece of rebar, didn't you?"

"No, I didn't." The smirk returned to Reynolds's face. "It wasn't me. And even if it was, you have no video showing me walking around the corner."

True.

Pete mimicked Reynolds's smirk. "The area shown in this video is small. You could have stayed behind the car, and walked in the shadows, without being seen."

"Afraid not."

"You'll get a better deal if you tell the truth."

"You're out of your mind."

Pete took it in stride. "Are you going to be around in a couple of weeks?"

"I'm not going anywhere."

"Good." He pointed his thumb at me. "We delivered a subpoena to your lawyer. We brought a copy for you. Mike needs you to testify at Freddie Alvarez's trial."

"I'm not sure that it was a great idea to go after Reynolds," I said.

Pete grinned. "I thought you might like a preview of his testimony."

We were standing in the parking lot between the Glamour Slammer and the Hall of Justice. The wind was whipping between the buildings.

"Did you consider the possibility that I might want to ambush him in court?" I asked.

"Yes. You can still go after him at trial. I thought you'd want to see what you're dealing with."

I did. "How do you think he'll present in court?"

"Poorly. He's arrogant. The jury won't like him."

Probably true. It may not matter. His lawyer will probably tell him to take the Fifth if I ask him any hard questions. "Who did you talk to at Northern Station about the A's cap?"

"Nobody." Pete's grin widened. "I wanted to see how he would react."

"Nice bluff."

"I thought so. Unfortunately, it doesn't prove that it was Reynolds in the video. Or that he killed Moriarty."

"We don't need to prove it, Pete. We just need to convince one juror that it's possible that it was Reynolds."

"You're a good lawyer, Mick. You'll find a way."

"Where to now?"

"Let's go see Freddie."

12

"TRY THE PRESIDIO"

Freddie studied the photo of the man in the A's cap that I showed him. "I don't know him."

"His name is Eddie Reynolds," I said. "The photo was taken around the corner from Moriarty's house on the morning that he died. He may have been looking to steal a car or break into a garage. He pled guilty and cut a deal for grand theft auto on an unrelated matter."

He looked at the photo again. "I didn't see him on the morning that Moriarty died."

The fluorescent light buzzed in the attorney-client consultation room in the basement of San Bruno Jail where Freddie, Pete, and I were sitting. I told Freddie that the guards could listen to us, so we had to be discreet.

"You sure you've never seen him?" I asked.

"If you think it would help my case, I'll testify that I did."

Afraid not. "I can't let you do that, Freddie."

"You mean that you *won't* let me do it." He looked at the photo again. "I think I saw him casing garages in the Marina."

"I don't believe you."

"It's the truth."

No, it isn't. "We'll discuss it again if it looks like we'll have to put you on the stand."

"I want to testify."

"It's too risky."

Pete showed Freddie a photo of Jack and Jill. "This was taken by the same security camera around the corner from Moriarty's house. Have you ever seen them?"

A look of recognition crossed Freddie's face. "Yes. They went by 'Jack' and 'Jill.' I don't know if those are their real names. They were together, but they might have been a 'street couple.'"

"What's that?"

"Two people who pair up and look out for each other, but it isn't necessarily romantic. Sometimes people do it for companionship and protection. I was part of a street couple for a few months. It was good until it wasn't."

"Did you ever talk to them?" Pete asked.

"Once. Jack was about twenty years older than Jill. He was a vet who served in Afghanistan and had PTSD. He was on heroin. She used to be a teacher who got hooked on crack. It looked like both of them had been living on the street for a while. They asked me if I knew where Jack could find heroin and Jill could get crack. I gave them some names in the Tenderloin."

"Did they have criminal records?"

"I don't know."

"Any evidence that either of them might have been violent?"

"I don't know that, either."

"Do you know where they were staying?"

"Try the Presidio."

"It's a big place."

"They were staying near the Lombard Street Gate. Start there and work west."

The Presidio extends from the Palace of Fine Arts to the Golden Gate Bridge. It was a military base from 1776 until 1994, when the Army transferred it to the National Park Service. Nowadays, most of the historic buildings have been restored and leased out as housing and offices. About five thousand residents live in the former officers' housing, and businesses and nonprofits fill the commercial space. The main post has been restored, and there are several hotels and restaurants along with a Disney Museum, a golf course, and a military cemetery. Lucasfilm built its corporate headquarters on the site of the old Letterman Military Hospital.

"Do you have any idea if they're still together?" Pete asked.

"Not a clue."

My phone vibrated as I was driving north on I-280 toward the office. Nady's name appeared on the display. I answered on the first ring using the hands-free.

"Did Freddie know Reynolds?" she asked.

"First, he said that he didn't recognize him. Then he changed his story when he thought it might help his case."

"Do you believe him?"

"No, and I'm not going to let him testify that he did."

"What about Jack and Jill?"

"He talked to them once." I summarized Freddie's description of the so-called "street couple." "I want to add Reynolds and Jack and Jill to our witness list."

"Do you want me to inform the DA?"

"Not yet. Let's wait until the last minute. I sent Pete down to the Presidio to look for Jack and Jill."

"How soon can you get to North Beach?"

"Twenty minutes."

"Meet me at Caffé Trieste. Moriarty's third ex-wife is willing to talk to us."

13

"HE WAS AN ANGRY DRUNK"

Moriarty's third ex-wife took a sip of her soy latte. "Frank was a complicated guy," she said.

The aroma of coffee and homemade pastries enveloped the paneled room of Caffè Trieste, which has anchored the corner of Grant Avenue and Vallejo Street in North Beach since 1956, when "Papa Gianni" Giotta introduced espresso drinks to the West Coast. The inviting café soon filled with the neighborhood's writers and beat poets, including Lawrence Ferlinghetti, Jack Kerouac, and Allen Ginsberg. Its walls are covered with yellowed black-and-white photos of the Giotta family, longtime customers, and celebrities such as Francis Coppola, who wrote parts of the screenplay to *The Godfather* at a table in the back. As always, opera music played through its sound system.

"How long were you and Frank married?" Nady asked.

"Not long." Wendy Klein took a bite of her pastry. "I realized that it was a mistake after six months. It was the third marriage for each of us. I don't think Frank was surprised when I told him that I wanted out. Our split was quick and amicable. We were both lawyers. We knew the importance of a good prenup."

Rosie and I didn't need one. There was nothing to split.

Klein, Nady, and I were sitting at a table in the back corner of Caffè Trieste at ten-thirty on Wednesday morning. According to the State Bar's website, Klein was sixty. Her shoulder-length hair was a frizzy bleached blonde, her eyes were crystal blue, and her figure reflected serious time at the gym. Her perfect skin suggested that she had invested in Botox. If you listened carefully, you could still detect a hint of her native Brooklyn as she spoke in the precise sound bites commonly used by lawyers. She had gone to college at Brandeis and graduated at the top of her class at Columbia Law. She moved to San Francisco after graduation and never left.

Nady kept her voice even. "How did you and Frank meet?"

"We were associates at the Brobeck firm years ago. We were married to other people at the time, but there was always an attraction. Frank was charismatic, charming, and funny. He was also an iconoclast, so he wasn't a great fit at a white-shoe law firm. Eventually, he went out on his own and became a wildly successful personal injury lawyer. I left Brobeck a few years later and started a boutique law firm to handle real estate, zoning, and land use matters. We stayed in touch over the years. About five years ago, we were both divorced again. We went out for a few months and decided to get married. I think both of us knew that it probably wouldn't last, but we had a lot of fun for a while."

I appreciated Klein's forthrightness, but I hadn't expected her to be quite so even-tempered about her divorce. Rosie and I were far more emotional.

"When did you separate?" Nady asked.

"Two years before Frank was killed."

"You moved in with him in the Marina?"

"Yes." Klein's eyes glowed. "It was a really nice house that Frank had remodeled from top to bottom." She said that while she was living with Moriarty, she rented out her condo on Russian Hill. "After we split up, I moved back in."

Nady spent the next ten minutes lobbing softballs at Klein, who enjoyed talking about herself. She had two grown children from her first marriage. One was an investment banker in New York. The other was a social worker in Oakland. She spent the summer at her villa in Tuscany, and December and January at her condo at Kiahuna Plantation in Kauai. All things considered, it sounded pretty good to be Wendy Klein.

Nady's expression turned serious. "How did Frank's children feel about your marriage?"

NEVER PLEAD GUILTY   75

"They weren't happy about it, but we never saw them. They didn't attend our wedding, and they spent the holidays with their mother. Frank didn't talk to them very much." She noted that her kids weren't crazy about her marriage to Moriarty, either.

Nady asked whether the divorce was acrimonious.

"Not really. Frank saw it coming. For all his bluster, he was pretty self-aware."

"It still must have been sad for you when he passed away."

"It was." Klein didn't elaborate.

"Do you know anything about what happened?"

"Only what I've read in the papers."

"Did you talk to the police?"

"Yes." She shrugged. "I was out of town when Frank was killed. I have no information about what happened. That's exactly what I told the police."

It's exactly what I expected you to say.

Nady looked my way, and I picked up the cue.

"You said that Frank was a complicated guy."

"He was."

"How so?"

"He was a world-class trial lawyer. He would do almost anything for his clients."

"Bend the rules?"

"A little. Most of the time he didn't need to. He was that good. I have never seen anybody relate to a jury as well as Frank did. He was a natural storyteller. He was hard-nosed when he needed to be and charming when he wanted to be. He made each juror think that he was talking only to them. It wasn't just natural charisma, either. He rehearsed everything—especially the stuff that sounded spontaneous. Nobody was better prepared. That's why he was so hard to beat."

"And in his personal life?"

Her face scrunched. "Same deal. He was charismatic and charming. He was also very demanding. He had a big ego. He was used to having things his way. He didn't play well with others. That's the primary reason that he left the big law firm. At times, he was condescending or flat-out insulting. It wasn't just a coincidence that he was divorced three times and his kids stopped talking to him."

"How did he act when he was under stress?"

"Badly. It was no secret that he had a temper. It was exacerbated when he drank."

"Did he drink a lot?"

"It got worse over the years. I didn't realize how bad it was until after we got married. He was an angry drunk."

"Abusive?"

"At times."

"Physically?"

"He put his hands on me twice. The first time, I called the cops. I told Frank that I wouldn't press charges if he promised never to do it again. The second time, I filed for divorce."

Good call. "Was he ever unfaithful?"

"Yes."

"Did you hire a private investigator?"

"Yes."

"Would you mind giving us his name?"

"I'll get you his information."

"How did he get along with his friends and neighbors?"

"Fine, most of the time. He was the life of the party at the Olympic Club. He could be very generous. He once paid for cancer treatments for his secretary's daughter. On the other hand, he could be litigious and nasty. He filed dozens of lawsuits against his neighbors. Everything was hand-to-hand combat. He sued his neighbor, Henry Keller, at least a dozen times. They fought about property line disputes, additions to their houses, noise, dust. Frank handled all of the suits himself. Most of the time, he got what he wanted."

"We understand that Mr. Keller found the body. Do you think he might have been involved in Frank's death?"

Klein smiled. "I wouldn't have blamed him after all the grief that Frank put him through, but I can't imagine he did. Henry is probably worth a billion dollars. He has a temper, too, but I don't think he would have risked everything to hurt Frank."

Nady spoke up again. "We heard that Frank had a problem with the homeless in the Marina."

"If you had a seven-million-dollar house, you would have gotten upset if homeless people were urinating on your garage door."

Fair point.

"Did he ever do anything about it?" Nady asked.

"He called the cops, but they didn't do anything. If he saw homeless people outside, he would go out and yell at them to leave. Frank was intimidating. Most of the time, they did."

"Did he ever get physical?"

"On several occasions when he saw a homeless person in his driveway, I saw him go outside with a baseball bat. As far as I know, he never used it."

"That was enlightening," Nady said.

"Some of the information that Klein provided may be useful," I replied.

We were still sitting in the back of Caffé Trieste. Klein had left a few minutes earlier. The line outside the door now extended down the block.

"Maybe Moriarty came after Freddie with a baseball bat," I said.

"There was nothing in the record about a bat at the scene. Even if there was, Freddie told us that he didn't act in self-defense. Are you heading back to the office?"

"I'm going to talk to the neighbor who found Moriarty's body."

14

"WAS HE A GOOD NEIGHBOR?"

"I love your office," I lied.

Henry Keller responded with a phony smile. "Thank you, Mr. Daley."

"Mike."

"Henry."

Fine. "I'm a little surprised that the headquarters of Keller Properties isn't located at the top of one of the big office towers downtown."

He pointed at the exposed brick wall in his corner office on the second floor of a refurbished post-Earthquake era building on Pacific Avenue in Jackson Square between the Financial District and North Beach. "I was in my office on the fiftieth floor of the Bank of America Building when the Loma Prieta earthquake hit in 1989. Since then, I've preferred to work closer to the ground. This was the first building that I bought forty years ago. In addition to the historic vibe, it has sentimental value."

I feigned admiration of the century-old flourishes in an historic building that was undoubtedly wired for the twenty-first century. "You did a nice job."

"Thank you. We have an excellent team."

Keller was a diminutive man in his late sixties with a cherubic face, a full head of perfectly-coiffed hair dyed an unnatural reddish brown, a salt-and-pepper goatee, and an impish smile. He reminded me of the partners at my old law firm who always had a smile and an off-color joke, played a wicked game of cribbage at the Pacific Union Club, and wouldn't hesitate to shiv you over a half percentage point during the annual battle over partner compensation. His clothing was high-end business casual: a Brunello Cucinelli navy blazer with a maroon pocket square, a powder-blue Ralph Lauren dress shirt, and a pair of Brooks Brothers khakis.

His immaculate office was furnished with meticulous attention to detail: a custom mahogany desk with matching credenza and chairs, a hand-carved conference table topped with a scale model of a century-old building near the Hall of Justice that his firm was remodeling, and a bookcase filled with first editions by Bay Area authors. The artwork was modern and expensive. The only personal item was a framed photo of a smiling Keller along with his perfect wife and their four perfect adult children.

I looked at the bookcase. "Impressive collection."

"Thank you. I'm a Bay Area history and literature aficionado. I'm a fourth-generation native of the City. My great-grandparents settled in the Mission. My grandparents and parents lived in Sea Cliff. I'm in the Marina."

I can play this game, too. "I'm second-generation. My grandparents lived in the Mission. My parents moved to the Avenues when I was a kid." I didn't mention that my dad was a cop who did a couple of tours in the Tenderloin and Chinatown to pick up enough "gratuities" from the local business owners to scratch together a down payment on our modest house in the Sunset.

We spent a few minutes going through the obligatory exchange of information about our respective high schools, colleges, and grad schools. When I told him that I went to S.I., he pulled trump by saying that he went to the private University High School. I went to Cal, he went to Stanford. We finally found common ground when I told him that I went to law school at Berkeley. He said that he got his MBA at Cal, although he roots for Stanford at Big Game. He was unimpressed when I told him that Grace graduated from USC and Tommy was at Cal. He quickly let me know that his four kids all attended Ivy League colleges. When I didn't ask which ones, he immediately volunteered that one went to Harvard, the second to Penn, and his twin daughters attended Brown. The Harvard grad worked for a private equity firm in New York. The Penn alum worked for Keller Properties. The Brown alums were a teacher and a social worker. He lamented the fact that neither made much money.

I finally capitulated. "Sounds like you have a wonderful family."

He was pleased at his triumph in the prestige battle. "Thank you."

I pointed at the model of the building on the table. "Looks like a big project."

"We're converting a pre-Earthquake blacksmith shop into offices. The building is currently used as a warehouse. Our team is doing an exceptional job."

"How big is your real estate portfolio?"

"More than a billion dollars' worth." He sat up taller. "It's a mix of office space and residential in major metropolitan areas. Our biggest footprint is here in the Bay Area. We also have properties in New York, Miami, Seattle, and Chicago." He said that his firm specialized in renovating older buildings. "It's more creative than building new office towers."

I played along. "It must be very rewarding."

"It is."

And very lucrative.

His fake smile and the phony grandfather's tone disappeared. "You wanted to talk about Frank Moriarty?"

"Yes." I explained that I had picked up the case on short notice. "You're on the prosecution's witness list."

"I know."

"I understand that you discovered Mr. Moriarty's body."

"I did."

"It must have been very upsetting for you."

"It was."

Keller's terse answers indicated that he would be a strong witness. He was smart, and he had been involved in litigation on many occasions. He had been coached to answer only the questions posed and not volunteer any additional information. It seemed unlikely that he would lose his composure under intense questioning.

"Would you mind telling me what you saw when you found Mr. Moriarty's body?"

"I gave the police a full statement."

That's undoubtedly true, but you didn't answer my question. "You found the body when you took your trash cans out to the curb?"

"Correct. Frank was lying face down on the driveway. The back of his head was bloody. Your client was passed out about two feet away. There was a bloody piece of rebar next to your client's right hand." He said that he called 9-1-1 immediately and tried to help Moriarty. "I did what I could, but I couldn't find a pulse."

"How soon did the police arrive?"

"Within ten minutes. The EMTs arrived shortly thereafter. It was chaotic. Obviously, I didn't see your client kill Frank."

Obviously.

He quickly added, "I gave my statement to Officer Dito and Inspector Wong. I was, of course, fully cooperative."

Of course.

I spent fifteen minutes asking detailed questions about what he saw at the scene. To his credit, Keller answered every one. He measured his words carefully, and he didn't become defensive.

I asked him how long he had known Moriarty.

"We were neighbors for twenty years. When he first moved into the house next door, I hired him to handle some legal work. He was tenacious, and he got an excellent result."

"Was he a good neighbor?"

"No." A hesitation. "Everything that made him a terrific lawyer made him a difficult neighbor. Frank was brilliant, strategic, gregarious, and funny. He was also the most combative person I've ever known. He responded to every perceived slight by filing a lawsuit." He eyed me. "You're a lawyer. You know how the system works. Anybody with a law degree and the money for the filing fee can file a lawsuit whenever they want."

I nodded in sympathy. "That's true."

"Frank was a smart lawyer who knew how to work the system to his advantage. He knew that it would cost thousands of dollars in attorneys' fees just to get a frivolous lawsuit dismissed. If you and I had a dispute over a property line or construction noise, we would sit down and work it out. Frank would file a lawsuit."

"I take it that you were on the receiving end of some of these legal actions?"

"He sued all of his neighbors. I lived next door, so I got hit the most."

"How many times did he sue you?"

He looked up at the ceiling as if to suggest that he was running a mental calculation. "At least a dozen times. He sued me over a property line dispute, construction noise, the location of a dumpster when I was having some work done, the removal of a tree, and the expansion of my backyard patio. When I wanted to put a deck on the roof, he tied me up in litigation for ten years. I finally got my deck, but the legal fees were a million dollars."

"That must have been infuriating."

"It was. It was especially upsetting for my wife." He flashed a conspiratorial grin. "You know how it goes. Unhappy wife, unhappy life."

"I know." *Seriously?* "Did you ever get tired of it?"

"Yes. About five years ago, I finally told Frank that he would have to communicate with me through my lawyer. It was expensive, but it made my life a lot easier."

"Was he as combative with your neighbors?"

"Absolutely. I don't think that anybody was still talking to him by the time he died."

Not surprising. I showed him a photo of Reynolds. "Do you recognize him?"

"Afraid not."

"His name is Eddie Reynolds. He was spotted in a video taken by Shreya Patel's security camera on the morning that Mr. Moriarty died. We think he was looking to steal a car or break into a garage. He's at County Jail serving time for grand theft auto."

He studied the photo. "I've never seen him."

I showed him the video of Jack and Jill. He said that he didn't recognize them, either.

"We understand that Mr. Moriarty had a serious issue with the homeless in the neighborhood," I said. "We heard that he would threaten them with a baseball bat."

"I heard the same thing, but I never saw him do it."

"Do you think he threatened my client?"

"I don't know."

Good answer. "Do you see a lot of homeless people in your corner of the Marina?"

"A few. I've been told that there's a substantial homeless population living in the Presidio."

"Is it possible that somebody from a homeless encampment came over and attacked Mr. Moriarty?"

"Anything is possible, Mr. Daley. On the other hand, I have no knowledge that somebody did. If you ask me about it in court, that's exactly what I plan to say."

Fair enough. I showed him a photo of Freddie. "Recognize him?"

"Yes. I've seen his photo in the papers."

"Did you ever talk to him?"

"No."

"Did you ever see him in the neighborhood?"

"Just once."

Uh-oh. "When?"

"A couple of nights before Frank died. Frank must have seen your client on his driveway. Frank went outside and yelled at him. The noise woke me up, so I went to see what was going on. Frank told your client to get the hell off his property. Your client told him that he would beat the crap out of him if he didn't leave him alone. Eventually, your client backed off and left."

"You're absolutely sure that it was Freddie?"

"Absolutely."

"It was the middle of the night. Is it possible that you might have mistaken him for somebody else?"

"Absolutely not."

Freddie's voice filled with anger. "Keller is lying."

I stared at him across the table in the attorney-client consultation room at San Bruno Jail. "You're sure?"

"I'm sure."

"Why would he lie?"

Freddie held up his hands in frustration. "To protect himself."

"You think he killed Moriarty?"

"I don't know. I do know that I didn't."

Freddie was more animated than I had ever seen him. The reality that trial was starting in less than two weeks was hitting him hard.

"It was late at night," I said. "Is it possible that he mistook somebody else for you?"

"Anything's possible, Mike. I have no idea how we can prove it."

Neither do I, unless we can find a witness to cast doubt upon Keller's claim.

"Let me see what else I can find," I said to Freddie.

"Right." His tone was skeptical. "Who are you going to talk to next?"

"Shreya Patel."

15

"HE HATED THEM"

"Thank you for making time to see me," I said.

Shreya Patel forced a smile. "You're welcome, Mr. Daley."

At three-forty-five that same afternoon, we were sitting in her antiseptic office in a mid-rise office building on Terry A. Francois Boulevard, which separated the new UCSF Mission Bay Medical Campus from the Bay. Her desk, credenza, file cabinet, and conference table were made of bleached wood. The chairs and sofa were black leather with steel frames. The artwork was garishly modern. The only personal item was a framed photo of Patel's twelve-year-old daughter, who bore a striking resemblance to her mother—minus the designer clothes and abundant makeup.

"I love your space," I lied. "When did you move in?"

"About six months ago. It's nice to be in a new building."

Patel's office was on the eastern edge of the steel-and-glass city-within-a-city that's sprung up south of downtown over the last thirty years in what used to be an empty expanse of rusted railyards. When the UCSF Medical Center ran out of room to expand its original complex on Parnassus Avenue below Mount Sutro, it partnered with the City and several private developers—including Henry Keller and the Giants—to build a new neighborhood of gleaming medical, biomedical research, office, and residential buildings bookended by the ballpark to the north and Chase Center to the South.

I admired her unobstructed view extending from the Bay Bridge to Chase Center. "Are you a Warriors fan?"

"I'm a part-owner."

I'm jealous. "Do you have courtside seats?"

"Two rows behind the Warriors bench."

Now I'm really jealous.

Patel's intense brown eyes sat between high cheekbones and a severe pixie cut. She was forty-two, divorced, with a twelve-year-old daughter. Her ex-husband was a scientist at Genentech.

We exchanged stilted small talk for a few minutes. She confirmed the basic biographical information that Nady and I had gleaned from the Internet. The Los Altos native was the daughter of a chemistry professor and a university administrator. Undergrad degree in biochemistry from Princeton followed by a Master's, PhD, and MBA from Stanford. She spent ten years at Genentech, followed by stints at Kleiner Perkins and Andreessen Horowitz. She had formed Patel Ventures five years earlier with former colleagues from Genentech.

"Why did you leave Andreessen?" I asked.

"I wanted something small, nimble, and focused on life sciences. We have only four partners. Everybody has an advanced degree in biochemistry. We're very selective in our investments. Our goal is to fund companies that will make a meaningful difference."

"Like finding a cure for cancer?"

"Exactly."

Very admirable. And you probably wouldn't be heartbroken if you also make boatloads of money. I pointed at the photo of her daughter. "Where does she go to school?"

"Hamlin."

I'm not surprised. Hamlin School for Girls in Pacific Heights is one of the most prestigious private schools in the Bay Area. Tuition runs about fifty grand a year.

"Is she showing signs of becoming a teenager?" I asked.

"I'm afraid so."

I gave her a sympathetic smile. "Nobody gets through the teenage years unscathed, but you'll be fine. Our daughter just turned twenty-seven. My ex-wife took the brunt of her high school years. It gets easier after they're out of college."

"Good to hear." She glanced at her watch—the signal that the chitchat was over. "You had some questions about Frank Moriarty?"

"Yes. I'm representing Freddie Alvarez. I understand that you live around the corner from Mr. Moriarty's house."

"I do. We were neighbors for about ten years. I didn't know him well. He lived by himself after his last divorce."

"Were you at home on the night that Mr. Moriarty died?"

"Yes." She lowered her voice. "I will tell you what I told the police. I didn't see or hear anything that night. Neither did my daughter." She said that she woke up at six AM and saw police cars on the street. "I made sure that my daughter was okay. Then I went outside to see what was going on. That's when I found out that Frank was dead."

"Did you see anybody or notice anything unusual during the night?"

"No."

"Did you ever see my client in the neighborhood?"

A shrug. "Once or twice. He never gave me any trouble."

"The police provided us with a security video taken by your camera on the morning that Mr. Moriarty died."

"They asked the neighbors for information, so I gave them my security video. Your client walked by my house around twelve-thirty AM."

"Did you see him?"

"Just in the video."

I pulled out my phone and showed her the video of Eddie Reynolds lurking in the driveway across the street. "His name is Eddie Reynolds. He was recently arrested for stealing cars and breaking into garages."

"I've never seen him."

I showed her the video of Jack and Jill. "Have you ever seen them?"

"Afraid not."

She was becoming impatient, so I moved in another direction. "Was Mr. Moriarty a nice guy?"

"He was fine."

"Did he ever give you any trouble?"

"Not really." She waited a beat. "He had a lot of work done on his house. There were always trucks, dumpsters, and portable toilets in front of his house. The contractors started early, and there was a lot of dust. The noise woke up my daughter. I talked to him about it a couple of times. He said that he would do something about it, but he never did."

"I take it that this didn't make him terribly popular with the rest of his neighbors?"

"Correct."

"Did anybody else ever complain?"

"Henry Keller got into it with Frank over the years. Frank sued Henry at least a dozen times. It was a running joke on the block. They finally stopped talking to each other."

"Do you know Mr. Keller pretty well?"

"Not really. He always says hello when I see him, but we don't socialize." She eyed me. "Are you suggesting that a billionaire real estate developer killed his neighbor over a bunch of nuisance lawsuits?"

"Seems unlikely." *You never know.* "Have you ever had any trouble with the homeless?"

"Occasionally. A guy was sleeping on my driveway a few months ago. I asked him to leave, and he did."

"How did Mr. Moriarty feel about them?"

"He hated them."

Don't feel compelled to sugarcoat it. "Do you know what set him off?"

"A series of incidents. He found a homeless man sleeping on his front porch after he got home from a trip to Italy. He yelled at the guy to leave, but he didn't. Frank went inside his house and came back with a baseball bat. I don't think he really intended to hit him, but he definitely wanted to scare him. The guy finally left. Then he got really upset after the Cybertruck incident."

"The Cybertruck incident?"

She couldn't hide a grin. "I'm surprised that nobody else mentioned it. Frank bought the first Cybertruck in San Francisco. He paid extra so that it was delivered a few weeks early. He drove it home and parked it in his driveway where everybody could see it. Later that night, he saw a homeless man urinating on his bumper. Frank was furious. I think he chased the guy all the way to the Marina Green, but he didn't catch him. He called the cops, but they couldn't find him."

It took all of my self-control not to laugh. I opted for understatement. "It must have been very frustrating."

"It was." She chuckled. "I think those cars are ugly, but I can understand why Frank was upset. After that, he made no attempt to hide his contempt for the homeless."

"Did he ever hit anybody?"

"Not that I saw. I think he just yelled at them." She glanced at her watch. "I have another meeting, Mr. Daley."

"I trust that the DA has informed you that you're on her witness list?"

"Yes. She wants me to confirm that I provided the security video showing your client walking by my house." Another look at her watch. "I guess I'll see you in court."

At eight-forty-five that same night, I was sitting in my office and reading draft jury questionnaires when Pete's name appeared on my phone.

"Did you get anything from Patel?" he asked.

"Not much." I summarized my conversation. "Did you hear about the 'Cybertruck incident'?"

"The Cybertruck incident?"

"Moriarty bought the first Cybertruck in San Francisco. He parked it in his driveway and saw a homeless guy pissing on his bumper."

My brother has an acerbic sense of humor, but he almost never laughs. In this case, he couldn't contain himself, and he let out a throaty laugh. "Moriarty bought a douchebag car, and a homeless guy pissed on it?"

"Yes."

He was still laughing. "Serves him right, although I suppose it could have been an honest mistake."

"How do you figure, Pete?"

"Cybertrucks look like urinals with wheels."

It was my turn to laugh.

His tone turned serious. "Meet me at Mel's on Lombard. I found Jack."

Progress. "Is he still together with Jill?"

"No."

"Any sign of her?"

"Still looking."

16

"I HAVE NO IDEA"

Jack Allen took a bite of his second cheeseburger, gobbled a handful of fries, and washed it down with a long draw of his chocolate shake. "Thanks for dinner."

Pete took a sip of coffee. "You're welcome, Jack. You want another burger?"

"Sounds good."

"Anything else?"

"The fried chicken is good."

Pete summoned our harried server and ordered a third burger for Jack to eat and a fourth one to take out along with an order of chicken.

Pete leaned forward. "I take it that you've eaten here?"

Allen nodded. "I know one of the dishwashers. He saves leftovers for me sometimes."

He was tall—at least six-two. I pegged him to be in his mid-fifties, but it's hard to tell with people who live on the street. His gray hair was cut short. His leathery face was covered with stubble. His left eye was bloodshot, his right eye twitched. His black Giants hoodie was old but clean, jeans worn, boots scuffed.

"How long have you lived on the street?" I asked.

"On and off for about ten years."

"We can help you get a room in a shelter."

"I don't do shelters anymore. Too many rules."

I tried.

At nine-forty-five PM, the aroma of burgers, fries, onion rings, and fried chicken enveloped us as Pete, Jack, and I sat in a booth in Mel's Drive-In, a Fifties-style diner on Lombard between Steiner and Fillmore, a short walk from Moriarty's house. Mel Weiss and Harold Dobbs opened their original drive-in in 1947 on South Van Ness, now the site of an upscale high-rise apartment building. It became famous as "Burger City" in *American Graffiti*. Mel's quickly expanded to two dozen locations, but by 1972, competition from fast-food chains led to a substantial drop in business. Weiss and Dobbs sold Mel's to Foster's, which went bankrupt shortly thereafter.

In 1985, Weiss's son opened the first new-generation Mel's on Lombard. The neon-lit retro diner has the obligatory counter, booths, and jukeboxes. The burgers and fried chicken are a cut above traditional diner fare. They now have locations on Van Ness and Geary and in L.A. I still think the burgers were better at the long-departed Zim's on Taraval, Clown Alley on Columbus, and Hippo Hamburgers on Van Ness, but that may reflect rosy memories of simpler times. In a nod to twenty-first century tastes, you can now get plant-based burgers and cappuccinos at the new Mel's.

Pete lobbed a softball to try to get Jack talking. "You from around here?"

"Vallejo. My dad was a mechanic at Mare Island Naval Base, but he died in an auto accident when I was eleven. My mom worked at the base until it closed in 1996. She passed away about ten years ago from cancer."

"I'm sorry."

"Thank you. I went into the Army after I graduated high school." He said that he served in Iraq and Afghanistan. "I was discharged in 2008 right before the Great Recession. I was dealing with PTSD." He said that he got hooked on heroin and ended up on the street. "Once you live without a roof, it's hard to recover."

Sad, but true.

"You still doing heroin?" Pete asked.

"Not as much as I used to."

"We can help you get into treatment."

"I'll get back to you." In response to Pete's question, Jack said that he had lived in Civic Center Plaza, Golden Gate Park, and the Tenderloin. "You try to find someplace safe, and you move when you have to."

"I found you in the Presidio."

"I had to get out of the TL. It's always been bad, but now the streets are flooded with fentanyl."

"You're able to get heroin in the Presidio?"

"You can get stuff almost anywhere nowadays."

Also sad, but true.

I listened as Pete and Jack conversed like old friends. Pete was masterful at putting people at ease. Jack liked talking about himself. He said that he was married once when he was in the Army, but it lasted only a year. No kids. No other family. He worked as a mechanic after he was discharged, but he had trouble keeping a job. He had stayed in shelters for short periods, but didn't like the rules. He was able to get clean twice, but it didn't last. He had a studio apartment in the Tenderloin for six months, but the building was torn down, and he ended up back on the street. He spent the Covid years living in his tent and staying away from people. He acknowledged that he was lucky to survive.

After another round of burgers, Pete decided to ease Jack into the matters at hand. "Mike is a Public Defender. He's representing Freddie Alvarez."

Jack's expression turned circumspect. "Uh-huh."

"Do you know Freddie?"

"I might have met him once or twice. You meet a lot of people on the street."

"He's accused of killing a man named Frank Moriarty, who lived on Baker Street across from the Palace of Fine Arts. Freddie's trial starts a week from Monday."

"I don't know anything about it."

Pete pulled out his phone and showed him a picture of Eddie Reynolds. "This was taken by a security camera around the corner from Moriarty's house on the night that he died. Do you recognize this guy?"

Jack put on a pair of scratched reading glasses and studied the photo. "Afraid not."

Pete showed him the video of himself and Jill. "This was taken a few minutes later by the same camera. That's you and Jill, isn't it?"

"Yes."

"What were you doing there at twelve-thirty AM?"

"Walking back to the Presidio. We got leftovers from Super Duper Burgers on Chestnut, and we collected some empty bottles to cash in at the recycling center."

"Does Jill have a last name?"

"Harris."

"Is that her real name?"

"As far as I know."

"Were you together?"

"Yes. It wasn't really a romantic thing. We looked after each other."

"Are you still together?"

"No." Jack took a drink of his shake. "We met in the Haight when I was living in Golden Gate Park. She grew up in the Fillmore. She said that she used to be a teacher, but I don't know if that was true. She got hooked on painkillers after she had surgery to fix a knee problem. Then she started doing crack and lost her job. She moved in with her sister in the Haight. The sister couldn't deal with Jill's crack habit, so she threw her out. We looked after each other for a few months, but it didn't last. I was doing a lot of smack, and she was doing a lot of crack. Neither of us was easy to deal with at the time. I was sad when she took off, but I understand why she did."

"Where did she go?" Pete asked.

"I have no idea. Somebody said that they saw her in the Tenderloin. Another person told me that she was going to live with her cousin in L.A."

"When was the last time that you saw her?"

"Almost a year ago."

Pete looked my way. It was my turn.

"The homicide inspector in charge of the investigation told us that she tracked you and Jill down in the Presidio to ask you about Moriarty's death."

"She did. I think it was an Asian woman. Inspector Wang, maybe."

"Wong?" I said.

"I think that was it. We told her that we didn't walk by Moriarty's house, and we didn't see anything. Jill and I walked through the park at the Palace of Fine Arts on our way back to the Presidio."

Pete spoke up again. "Did you know Moriarty?"

"No."

"We heard that he was hard on the homeless. Somebody said that he used to chase them out of his driveway with a baseball bat."

A hesitation. "Word was out on the street to avoid his house."

"Did he ever come after you and Jill?"

"No."

I lowered my voice. "I need you to testify at Freddie's trial."

"I don't do trials."

You do now. I slid a subpoena across the table. "You are legally required to appear in court."

He glared at me. "I agreed to talk to you tonight out of the goodness of my heart. And now you're serving me with a subpoena?"

Yes. "I would really appreciate your assistance, Jack."

"And if I don't show up?"

"The judge can hold you in contempt." *And throw you in jail until you show up.* "If you cooperate, I might be able to pay you for your time in court."

"How much?"

"A hundred dollars plus cab fare."

"Not enough."

"You understand that we are under no obligation to pay you, right?"

"Not enough."

"I might be able to get you two hundred."

"Still not enough."

You have no choice, but I don't want to antagonize you more than I have to. "We'll get you a place to stay and provide you with meals until you need to be in court."

"I don't do shelters."

"We'll get you a room in a motel."

"You'll pay for it?"

"Yes." *It helps that I'm in charge of the budget for the PD's Office.*

"A nice one?" he asked.

Not the Four Seasons. "A decent one. It won't be fancy, but it will be clean."

"I need to bring my stuff with me. I don't want anybody to hassle me."

"Pete will help you move your belongings. One of his associates will make sure that you have what you need and take you to court." *And keep an eye on you.* "And you can't bring smack into the motel."

"I won't." Jack was now engaged. "I'll need a cell phone, too."

Pete slid a disposable "burner" phone across the table. It was wrapped in five twenty-dollar bills. "You can use this one."

"Thank you." Jack looked my way. "What do you want me to say in court?"

"That Frank Moriarty had a reputation for being abusive and violent to the homeless people in the neighborhood."

"That's it?"

"That's it." *I may also take the opportunity to accuse you of murder.*

Jack stuffed the phone and the bills into his pocket. "I think I can do that."

17

"I MAY NEED THE NAME OF A GOOD JEWELER"

The gregarious bartender tossed his dish towel over his shoulder, smiled broadly, and spoke to me in a phony Irish brogue. "What'll it be, lad?"

"Have I ever ordered anything other than a Guinness, Joey?"

"Nope." His grin widened. "Coming right up, Mike."

At eleven o'clock on Wednesday night, the aroma of fish and chips and Guinness wafted through the cozy pub at Twenty-third and Irving, around the corner from the house where I grew up. My uncle, Big John Dunleavy, opened Dunleavy's Bar and Grill sixty-five years ago. His photo is mounted above the weathered bar that my dad helped him build. As always, Big John had a smile on his face, a cigarette in his mouth, and a Guinness in his mug.

When Dunleavy's first opened, it catered to the Irish, Italian, and German families who had decamped from the apartments of the Mission, the Castro, and Noe Valley in search of single-family houses for their growing families. It later served the Chinese community who moved in from Chinatown. Nowadays, Dunleavy's is a second home to a neighborhood that still skews Asian, although young tech workers have made inroads in search of slightly more affordable housing.

Except for the flat-screen TVs and the Wi-Fi password on the blackboard, the wood-paneled watering hole looks the same as it did when I drank my first beer at fourteen and tended bar on weekends when I was in college. Twenty years ago, Big John handed over the day-to-day operations to his grandson, my cousin Joey, but he kept coming to his beloved saloon to make his fish and chips and visit with his regulars.

He died of a heart attack two years ago as he was counting the day's receipts and sipping a twenty-five-year-old single-malt Irish whiskey. Joey inherited the bar and Big John's house around the corner. He's been in charge ever since.

Joey filled Pete's cup with Folgers. Big John steadfastly refused to serve fancier coffee. Then he turned to the third person sitting at our table. "More coffee, Roosevelt?"

The most decorated homicide inspector in SFPD history pointed at his empty mug and spoke in a raspy baritone. "Thanks, Joe."

Joey topped off his cup. "You okay?"

"Not bad for an eighty-seven-year-old." My father's first partner took off his aviator-style glasses and wiped them with a napkin. He spoke in the familiar voice that I heard on Sunday nights when he and his family used to come over for dinner. He reported that he was healthy, but an old knee injury required him to walk with a cane. His wife, Janet, had passed away a couple of years earlier. He was immensely proud of his five grandchildren and three great-grandchildren. He smiled. "I hope I'm around long enough to see a great-great grandchild."

Joey's tone was respectful. "Your fish and chips are ready. I'll pack them up for you." He headed to the kitchen.

Roosevelt turned to us. "You boys okay?"

Pete and I nodded in unison. "Fine, Roosevelt," I said.

"I heard you picked up the Freddie Alvarez case."

"I did."

"Seems pretty clear-cut to me."

"I'm not so sure. What have you heard?"

"Not much."

He knew more than he was letting on. Roosevelt retired twenty years earlier, but he was still tuned in to SFPD gossip. From time to time, he worked on cold cases.

My dad's longtime partner put on his glasses. "Did he do it?"

"He says he didn't."

"Do you believe him?"

"I'm not sure." I never BS Roosevelt. "He was high on heroin. He doesn't remember much about what happened, but he said that he didn't kill Frank Moriarty."

"Maybe you should try a 'diminished capacity' defense."

"I suggested it to our client, but he insisted that he didn't do it."

"Who's the judge?"

"Betsy McDaniel."

"She's good. From what I gather, Moriarty was a great lawyer, but a difficult guy. Either way, it didn't give your client an excuse to whack him. Any witnesses?"

"No."

"You going to be able to get him off?"

"We'll see."

Pete took a sip of coffee and replaced the white cup in its saucer. "I've been looking for witnesses in the Marina. Maybe I'll find somebody who saw something."

"Maybe." Roosevelt's expression turned skeptical. "If not?"

Pete grinned. "You know how it goes. Mike will flood the zone with forensics experts and potential alternative suspects. Maybe something will stick. Maybe not." He pointed my way. "Mike is very adept at creating confusion among jurors."

"That he is." Roosevelt's expression turned serious as he turned my way. "Melinda Wong is an excellent homicide inspector. She's very meticulous."

Just like you.

He added, "Catherine O'Neal is a fine prosecutor. A bit strident for my taste, but she's good on the law, and she presents well in court. You're going to have your hands full."

"I know."

His eyes twinkled. "This is going to be an interesting battle. It's been a while since I watched you try a case. It's been even longer since I answered your questions in court. Maybe I'll stop by and watch some of the trial."

"I'd love to see you there."

Joey returned with Roosevelt's takeout order of fish and chips. The old warhorse thanked him, excused himself, and headed to the door.

Joey dropped the phony brogue. "I have more fish and chips in the kitchen. You interested?"

"No, thanks, Joey," I said. "We had dinner at Mel's."

"The food is better here," he said.

"That it is. We were interviewing a witness."

"Next time bring him here."

"We will. How's business?"

"Good. We're down a little in-house, but our takeout is up. The young people prefer to order from Uber Eats or Door Dash and eat at home while they stare at their phones."

Pete looked up from his phone. "You got a problem with that?"

"Not at all." Joey looked at Big John's photo. "Grandpa used to say that money is money. As long as our customers pay us, it doesn't matter to me how or where they choose to consume our food and drinks. He knew what he was doing."

He sure did. Dunleavy's had put Big John's children and grandchildren through college and paid for his house around the corner and a condo in Palm Springs. I thought about the old days when Roosevelt and my dad would come in after their shifts and have a beer and fish and chips at their regular table in the back room. Big John's German shepherd, Lucky, always sat with them. Lucky knew that my dad always brought him a Milk-Bone. Herb Caen, the *Chronicle*'s legendary gossip columnist, used to stop in for a martini and to play liar's dice. He provided free publicity when he reported on the goings-on at Dunleavy's. Big John never charged him.

"How is Margarita?" I asked Joey.

"Fine."

He had just turned forty. At six-four and two-forty, he had continued our family tradition of playing football at St. Ignatius. The one-time offensive lineman was still imposing, although he was getting a little soft in the middle. His thinning red hair had turned gray, and his jowls had expanded along with his girth. He almost got married to his high school sweetheart, but it didn't work out. A year ago, Rosie's mother introduced him to the granddaughter of one of her neighbors. Margarita Mares worked for a start-up. She was smart, ambitious, and independent. Joey and Margarita had recently moved in together at Joey's house. Rosie and I were hoping that they would make their relationship permanent.

"You're adapting to living together?" I asked.

"So far, so good."

I arched an eyebrow. "Any additional news that you might want to share?"

"Nothing official, Mike." He flashed his bartender's grin. "I may need the name of a good jeweler in the not-too-distant future."

Excellent. "I'll get you a couple of names."

"Much appreciated. Keep this to yourself for now, okay?"

"Attorney-client privilege," I said.

Joey pointed at Pete. "He's not an attorney."

"He's better at keeping secrets than I am."

We exchanged gossip for a few minutes. He invited me to the bar's annual Thanksgiving weekend football-watching marathon. I invited him to join us for brunch on Sunday after church. We've been having the same conversations for the last forty years.

He lowered his voice. "I hear you picked up the Freddie Alvarez case. Is Jeff Henderson going into rehab again?"

San Francisco is still a small town where there are no secrets. "He says he is."

"I hope it works out. Are you going to try the case yourself?"

"Yes. I'm taking the lead. Nady is sitting second chair. Pete is helping us with the investigation. Trial starts a week from Monday."

"That's tight."

"Freddie wants to proceed ASAP."

"Did he do it?"

"He says he didn't."

"Do you think he did?"

I never BS Joey, either. "I don't know."

Joey waved to a regular who came in the door. "I need to deal with this for a few minutes." He headed toward the bar.

Pete looked up from his phone. "You going home?"

"Yes. You?"

"I need to check in with my guy who is helping Jack move his stuff into a motel on Lombard. Then I'm going to ask around to see if I can find Jill."

"You want company?"

He stood up and put on his bomber jacket. "No."

18

"YOU'RE HOME LATE"

Rosie took a sip of Cab Franc from a Crate and Barrel goblet that was one of our few remaining souvenirs from our wedding almost thirty years earlier. "You're home late."

"I had a beer with Pete at Dunleavy's. Roosevelt was there, too. He's getting along okay. He finally gave in to reality and is using a cane. He's even considering the possibility of moving into independent living."

"You do what you need to do."

"Will you ever be able to persuade your mom to move into independent living?"

"Not a chance."

At eleven-forty-five on Wednesday night, we were sitting at opposite ends of the sofa in the living room of Rosie's post-Earthquake bungalow in Larkspur, a leafy suburb ten miles north of the Golden Gate Bridge. Rosie rented the house after we split up, and I moved into an apartment a couple of blocks away. Since the Public Defender is required to have an "official" residence in San Francisco, Rosie also leases a studio apartment a few doors from her mother's house in the Mission. We became the proud owners of the Larkspur house when a grateful (and well-heeled) client bought it for us after we got his murder conviction overturned. We could probably sell our little piece of the American Dream for somewhere close to two million dollars, but it would cost more to buy a replacement in the Bay Area's supercharged real estate market. Over the years, Rosie added a third bedroom and a second bathroom. She updated the kitchen after she was re-elected for her second term. I spend most nights here with

Rosie, but I've kept the apartment for those occasions when we need a little space. It also served as our quarantine location during the Covid years.

"How's Joey?" she asked.

"Fine. Business is good." I arched an eyebrow. "I think he's going to ask Margarita to marry him."

Her eyes gleamed. "Excellent news. Mama will be pleased."

"Don't say anything for now. Joey hasn't bought a ring."

"I hope that he's going to do a better proposal than you did."

"I took you to Napa for the weekend. I popped for a room at Auberge du Soleil and took you out for dinner at Bouchon."

She grinned. "You should have taken me to the French Laundry."

Thomas Keller's exquisite restaurant in Yountville is still the Bay Area's toughest reservation. It's also insanely expensive.

I feigned exasperation. "I was trying to make ends meet on the salary of a baby Public Defender. I was living in a studio apartment above Big John's garage. He gave me a family discount on the rent. I spent a month's salary on that weekend and six months' salary on your engagement ring."

Her smile broadened. "I'm worth the French Laundry."

Yes, you are. "Do you ever miss the days when we were young and broke?"

"Young, yes. Broke, no. I like nice things. Did you stop at the apartment on your way home?"

"Briefly. I made sure that Wilma and Betty had food and water and a clean box."

"You're a good cat dad."

About five years ago, I adopted a sweet snow-white cat named Wilma, who used to live in the apartment next door. When my neighbors had twin boys, Wilma started coming over to my place for peace and quiet. It turned out that the twins were allergic to cats, so my neighbors asked me to adopt Wilma. I was happy to do so—especially since Wilma had already moved in. Betty is a tortoiseshell tabby who wandered into my apartment about a year ago, liked what she saw, and decided to stay. I checked with the Humane Society (Betty had an identification chip). Her owner had died, and they had no record of anybody adopting her. Betty and Wilma get along fine during the two hours a day when they're awake, and they keep each other company. Wilma spends most of her time sleeping on the sofa, and Betty has taken up permanent residence on the recliner. So far, so good.

Rosie's expression turned thoughtful. "Do you think we need to keep the apartment?"

Probably not. "It's good when we need a little space. And the cats like it."

"You can't give it up, can you?"

"Not yet."

"You've been giving me the same answer for years."

"I'm superstitious, Rosie. We started getting along better after I moved into the apartment."

"We're older and wiser now. You spend almost all of your time over here. The cats would like it here, too. It's sunny, warm, and quiet."

True. "Let me think about it."

"Fine. Did Pete find anything that will help with Freddie's case?"

"Working on it."

"In other words, he's found nothing."

"He just started looking."

Her eyes reflected the embers in the fireplace. "Are you going to get an acquittal?"

"Can we talk about business in the morning?"

She placed her empty goblet on the table. "It's my responsibility to monitor my subordinates."

Here we go. "Nady and I went through the police reports and transcripts from the preliminary hearing. There are security videos from a neighbor's house placing some people in the vicinity around the time that Moriarty died, but we don't have anything that would lead to a slam-dunk acquittal."

"What does Nady think?"

I no longer take it personally that Rosie is more interested in Nady's opinion than mine. "She isn't wildly optimistic, either." I filled her in on our conversations with Freddie, the DA, Inspector Wong, the ME, Sergeant Dito, and Moriarty's neighbors. Then I described my conversations with Eddie Reynolds and Jack Allen. "There are some possibilities, but no eyewitnesses."

"Sounds like Reynolds may be your best alternate suspect. He's already in jail, and he won't play well to the jury. Any chance the neighbor who found the body might have killed Moriarty?"

"Keller and Moriarty had an acrimonious relationship for years. We'll bring it up at trial, but we have no hard evidence that Keller killed him."

Rosie flashed a catlike grin. "You can suggest it."

"We will. It seems like a stretch that a billionaire would have killed his neighbor in a fit of anger, but you never know. Unless we find some new witnesses or additional evidence, our strategy may boil down to muddying the waters and suggesting that other people had motive and opportunity to kill Moriarty. It might be just enough to get one juror to reasonable doubt."

"Are you going to put Freddie on the stand?"

"Only if we're desperate."

"Sounds like you might be by the time trial starts. Anybody else?"

"Maybe it was personal. Moriarty was divorced three times."

"Were any of his exes in the vicinity on the night that he was killed?"

"No."

She scowled. "It doesn't sound very promising, but you always find a way, Mike."

Not always.

She refilled her wine glass. "Our DA is also running for re-election and could use a victory at trial. She's spent the last year blaming the City's problems on her predecessor. The drug dealing and the homelessness in the Tenderloin are happening on her watch now. The fentanyl epidemic is still killing people. People are pointing fingers at her."

"That's why she tapped O'Neal to try this case."

Rosie stared at the embers in the fireplace. "What's Plan B?"

There is none. "Blowing smoke and making wild and unsubstantiated accusations."

Her whimsical smile reappeared. "Any evidence to support those wild and unsubstantiated accusations?"

"That's why we have Pete." I pointed at the framed wedding photo of Grace and Chuck taken two years earlier. "Everybody okay?"

"Fine. Grace is finishing a short film. Chuck is busy working on story development for the next feature."

I shifted my gaze to Tommy's high school graduation photo. "All good at Cal?"

"Status quo. Med school applications are finished. It's even more competitive than undergrad." She touched her heart. "Your ticker okay?"

"Everything's working fine."

Three years ago, I developed an extra heartbeat called a ventricular bigeminy. It's fairly common even among people like me who aren't overweight, have low cholesterol, and exercise pretty regularly. My cardiologist did a high-tech procedure called an ablation where she sent a tiny probe into my heart, did a detailed map, and zapped the spot causing the extra beat. I felt like I was in a video game. I was in and out of the hospital the same day, and I didn't feel a thing. Thankfully, the procedure was successful, and my heart is back to normal.

Rosie's voice turned serious. "I know that I dumped Freddie's case on you on short notice, but I don't want you to overdo it. I need you to be at full strength for the next four years after I win the election."

"I'll be careful."

"You should walk the steps with Zvi tomorrow."

"I will."

Our friend, neighbor, and hero, Zvi Danenberg, is a relentlessly upbeat ninety-nine-year-old retired science teacher who stays in exemplary shape by climbing the one hundred and thirty-nine steps connecting Magnolia Avenue in downtown Larkspur with the houses on the adjacent hill. He used to do it every day, but his doctors persuaded him to slow down to twice a week after he turned ninety-five. I join him from time to time. After we finish, I take Zvi out for a chocolate donut at Donut Alley, the beloved hole-in-the-wall donut store across the street from the even more beloved Silver Peso dive bar.

Rosie eyed me. "I don't want you taking Zvi to Donut Alley. It's bad for both of you."

"Fine, Rosie," I lied.

"You're going to do it anyway, aren't you?"

Yup. "The old-fashioned chocolates are very good. Are you going to spin class tomorrow?"

"Yes." She grinned. "I got into Attila's class."

"Excellent."

Rosie's new spin instructor, Attila Fruttus (yes, that's his real name), is a former member of the Hungarian national cycling team. The chiseled Adonis moved to the U.S. when he was in his twenties, became a commercial photographer, and got a few minor roles in some B-movies. Now in his fifties, he cycles in the senior road racing circuit, continues to do photography, and makes six figures as the most popular spin instructor in Marin County and, perhaps, the entire Bay Area.

I grinned. "Do you go for the workout or just to gawk at Attila?"

"Both. You should try it, Mike."

"You know that I don't like being yelled at while I'm exercising."

She shook her head. "What time are you going into the office tomorrow?"

"Not too early. Nady and I are meeting with Judge McDaniel at ten AM."

"Good. I'm going to need more details on your case."

"Now?"

"In the bedroom." She grinned. "If your heart is up to it."

"You just told me not to overexert myself."

"I'll go easy on my cross-examination."

19

"PERHAPS YOU COULD WORK SOMETHING OUT"

At ten o'clock the following morning, a Thursday, the Honorable Elizabeth McDaniel smiled broadly and pointed at the two empty chairs opposite her polished redwood desk in her well-appointed chambers on the third floor of the Hall with a view overlooking the slow lane of the I-80 Freeway. "Have a seat."

"Thank you, Your Honor," I said. Nady and I took our seats. I nodded at O'Neal, who was sitting in the chair next to mine. "Nice to see you, Catherine," I lied.

Her voice oozed with insincere honey. "Nice to see you, too, Mike."

Betsy McDaniel is an elegant woman of seventy-five with stellar credentials, a razor-sharp mind, and a thoughtful presence. The Hall's resident mother hen has a ready smile and a cheerful demeanor. Nevertheless, the former prosecutor won't hesitate to verbally emasculate you if you're unprepared or your arguments are intellectually sloppy.

I admired the framed photos of her grandchildren on her credenza between her laptop, multiple volumes of California Jury Instructions, and several signed first-edition Donna Leon novels. "Grandkids okay, Betsy?"

"Fine, Mike. I just took my youngest to Barcelona and Madrid." Although she had lived in the Bay Area for almost a half-century, you could still hear a trace of her native Alabama in her voice. "I saw Rosie at Pilates yesterday. She seems to be doing well."

"She is."

She asked about Grace and Tommy.

"All good. Grace is still at Pixar. Tommy is a senior at Cal. He's applying to med school."

She gave me a bemused smile. "Neither of your children wants to be a lawyer?"

"Afraid not. They saw a lot of lawyering as they were growing up. I guess they didn't like what they saw."

"It will be nice to have a doctor in the family. Is Grace going to make you and Rosie grandparents anytime soon?"

"Maybe in another year or two. Rosie's mother isn't shy about expressing her desire."

"Neither is Rosie." Her smile broadened. "The Fernandez clan has many redeeming qualities, but patience isn't at the top of the list."

Quite right.

She turned to Nady. "Is Luna okay?"

"Fine, thank you, Your Honor."

"Good to hear. It might be good if more people involved in the justice system kept dogs in their offices. They have a calming influence." She looked at O'Neal. "How is your mother, Catherine?"

"She's still in remission. Her next MRI is in two weeks."

"Good. Please give her my best." The judge glanced at her computer, signaling that the social portion of our meeting was over. "Freddie Alvarez," she said to nobody in particular. She turned my way. "I understand that Jeff Henderson has left the PD's Office. I hope that he is going to get some help with his, uh, issues."

"He is."

"I wish him well. The Alvarez trial is scheduled to start a week from Monday. Are you prepared to move forward?"

"Yes."

She played with the reading glasses sitting on her desk. "Do you think that's wise?"

"It isn't ideal timing, but Freddie wants to proceed."

"If things don't turn out the way you hope, I trust that you are not setting up an appellate claim that the verdict should be overturned because you didn't have adequate time to prepare for trial."

"No, Your Honor." *Well, maybe.*

"Good to hear." She turned to O'Neal. "I presume that you'll be ready?"

"Yes, Your Honor."

"How much time will you need?"

"A couple of days for jury selection. Then our presentation should take no more than two court days. The evidence is straightforward. We will have just a few witnesses."

"How about you, Mr. Daley?"

It did not go unnoticed that I was once again "Mr. Daley." "Two or three days. The evidence isn't as straightforward as Ms. O'Neal has suggested." *Well, yes, it is. Time to start working the ref.* "It is incomprehensible that Ms. O'Neal is charging my client with first-degree murder. There is no way that she'll be able to prove premeditation."

Judge McDaniel wasn't buying. "That's up to her."

I glanced at O'Neal. "At the very most, this is a manslaughter case."

"It's murder, Mr. Daley."

The judge feigned disinterest as O'Neal and I volleyed back and forth for five minutes. Betsy was a skilled mediator and a patient soul, but she finally cut us off. "Is there any possibility that we can resolve this before trial?"

O'Neal raised her voice over mine. "Not unless Mr. Daley's client is willing to change his plea to guilty."

Come on. "Ms. O'Neal is being unreasonable."

O'Neal fired back. "We found a bloody steel rod next to your client. Rust on that rod matched rust on your client's gloves."

"He may have touched it, but it doesn't mean that he used it to kill Moriarty."

"He was close to the body."

"He was unconscious, and there was no blood on Freddie's hands or clothing."

"Moriarty turned away from him."

"Somebody else hit him."

Judge McDaniel's voice remained even. "Sounds like we aren't going to resolve this matter today." Her expression turned hopeful. "Perhaps you could work something out over the next week and a half."

Perhaps. "We'll try, Your Honor."

"Thank you, Mr. Daley. I reviewed your motions. First, your request to exclude the steel rod is denied. There is no evidence that the chain of custody was breached.

"Second, I am ordering Ms. O'Neal to provide any remaining police reports, crime scene photos, video, the autopsy report, and other relevant evidence that may tend to exonerate Mr. Alvarez by the close of business on Monday.

"Third, I expect you to exchange final witness lists at the same time. That gives each of you a week to interview any remaining witnesses—if they're willing to talk to you.

"Fourth, I am going to continue Judge Stumpf's gag order on all parties and counsel. I don't want you talking to the press or trying this case in traditional or social media. If you talk, tweet, or post, it will cost you.

"Finally, I want to make it clear that I will not allow the trial to be televised."

"But, Your Honor—," O'Neal said.

"You know as well as I do that people change their behavior when the cameras are on. And it isn't for the better."

"Yes, Your Honor."

Judge McDaniel leaned back in her leather chair. "I have worked with all of you. I know that you are good lawyers and reasonable people. I encourage you to go back to your respective offices, take a deep breath, and give some serious thought to this case. Then I would suggest that you go out for a cup of coffee and see if you can work something out." She arched an eyebrow. "Maybe you should bring Luna with you to keep everybody civil. Otherwise, I'll see you a week from Monday."

I was walking down the front steps of the Hall when I heard the familiar smoker's hack behind me. "Michael Daley," the voice rasped. "I haven't seen you in a while."

I turned and looked into the bloodshot eyes of Jerry Edwards, the *Chronicle*'s award-winning political columnist. At seventy-five, he remains pugnacious after three acrimonious divorces and periodic trips to rehab for a decades-long battle with alcohol. I respect him for his verbal dexterity and willingness to speak truth to power. On the other hand, Rosie and I have been on the receiving end of his well-crafted barbs on several occasions. It wasn't fun.

"Good to see you, Jerry," I lied. "I thought you retired."

"It lasted three months. I was bored out of my mind."

"Maybe you should take up a hobby."

"I hate hobbies."

"There must be something that you like to do."

"There is. I like to raise hell." The stubble on his leathery face and his faded trench coat gave him the appearance of one of the homeless people in the Tenderloin. "The *Chronicle* wouldn't put me back on staff, so now I'm an independent contractor. I only get paid if I write something controversial enough to generate a lot of clicks."

Welcome to the world of local newspapers in the twenty-first century. "I can't help you, Jerry."

"Maybe you can. I understand that you paid a visit to Judge McDaniel this morning regarding the Freddie Alvarez trial."

You still have your ear to the ground. "Trial starts a week from Monday. We were going over pretrial motions."

"Did your client do it?"

"No."

"That's not what I've heard."

"From whom, Jerry?"

"Informed sources."

"They aren't so informed."

He pushed out a fake laugh that immediately turned into a cough. "Yes, they are. They said that they found the murder weapon in your client's hand."

"Not true."

"And it was covered in blood."

"No comment."

He pulled out his leather-bound notebook. "Do you wish to provide a comment for my loyal readers, many of whom will be members of the potential jury pool?"

"We are very confident that our client will be exonerated."

"You always say that."

Yes, I do. "In this case, it happens to be true." I grinned. "It must be a slow news day if you're hanging out at the Hall of Justice."

"My editor tells me that true crime stories are very popular."

"So I've heard."

"People are tired of reading about the homeless and the dirty streets, Mike."

"That's the mayor's issue."

"The DA is taking a lot of heat. If her office convicts Freddie Alvarez, it will help her re-election prospects."

"That's the DA's issue."

"If you get an acquittal, it will help your ex-wife's re-election prospects, too. That's *your* issue."

"I'm just defending my client, Jerry. I leave the politics to the Public Defender, who is very capable of taking care of herself. Did you ever meet Frank Moriarty?"

"A couple of times. He was a terrific lawyer and a complete asshole."

"We've heard that he had a vendetta against the homeless."

"Wouldn't surprise me. He had anger management issues."

"Any chance you can help us find a witness who saw what happened in front of Moriarty's house at one o'clock in the morning on September fifth of last year?"

"That's your job." The bombast disappeared from his voice. "You've always been a straight shooter. Off the record, how do you think this is really going to go?"

"It's like every other case. I like our chances of getting at least one juror to reasonable doubt, but you never know what's going to happen in court."

"Good luck, Mike. I'll see you at the trial."
"Thanks, Jerry."

20

"IT'S TIME TO PULL THE GOALIE"

Sylvia Fernandez sat at the head of the table in her cramped dining room at eleven-thirty on Sunday morning. Rosie's mother took a sip of coffee, placed the porcelain cup in its saucer, and looked my way. "Father Lopez gave a lovely sermon this morning, Michael."

"He did." I took a bite of the chicken enchilada that Sylvia always made for our post-Mass brunch. "He's very good."

The sweet aroma of Sylvia's enchiladas wafted in from the tiny kitchen in the two-bedroom, one-bath century-old bungalow where the plaster walls were covered with photos of four generations of the Fernandez family. On most Sundays, Rosie and I joined Sylvia after church in the stucco house in the heart of the Mission. On occasion, Grace and/or Tommy joined us. Rosie's older brother, Tony, was also a regular.

Sylvia is an older, stockier, and equally intense version of Rosie and, by extension, Grace. She is still razor-sharp and pretty spry for someone with two artificial knees and an artificial hip. She lives around the corner from the apartments on Garfield Square where my parents grew up. When I was little, my mom and dad, two brothers, baby sister, and I squeezed into a two-bedroom apartment around the corner from here until we moved into a house a block from Big John's saloon.

Sylvia adjusted the white apron that she wore over her going-to-church dress. "Do you ever miss being a priest, Michael?"

"Sometimes. I still like going to church. I don't like being the star of the show."

"You seem to like being the star in court."

"The stakes are lower. In court, I talk to jurors. In church, I was expected to talk to God."

"Suit yourself." She turned to Rosie, who was checking messages on her phone. "Have you heard from Tony?"

"He's in Marin with Rolanda and the kids."

Tony has owned a successful produce market on Twenty-fourth Street for almost thirty years. He bought the store after he returned from active duty in the Marines. He's adapted to the changing demographics as the Mission's working-class Latino population has given way to an influx of affluent young tech people. Half of his store is devoted to traditional fresh produce. The other half is stocked with organic fruit and vegetables. He supplies several of the Mission's upscale restaurants in the trendy Valencia Street corridor.

Rosie added, "He and Rolanda will bring the kids over to see you this afternoon."

Sylvia beamed. Her great-granddaughter, Maria Sylvia Teresa Fernandez Epstein, just turned two. She is smart as a whip and is as opinionated as her great-grandmother. Her great-grandson, Antonio Eduardo Fernandez Epstein, is six months old. He looks like Tony, and he has a forceful but empathetic personality like his grandfather.

Grace was sitting next to Sylvia. At twenty-seven, she bore a striking resemblance to Rosie when I first met her. Sylvia, Rosie, and Grace are so similar in appearance and temperament that it's like looking at a series of time-lapse photos.

Sylvia touched Grace's hand. "Did you finish the final edits on your short film?"

"Yes, Grandma. I'll get you a preview copy soon." She reported that her husband, Chuck, was working on the latest version of his new script.

"On Sunday?"

"He's on a tight deadline."

"You kids work too hard."

"Not as hard as you and Grandpa did."

"That's probably true."

When Eduardo and Sylvia arrived in San Francisco, they routinely worked sixty- and seventy-hour weeks.

Sylvia smiled. "Eduardo and I wanted our children and grandchildren to go to college so they wouldn't have to work such long hours. Now you and your mother and father work as hard as we did."

Rosie held up a hand. "It comes with the job, Mama."

"After all these years, perhaps you could set boundaries, Rosita."

I learned long ago to keep my mouth shut when Sylvia and Rosie get into it.

Rosie elected to keep the peace. "I'll try, Mama."

Sylvia turned back to Grace. "Have you and Chuck given any more thought to starting a family?"

And here we go.

Rosie interjected again. "Leave her alone, Mama. They'll do it when they're ready."

"I was just asking her a question, Rosita."

Grace re-entered the fray. "We're thinking about it, Grandma."

"Perhaps you could think a little faster."

Rosie spoke up again. "Mama, please."

I am not bursting with pride about this, but I do enjoy watching three generations of the Fernandez clan do their thing to each other.

Sylvia's tone remained even. "Just asking another question, Rosita. Grandmothers are granted certain privileges in deference to our advanced age."

Grace tried again. "We're getting closer, Grandma."

"I'm eighty-seven, honey. I already have two great-grandchildren. A third would be nice while I still have the capacity to spoil them."

"You aren't going anywhere, Grandma."

Sylvia touched Grace's cheek. "It's time to pull the goalie, dear."

Rosie's voice filled with exasperation. "Where on earth did you hear that expression, Mama?"

Grace gave her mother a sly smile. "From me."

Rosie rolled her eyes. In the three decades that I've known her, it was one of the rare occasions where I've seen her flustered. "That's not something you should say to your grandmother, Grace."

Sylvia rushed to her defense. "It's fine, Rosita."

"I cannot believe that I am having this discussion with my mother and daughter." Rosie looked my way. "What are you grinning about?"

Busted. "Nothing, Rosie."

Grace tried to keep the peace. "Grandma, I promise that you'll be among the first to know when Chuck and I decide to try to start a family."

"Thank you, dear. That's all that I can ask for."

"Mom, I promise that you and Dad will know right after Chuck and I know."

"Fine," Rosie said.

"Can we talk about something else now?"

Relief. We discussed plans for Thanksgiving and Christmas. Sylvia still wants to organize the big holidays, but we finally convinced her to move the celebrations to Rosie's house. Sylvia always feigns disappointment, but she acknowledges that her house is too small to fit our expanding tribe.

Sylvia moved to another topic. "I talked to Margarita's grandmother." She winked at me. "She thinks that Joey is going to propose soon."

"I have no information at this time," I said.

"You aren't exactly denying it, Michael."

If she had been born twenty years later, Sylvia would have been the managing partner of the big law firm where I worked after Rosie and I got divorced.

"I have no information at this time," I repeated.

"Do you know something that you aren't allowed to tell me?"

"Possibly." *That's all that you're going to get from me.*

"Fine." Her expression turned serious. "I understand that you're handling the Freddie Alvarez case. Did he kill Frank Moriarty?"

"He says that he didn't."

"Do you believe him?"

"I'm not sure, Sylvia." I never BS my ex-mother-in-law.

"Jerry Edwards at the *Chronicle* says your client is guilty."

"That's why we have trials."

"If he didn't do it, who did?"

Good question. "There were other people in the area. Maybe one of them did it."

Sylvia displayed Rosie's customary skeptical expression. "Maybe."

Rosie placed her phone face down on the table and softened her voice. "Do you need anything, Mama?"

"I have more than I need. I think I'm getting addicted to online shopping."

Sylvia weathered Covid at home by chatting with her family and friends on FaceTime and Zoom and ordering copious amounts of food and drink from her favorite stores in the Mission. Tony provided fresh fruit and vegetables. She doesn't get out as much as she used to, but she still goes to Mass at St. Peter's every Sunday.

"How's your knee?" Rosie asked.

"Fine."

"And your back?"

"Also fine."

Sylvia would never admit that she was getting older. Rosie finally convinced her to get hearing aids for her FaceTime visits with her great-granddaughter.

"Are you playing tonight?" Rosie asked.

"Of course, dear. It's Sunday."

Sylvia and a rotating cast of her friends have been playing mah-jongg on Sunday nights since Rosie was a kid. When Covid hit, they started playing online. Since the average age of the participants is well north of eighty-five, and nobody lives within easy walking distance of Sylvia's house anymore, several of them still play online. Sylvia is the second youngest of the group. Jan Harris is the baby at eighty-six. Mercedes Crosskill is eighty-eight. Marge Gilbert and Flo Hoffenberg are in their early nineties. Char Saper and Yolanda Cesena clock in at ninety-five. A few years ago, at the suggestion of Ann-Helen Leff, a nonagenarian hippie, great-grandmother, and lifelong rabble-rouser, they switched the refreshments from sherry to marijuana. Sylvia receives a weekly delivery of edibles from a woman who runs a designer dispensary on Valencia and takes orders after Mass at St. Peter's.

Sylvia gave Rosie a knowing look. "I have some edibles that you should try, Rosita. They're exquisite."

"I'm sticking to wine, Mama. So is Mike."

"Don't be such a prude. It'll take the edge off. Besides, it's legal now." She finished her coffee. "How's the campaign?"

"We're going to win."

"I know. Do you promise that this will be your last term?"

"Yes, Mama."

"Good." She shot a loving glance at Grace, then she turned back to Rosie. "You'll want to have time to play with your grandchildren."

An hour later, my phone vibrated as Rosie and I were driving north on the Golden Gate Bridge. I answered on the second ring.

Pete got right to it. "Meet me at Original Joe's at eight o'clock tonight. Wendy Klein provided the name of the PI she hired to tail Moriarty to see if he was cheating on her. We're having dinner with him tonight."

21

"I LIKED THE OLD PLACE BETTER"

The diminutive PI tied a white cloth napkin around his neck in the traditional San Francisco manner, looked approvingly at his double order of veal parmigiana, adjusted the fresh red rose on the lapel of his top-of-the-line Italian suit, and held up his hands. "Enjoy."

"Thanks, Nick," I said.

He smiled at Pete. "How the hell are you?"

"Couldn't be better. You okay?"

"Indeed I am."

Nick "The Dick" Hanson was still wildly energetic at ninety-five. He founded the Hanson Investigative Agency seventy-five years ago in an office above the Condor Club on Columbus Avenue. Nowadays, he is the chairman emeritus of the biggest private eye operation on the West Coast.

Nick is the son of Russian immigrants who became small-time vaudeville stars. Weary of the endless travel, they moved to San Francisco, where Nick's uncle was a longshoreman. Nick's father opened a magic shop next door to the Tosca Café. Nick played baseball with Joe DiMaggio on the North Beach playground. During the Great Depression, he helped his father make ends meet by sweeping up at the Valente, Marini, Perata Funeral Home on Green Street, handing out towels at the Italian Athletic Club on Washington Square, and bilking tourists at three-card monte.

He pointed at the young woman sitting next to him. Her face bore a slight resemblance to Nick's, but she towered over him by a foot, and her jet-black hair had a magenta streak. "You remember my great-granddaughter, Nicki?"

"Of course," I said, shaking her hand. "Nice to see you again."

"Same here." She exchanged greetings with Pete.

Nicole "Nicki" Hanson is the head of the agency's cybersecurity group. The thirty-year-old hacker has a computer science degree from UC San Diego and a Master's in data analytics from UCLA. She is one of dozens of Nick's children, grandchildren, and great-grandchildren who work at the agency.

At eight o'clock on Sunday evening, the aroma of tomato sauce, garlic, and parmesan filled the room as we sat in a traditional red-leather booth at Original Joe's, a San Francisco classic now located at Stockton and Union in the heart of North Beach. In 1937, a Croatian immigrant named Ante "Tony" Rodin opened a fourteen-stool diner with sawdust on the floor in the Tenderloin. Tony ran his beloved restaurant for the next sixty-nine years until he passed away in 2006 at the age of ninety-three. He expanded Original Joe's into a San Francisco institution where mayors, judges, athletes, actors, hookers, and homeless mingled amiably and dined on huge steaks and gigantic portions of pasta at reasonable prices, even though they sometimes had to make their way around people smoking crack outside the door.

You won't find artisan cheese or organic kale at Original Joe's. The line cooks still slam halibut into blackened sauté pans, and tuxedoed waiters whip up zabaglione with cheap Chablis. Joe DiMaggio was treated like royalty by his favorite waiter, Angelo Viducic, who sweated it out in his black tux for decades. Back in the Seventies when my dad and Roosevelt Johnson were patrolling the Tenderloin, they used to stop in at Original Joe's when they were a little flush. Pop always got the Joe's Special, a cholesterol bomb made of scrambled eggs, ground beef, spinach, onions, and whatever leftover vegetables were available in the kitchen. Roosevelt always ordered the liver and onions. In 2007, a fire at the Tenderloin location closed Original Joe's for the better part of a decade. It reopened in 2016 in North Beach in a sleeker space that retained the booths and tuxedoed waiters. The menu has been updated a little, but you can still order the Joe's Special, the liver and onions, and the magnificent hamburger—a twelve-ounce patty mixed with onions and mesquite-grilled on a buttered, toasted baguette.

Nick's rubbery face transformed into a thoughtful expression as he surveyed Tony Rodin's legacy. "This is very nice, but I liked the old place better. It had ambiance."

That it did.

Pete looked up from his burger—the only thing he had ever ordered since our dad took us to the old place on Taylor Street when we were kids. "There was only one Tony."

I looked across Washington Square at the towers of Saints Peter and Paul. North Beach has changed over the years, but you can still smell pizza, spaghetti, meatballs, and garlic as you walk down the narrow streets. Times change, but certain magical parts of my hometown are timeless.

Nick raised a glass of high-end cabernet. "I hope you're hungry."

I touched my glass to his. "We are."

I had consumed a filling brunch at Sylvia's house a few hours earlier, but I was prepared to indulge. Dinner with Nick is a commitment—at least three hours. Hopefully, my stomach would recover in a couple of days.

Without being asked, a waiter brought Nick a double order of linguine with clam sauce. He refilled Nick's wine glass for a second time. At barely five feet tall and a hundred and twenty pounds, he never gains an ounce. He lives a few blocks away in an Earthquake-era mansion just below Coit Tower near the top of Telegraph Hill. A savvy businessman and astute investor, he has accumulated a portfolio of apartment buildings rumored to be worth a cool fifty million. In his spare time, he writes mystery novels that are loose embellishments of his cases. Danny DeVito plays Nick in a long-running Netflix series.

There is a protocol for dining with Nick. You never bring up business until he does. And you have to let him expound on whatever is on his mind. It isn't difficult. Nick is the best storyteller I've ever met.

Here goes. "How's life?" I asked.

His eyes lit up. "We're having our best year ever." He said that the agency was expanding into Artificial Intelligence. His real estate portfolio was also growing. He had just acquired the building housing Caffé Trieste. "I'm trying to buy this building, but the owner is being difficult."

"You're very persuasive," I said.

"Indeed I am. More important, I'm very persistent. Eventually, I'll wear him down."

Yes, you will. Nick will probably live to 110. I asked about the TV series.

He took a bite of linguine. "We're going to wrap up at the end of the season. Danny is game to do one more, but the network doesn't want to pay him. It may be just as well. My dad always said that you should get offstage when the audience still wants a little more."

"Were you at the Triple-I on Columbus Day?"

"Indeed I was. I haven't missed one in sixty years. I saw you on the other side of the banquet hall. I'm sorry that I didn't make it over to say hi."

The San Francisco Irish-Israeli-Italian Society, affectionately known as the "Triple-I," was hatched in the Fifties by George Reilly, a gregarious member of the Board of Supervisors who twice ran for mayor (and lost), and Nate Cohn, a theatrical trial lawyer whose clients included Frank Sinatra, Melvin Belli, Duke Ellington, and the Birdman of Alcatraz. The "Society" has no dues, no website, and almost no organization. Its members don't need to be Irish, Jewish, or Italian. Its sole purpose is organizing boisterous luncheons at the Italian Athletic Club on St. Patrick's Day, Israeli Independence Day, and Columbus Day, where politicians, cops, lawyers, labor leaders, business execs, and other hangers-on rub elbows for old-fashioned civic bonhomie. I used to accompany my dad and Big John to the festivities every year. Nowadays, I go with Rosie.

We stuffed ourselves with pasta and shot the breeze for another hour. Nick is never in a hurry, and Nicki was content to nibble at her Petrale sole and let him talk. Nick was gifted at spinning yarns, and he was always the hero in his stories. The mayor stopped by our table to say hello. A couple of people asked for selfies, and Nick was happy to oblige. Most private eyes are loath to have their pictures taken, but Nick has two million followers on Instagram.

He finally turned to business. "I heard you picked up the Freddie Alvarez case."

Nick knows everything. "Trial starts next week. Pete is helping with the investigation."

Nick smiled at Pete. "You're a good brother." He turned back to me. "Did your client do it?"

"He said that he didn't."

"You believe him?"

"That's what we're trying to find out."

He darted a glance at Nicki, who was listening intently, but hadn't said anything in over an hour. He looked my way again. "How can I help you?"

"The decedent is Frank Moriarty. We understand that you did some work for his ex-wife."

He corrected me. "Ex-wives."

"How many?"

"All three." Nick arched a bushy eyebrow over his thick glasses. "They suspected that Frank was cheating. It didn't take us long to confirm it." Nick said that he worked on the first two cases himself. "Nicki handled the third one."

She nodded. "Wendy did very well in the divorce."

"So did the first two ex-wives," Nick said.

"How would you describe Moriarty?" Pete asked.

Nick answered him. "He was a phenomenal personal injury lawyer. Charismatic. Aggressive. Likeable. He owned the courtroom. He stretched the rules to the limit, but he was never disciplined by the State Bar. He worked at a big law firm for about ten years. They finally got tired of him asking for more money, so they cut him loose. He opened his own shop and did very well. He struck me as the sort of guy who was better suited to working solo. He didn't play nicely with his friends in the sandbox."

"Greedy?" I asked.

Nick smiled. "He's a lawyer."

"Arrogant?"

"Comes with the territory."

"Litigious?"

"Absolutely. He sued his neighbors dozens of times. It was a game to him."

"What did his friends think of him?"

"As far as I could tell, he didn't have any. He was the life of the party at the Pacific Union and Olympic Clubs, but it wasn't easy to be his friend or neighbor."

Or wife.

"What about his kids?" Pete asked.

"They stopped talking to Moriarty years ago. They blamed him for the divorce with his first wife. He was cheating on her, after all. His behavior got worse over time, especially after he started drinking heavily. Wendy called the cops a couple of times when he got physical. It was pretty bad toward the end."

Nicki chimed in. "They were married for a short time before she bailed. He started stalking her. She got a restraining order. It must have been very difficult."

I spoke up again. "We've been told that Moriarty had a problem with the homeless in the Marina."

"If somebody was smoking crack in your driveway, you would have been upset, too. He went nuts after a homeless guy broke the windshield on his Maserati. He was really angry when a homeless guy pissed on the bumper of his Cybertruck. I don't know what Elon was thinking when he designed that ugly piece of crap, but rich egomaniacs like Moriarty seem to like them. And I saw him threaten a homeless guy with a baseball bat."

"Did he hit him?"

"No."

"Do you think that he was capable of hitting him?"

"Absolutely."

I looked at Nicki. "You said that you caught Moriarty cheating with another woman. Do you have a name?"

"Yes. It was Moriarty's neighbor, Shreya Patel."

Pete grinned. "Nick was in good form."

"He always is," I said. "I'm not going to eat for a week."

North Beach was quiet as we stood outside Original Joe's at eleven-thirty on Sunday night. The restaurant was closed, but a few customers were lingering over after-dinner drinks. Our dinner with Nick had lasted three and a half hours. I finally cried uncle when Nick ordered the second round of zabaglione and tiramisu.

"We need to talk to Patel again," I said.

Pete nodded. "I'll find her."

22

"IT WASN'T SERIOUS"

Shreya Patel lowered the driver's side window of her Tesla Model S as she pulled into her driveway at six-fifteen the following evening. "I don't appreciate being accosted in my own driveway," she snapped.

I opted for a low-key response. "We're sorry to trouble you again."

Pete and I hadn't accosted her. We had been sitting in Pete's car across the street waiting for her to come home. When we saw her approaching her house, we got out and waited—respectfully—in her driveway.

Her eyes were on fire. "I need to take my daughter to dance class. I've told you everything that I know about Frank Moriarty."

She raised the window and drove into her garage. Pete and I remained outside the garage, mindful that trespassing is still a crime.

She exited her car and attempted to freeze us with a glare.

Pete tried a soft approach. "Please, Ms. Patel. If you give us a moment now, Mike will make your life easier in court. In fact, he may not need you to testify at all."

Not a word of that was true, but his delivery was perfect. Our dad used to say that people are more likely to respond to sugar than vinegar.

"I'll give you a minute," Patel said.

Pete smiled. "Mind if we come inside?"

"We'll talk out here."

"Fine. We confirmed the identities of the people in the security videos that you provided to the police. The man across the street was Eddie Reynolds. He's currently doing time for grand theft auto."

"I've never met him."

"The man and woman who walked by your house were a homeless couple known as Jack and Jill. Jack's full name is Jack Allen. Jill's last name is Harris."

"I never met them, either."

"Did you ever see them on your security video other than on the night that Mr. Moriarty died?"

"Not that I recall." She glanced at her watch. "Anything else?"

Pete glanced my way.

"Ms. Patel," I said, "we spoke to Mr. Moriarty's third ex-wife, Wendy Klein. Did you ever talk to her?"

"I met her briefly once or twice. She was always polite."

"She said that Mr. Moriarty was physically and emotionally abusive to her—especially after he had too much to drink. She told us that she called the police on a couple of occasions after Mr. Moriarty got physical."

"I don't know anything about it."

"Did you ever see any evidence of such behavior?"

"No." Another glance at her watch. "If you don't have anything else, I need to help my daughter get ready for dance class."

"Just one more thing," I said. "Ms. Klein gave us the name of a private investigator that she hired to confirm that Mr. Moriarty was having an affair."

Patel froze.

"We talked to the PI," I said. "He informed us that you and Mr. Moriarty had a relationship."

Patel's lips tightened into a tiny ball. "Mr. Moriarty and I went out for dinner a couple of times. It wasn't serious."

"Was he still married at the time?"

"He told me that he and his wife had separated. It was casual. Frank could be very charming."

And now he's "Frank." "You didn't pursue this relationship?"

"There wasn't any chemistry. Frank was a lot older than I was. I have a young daughter. It would have been very complicated."

"Did he ask you out again?"

"Yes. I told him that I didn't think it was going to work."

"How did he take the news?"

"He was a perfect gentleman." She folded her arms. "I know that you're just doing your jobs, but if you're trying to get me to say anything bad about Frank, you're out of luck."

"Is there anybody else that we should talk to?"

"Talk to Henry Keller. He and Frank were at each other's throats for years. Maybe he'll tell you something that you don't already know." Without waiting for an answer, she turned around, headed into her garage, and closed the door behind her.

Pete gave me a crooked smile. "I think we may have pissed her off, Mick."

"Comes with the territory. Shall we knock on Keller's door?"

"He isn't home."

"How do you know?"

"You pay me to know stuff like that."

"Do you know where he is?"

He glanced at his phone. "Yes."

23

"I'VE TOLD YOU EVERYTHING"

I pushed my way through the crowded doorway, filled my lungs with the aroma of upscale burgers, pasta, and pork chops, and scanned the packed bar. "Are you sure that Keller is here?" I shouted to Pete, who was standing next to me.

He surveyed the scene. "Over by the bar, Mick."

At seven-thirty PM, Keller was surrounded by three attractive twenty-something women who towered over him. They were pretending to be entranced by an older guy who was desperately trying to impress them. Keller had the full repertoire down pat. He ordered another round of drinks from one of the four bartenders who worked with Broadway-level choreography. Keller toasted the women, downed his espresso martini, flashed a grin, and told a bawdy joke. The women acted as if he was the funniest guy in the world.

Pete shook his head. "The dance never changes, Mick."

"Do you think his wife knows that he's here?"

"Probably. She's in Cabo with her tennis instructor."

I remain in awe of Pete's ability to dig up dirt. I pointed at the women who were still feigning interest in Keller. "Do you think they know that he's married?"

"Absolutely. Just because they're pretty doesn't mean that they're stupid or naïve. They probably work for the big tech companies."

"What do accomplished young people see in an old guy like Keller?"

"Money."

San Francisco's hottest bar—for now—is also one of its oldest. At 112 years and counting, the Balboa Café doesn't look trendy with its dark wood paneling, crisp white tablecloths, and an old-school green neon sign above the door. Over the years, it's run hot and cold, and it has remade itself several times. In various eras, it has been a saloon for blue-collar workers, a training ground for star chefs, a place for the Pacific Heights crowd to exchange gossip, and a mecca for singles looking to hook up. Nowadays, a new generation of young and beautiful people have made it a place to be seen. It reminds me of the Balboa's last golden era in the Eighties, when it was a socialite hub during the day, and a pickup spot at night. The *Chronicle*'s society columnist at the time reported frequent appearances by Boz Scaggs (who owned the Blue Light Café around the corner), Oscar de la Renta, Judge William Newsom, and billionaire Ann Getty, who went for hot fudge sundaes at midnight.

The Balboa was the linchpin of what came to be known as the Bermuda Triangle, a cluster of upscale bars that then included Pierce Street Annex and Dartmouth Social Club. Only the Balboa remains. The pub had lost some of its luster by the mid-Nineties, when an up-and-coming entrepreneur named Gavin Newsom (Judge Newsom's son) partnered with an old-money heir to an oil fortune named Gordon Getty (Ann's husband) to buy the Balboa in 1995. It was the first investment by the PlumpJack Group, which now owns an upscale wine shop across the street along with high-end restaurants and resorts in Napa and Lake Tahoe.

"Maybe we should talk to Keller after he leaves," I said.

Pete disagreed. "That won't happen if he departs with one of those women. Freddie's trial starts a week from today. There's no time like now."

He followed me through the crowd of well-dressed, well-behaved young people. I darted between two of the young women and made a beeline for Keller. I got his attention by jostling him, whereupon I smiled and apologized profusely.

The fake grin was still plastered on his face. "No worries."

I feigned surprise. "Mr. Keller?"

"Uh, yes."

"Mike Daley." I extended a hand. "We met earlier this week."

"Uh, right."

I pointed at Pete, who smiled. "This is my brother, Pete. Do you come here often?"

"Occasionally."

"Who are your friends?"

Keller froze—the tell that he didn't know the names of the women that he was trying to bed. "Ladies, please introduce yourselves to Mike and Pete."

They smiled graciously and rattled off their names and occupations. As Pete had predicted, one worked for Facebook, the second worked for ChatGPT, and the third for Google.

Time to start lying. "I'm sorry for interrupting you," I said to Keller. "I wonder if I could ask you a couple of quick questions."

He frowned, but he didn't want to come off as a jerk in front of three beautiful women. "Could you call my office?"

"I left you a message, but I didn't hear back from you."

"You should have waited until I called you back."

I probably should have—especially since I just lied about calling you. "I'm sorry."

Keller looked over my shoulder—a sign that the women were getting distracted by some of the younger and more muscular men at the bar. "I've told you everything that I know about Frank Moriarty."

Well, maybe not everything. "We've been following up with your neighbors. I wonder if I might show you a couple of photos. Then we'll let you get back to your friends."

His expression turned sour as the woman who worked at Facebook started talking to a young man wearing a Patagonia jacket. "Okay," he said to me. "Make it quick."

I took out my phone and showed him a photo of Reynolds. "His name is Eddie Reynolds. He is in jail on a grand theft auto charge. Have you ever seen him?"

Keller pretended to study the photo. "I'm sorry."

I showed him the video of Jack and Jill.

A look of recognition crossed his face. "I may have seen them once or twice. I think they asked me for money. I turned them down and told them to leave."

"Were they on drugs?"

"It wouldn't surprise me."

"Were they aggressive?"

"Not to me." He said that he didn't know where they were staying.

"Did you ever talk to Mr. Moriarty about them?"

"Frank and I stopped talking years ago."

"Mr. Keller," I said, "we spoke to your neighbor, Shreya Patel. She told us that she got into an argument with Mr. Moriarty over the noise and dust from one of his frequent remodel projects."

"All of Frank's neighbors argued with him over the noise. The lucky ones—like Shreya—just got yelled at. The unlucky ones—like me—got sued. Frank's contractors used to arrive early and wake up Shreya's daughter. It went on for years." Keller's voice filled with indignation. "I hope you aren't suggesting that Shreya had something to do with Frank's death. Do you really believe a prominent VC killed her neighbor because his contractor made too much noise? You can't be serious, Mr. Daley."

No, I'm desperate. "Were you aware that Mr. Moriarty and Ms. Patel were seeing each other socially before his death?"

"Uh, no." He was now intrigued. "For how long?"

"Not long. Mr. Moriarty was still married at the time. His relationship with Ms. Patel ended badly."

"His marriages didn't end well, either. I still can't imagine that she would have killed Frank."

You never know.

He turned and spoke to one of the young women. "Can I buy you another drink?"

"Thank you. Remind me of your name again."

"Henry." He turned back to me. "Nice to see you again, Mr. Daley." He brushed me aside and headed to the bar.

"Thank you for your time, Mr. Keller," I said to his back.

I inhaled the cool evening air. "The Bermuda Triangle isn't as busy as it used to be," I said.

Pete nodded. "It's still early, Mick." He glanced at the people huddled under heat lamps in the outdoor seating area of the Balboa Café. "Do you think Keller is going to get lucky tonight?"

"Wouldn't surprise me." I clutched a paper bag holding two burgers that we had ordered to go. "Do you think he had anything to do with Morarity's death?"

"Probably not. Billionaires don't kill people. They hire out."

"Maybe he got fed up and lost his temper."

"Maybe." His expression was skeptical. "We have a better chance of getting an acquittal if we give the jury a plausible alternate suspect—preferably one that they won't like."

Good advice. "I'll take another run at Eddie Reynolds in the morning."

24

"TALK TO MY LAWYER"

Eddie Reynolds glared at me through the scuffed Plexiglas and spoke into the phone attached to the wall by a threadbare cord. "Talk to my lawyer," he snapped.

"I already did," I said. I held up the subpoena that I had delivered to him the last time I saw him. "I gave him another copy of this subpoena. It requires you to testify at Freddie Alvarez's trial next week. Your attorney will be coming over to talk to you about it later."

The visitors' area at the Glamour Slammer was full at ten o'clock the following morning, a Tuesday. The seats on my side of the divider were occupied by family members, friends, and a couple of defense lawyers. The windowless room smelled of mildew and sweat. A couple of bored guards monitored the proceedings. It wasn't unusual for people to become emotional in the visitors' area. It was less likely, but not unheard of, for people to become disruptive.

Reynolds squeezed the phone more tightly. "Just because you deliver a piece of paper doesn't mean that I have to show up next week."

"Talk to your lawyer," I said. "He will explain that if you fail to appear, you can add a contempt of court citation to your other legal issues."

"I'm already in jail."

"Your stay may be extended."

"I may get sick."

"We'll wait for you to feel better. Our judge isn't the most patient person in the world. If I were in your shoes, I wouldn't piss her off."

"I wasn't there on the night that Moriarty died."

"Yes, you were. We have witnesses who identified you." It was a bluff.

"They're mistaken."

"No, they aren't."

He started to become more agitated. "Yes, they are."

"We can talk about it in court."

"My answer isn't going to change."

"It might." I leaned closer to the Plexiglas. "We subpoenaed your phone records. Your phone was located within a hundred feet of Moriarty's house on the morning that he died."

"You're bluffing."

"No, I'm not." *Yes, I am.* "In addition to the potential contempt of court citation, you should tell your lawyer that he needs to be ready to defend charges of obstruction of justice and perjury."

"You're lying."

No, I'm bluffing. "Ask your lawyer to explain your obligation to testify."

He responded by unleashing a string of profanities.

I waited until he finished venting. "You can save yourself from potential embarrassment and a perjury charge if you would just admit that you were there."

No answer.

"Suit yourself," I said. "I'll see you in court."

Nady was standing next to Terrence's cubicle when I returned to the office. "Were you able to rattle Reynolds?" she asked.

"A little," I said. "He still insists that he wasn't the person in the video taken by Patel's security camera on the night that Moriarty died."

"Maybe he'll remember things differently in court."

25

"I NEED YOU TO TRY"

At ten-fifteen on Friday morning, Judge McDaniel pushed her reading glasses to the top of her head. "Thank you for coming in on short notice," she said to nobody in particular.

O'Neal, Nady, and I nodded.

The judge leaned forward. "I trust that you are prepared to start the Freddie Alvarez trial on Monday morning?"

Another nod.

Her eyes shifted my way. "Are you sure that you want to move forward, Mr. Daley?"

No. "Yes, Your Honor."

"I would be inclined to rule in your favor if you wish to request a delay."

"My client wishes to exercise his right to a speedy trial."

"Fine." Her eyes moved to O'Neal. "You're good to go?"

"Yes, Your Honor."

"Any last-minute issues?"

"None."

"You've exchanged witness lists?"

"We have."

"Any last-minute additions?"

"None from us."

"None from us, either," I said. "We are still looking for additional witnesses. We will let you know immediately if we plan to include any additions."

"Thank you." She turned back to O'Neal. "You've provided all relevant information as required by law to Mr. Daley?"

"Of course, Your Honor."

"We were hoping for more," I said.

O'Neal feigned irritation. "You are entitled to evidence that would tend to exonerate your client, Mike. We have complied with our legal obligations."

"You can do better, Catherine," I said, looking to tweak her.

"We have complied with our legal obligations," she repeated.

Betsy McDaniel's eyes moved back and forth as O'Neal and I took turns sniping at each other. Finally, she spoke in a voice sounding as if she was lecturing her teenage grandchildren. "Mr. Daley, if you have reason to believe that Ms. O'Neal is withholding relevant evidence, you can file a motion explaining your concerns."

"Yes, Your Honor."

She turned to O'Neal. "I would like you and Mr. Daley to get together before Monday to try to resolve this matter."

"Mr. Daley isn't listening to reason."

"I have always found Mr. Daley to be reasonable."

Nice to hear.

"Perhaps you and Mr. Daley can sit down and see if you could work something out."

"It's a waste of time."

"I need you to try."

O'Neal's voice was flat. "Yes, Your Honor."

The judge looked my way. "You'll confer with Ms. O'Neal?"

"Of course, Your Honor."

Terrence "The Terminator" was sitting in his cubicle when Nady and I returned to the office. "How did it go with the judge?" he asked.

"About what I expected. We're still going to trial on Monday. Any word from Pete?"

"No."

"Anything else that we need to know?"

"I just got a text from O'Neal. She wants to see you in her office at two o'clock this afternoon."

26

"ONE LAST CHANCE"

O'Neal sat behind her desk, eyes focused on mine, expression dour. "Thank you for coming in."

Don't react. "You're welcome."

Nady nodded.

The DA's Office was quiet at two o'clock on Friday afternoon. O'Neal's door was closed. The lights buzzed. We were sixty-eight hours from the start of Freddie's trial.

O'Neal gave me an icy glare. "Are you ready to go on Monday?"

"Of course."

"I won't object if you want to ask for a continuance."

"No, thanks." *Why are we here?*

Nady spoke up. "You wanted to talk to us?"

"Yes." O'Neal's expression didn't change. "Judge McDaniel asked us to try once more to resolve the Alvarez case." She looked my way. "She said you would be reasonable."

Always. "Of course."

"I had a long talk with Vanessa after I got back from our meeting with the judge. I persuaded her to authorize me to offer your client a deal for second-degree murder."

Let's hear the rest of it.

O'Neal added, "No enhancements. Credit for time served."

That's a little more than a year. "Recommended sentence?"

"High end of the scale."

The scale is fifteen to life. "How high?"

"Twenty." She waited a beat. "It's a good deal."

No, it isn't. "No deal."

"It took all of my persuasive powers to get Vanessa to go down to second-degree."

No, it didn't. "No deal."

"I can't do any better."

"Yes, you can."

"No, I can't."

You aren't being serious. It's a token so that you can tell Judge McDaniel that you offered something.

She tried again. "One last chance. There was rust from the murder weapon on Freddie's gloves. The jurors will be able to connect the dots."

If I were in your shoes, I would make the same argument. "I won't recommend it."

She decided to try Nady. "This is a gift. Ninety-nine times out of a hundred, we wouldn't be talking about a deal this close to the start of trial."

Nady kept her voice even. "That's because you haven't been serious for the past year. No deal."

"How do you explain the rust on your client's gloves?"

"He sat down on the driveway where there were a dozen rusty steel rods. There wasn't any blood on his gloves or his clothes."

"He hit Moriarty as he was walking away."

"You would have found traces of blood if he had hit Moriarty at close range."

Sensing that she wasn't making any headway with Nady, O'Neal decided to plead her case to me once more. "I won't be able to give you a better deal after today."

Probably true. "No deal."

"You're going to regret this decision."

Maybe. "I don't think so. I might be able to sell Freddie on involuntary manslaughter with a sentence at the shorter end of the spectrum."

"How short?"

The minimum sentence for involuntary manslaughter is two years, the maximum is four. "Two, with credit for time served."

"No."

"Three."

"No."

"Four."

"I'll never be able to sell it to Vanessa."

"Then I think we're done."

"You have a legal obligation to take my offer of second-degree murder to your client."

"We will, but we won't recommend it."

"Then we'll see you in court on Monday."

Freddie didn't hesitate. "No deal."

"I don't think they'll offer us something better," I said.

His voice became more emphatic. "No way."

Nady gave him one more chance. "You sure?"

"I didn't kill Moriarty. I'm not going to cut a deal saying that I did."

The anger in his voice was genuine, his resolve absolute. Rosie always says that the hardest cases are those where you think your client may be innocent.

I looked across the dented table in the consultation room in San Bruno Jail. "Trial starts on Monday at ten AM. Nady and I will bring you a suit and a tie. We need you to be alert and ready. It will play better with the jury if you're clean-shaven."

"Okay."

"Judge McDaniel is a stickler for decorum. I need you to be respectful. You shouldn't show any emotion or say anything unless Nady and I tell you to do so."

"Fine."

"The jury will be watching every move. I want you to sit quietly and take notes. It's okay to look at the jurors, but you can't appear arrogant or smug. Every nuance counts."

"Understood. What's the plan?"

I explained that it will take us at least a day or two to pick a jury. The prosecution would present its case first. Then it will be our turn. "The prosecution needs to prove beyond a reasonable doubt that you killed Moriarty. We don't need to prove anything. We will challenge everything the prosecution says. We'll do a hard cross-exam of O'Neal's witnesses. If things go exceptionally well, we won't need to put on a defense."

"What are the chances?"

"Slim. Our narrative is simple: O'Neal hasn't been able to prove her case beyond a reasonable doubt."

"And if we need to put on a defense?"

"We'll start with a blood spatter expert to testify that the police should have found blood on your gloves and clothes. We'll call a DNA expert to confirm that she didn't find your DNA on Moriarty's body. We'll hammer Inspector Wong."

"And if that isn't enough?"

"We'll put Eddie Reynolds and Jack Allen on the stand and suggest that they had motive, means, and opportunity to kill Moriarty. If it looks like the jury isn't convinced, we'll also put on Moriarty's neighbors. With a little luck, we'll create enough doubt in the minds of a couple of jurors to get us to reasonable doubt."

"I need you to prove that I'm innocent."

"That isn't our job."

"Do I get to testify?"

"Only if things aren't going our way and we absolutely need you to do so."

"I want to tell the jury that I'm innocent."

"It's very risky," I said. "We'll make that decision as the trial progresses. In the meantime, I want you to keep eating and try to get a good night's sleep."

His expression indicated that the gravity of the situation was becoming real. "Bottom line?"

I went with my standard lawyerly answer, which is never satisfying. "We have some good arguments, Freddie. We have a path to reasonable doubt."

27

"JUST ONE JUROR"

"I just got a text from Pete," I said to Nady. "He has somebody keeping an eye on Jack Allen at the Presidio Motel on Lombard. Still no luck finding Jill."

Her expression was somber as she sat in the chair opposite my desk. "We can't call her as a witness if we can't find her."

The PD's Office smelled of leftover pizza and salad at ten o'clock on Sunday night. Terrence was sitting at his computer and updating our jury questionnaires. Dazzle was organizing our trial exhibits in the conference room down the hall. We had been working all weekend. It comes with the territory when you're in the final countdown to trial.

"Any updates to the prosecution's witness list?" I asked.

Nady glanced at her laptop. "None."

As expected, O'Neal's final list was short: Keller, Patel, the first officer at the scene, the Chief Medical Examiner, a forensic evidence expert, and a DNA expert. She would call Inspector Wong at the end to tie a bow around her case.

"It's going to be a short presentation," Nady said. "We'll need to be ready to start our defense later this week."

Our witness list would include blood spatter and DNA experts, followed by people who were in the vicinity on the morning that Moriarty died: Keller, Patel, Reynolds, and Jack Allen. And if Pete can find her, Jill.

"Any change in the narrative?" she asked.

"No."

It was always the most important question in trial preparation. Lawyers are storytellers. Everything you do in court is in support of that story. Rosie taught me to begin trial preparation by writing my closing argument and then working backward to my opening statement. It helps me focus on the narrative.

I summarized our storyline yet again. "Insufficient evidence to prove their case beyond a reasonable doubt. They can place Freddie at the scene, but they can't prove that he hit Moriarty."

"What about the rust on his gloves?"

"He touched a rusty piece of steel at some point. It doesn't mean that he hit Moriarty with the bar with Moriarty's blood on it."

She played devil's advocate. "It was within a foot of Freddie's hand."

"If Freddie had hit him, they should have found Moriarty's blood on Freddie's gloves or clothing. They didn't."

"Moriarty was hit in the back of the head. They'll argue that he was walking away from Freddie when he hit him."

"Freddie would have been inches from Moriarty's head. It's impossible that some of his blood didn't find its way to Freddie's gloves."

"Maybe they didn't look."

I grinned. "It will not help their case if they admit it."

Nady returned my smile. "True. And if that isn't enough?"

"Rush to judgment," I said. "The DA and Inspector Wong ignored other potential suspects who had motive, means, and opportunity. Reynolds is probably our best alternative, and he isn't likeable."

"It's still a stretch, Mike. How do you feel about putting Freddie on the stand to issue a short and strong denial?"

"I don't like it. O'Neal will go after him with a sledgehammer. Let's see how things go at trial."

"Do you think Pete will find Jill?"

"Never underestimate my brother."

Her expression turned thoughtful. "How do you think this is going to go, Mike?"

"Rosie always says that you should never second-guess yourself when you're preparing for trial."

"Gut feeling?"

"My gut isn't feeling very good."

"Neither is mine." Her expression brightened. "I ran your opening through ChatGPT and asked the robot to punch it up."

"Seriously?"

"You take advantage of the tools that are available. I think there's some stuff that we can use."

Brave new world. "Let's give it a look."

28

"YOU'LL FIND A WAY"

Rosie's voice was filled with disbelief. "You let Nady run your opening statement through ChatGPT?"

"Yes. She asked it to tighten it up."

"Did it help?"

I flashed a sheepish smile. "I don't think that it will replace human lawyers anytime soon, but it gave us a few useful suggestions."

She shook her head. "It's probably good that I'm only going to serve one more term. Maybe ChatGPT should run for Public Defender."

"The robot wouldn't stand a chance against you."

Rosie handed me a glass of Cab Franc as I sat down on the sofa in her living room at eleven-fifteen on Sunday night. "You look like you could use a glass of wine."

"I could."

"Are you going to be able to get an acquittal for Freddie?"

I took a sip of wine. "I wouldn't bet on it."

"You always say that."

"Being a Public Defender means you have to manage your clients' expectations."

"I'm not your client. I'm your boss."

You never let me forget. "And your boss's expectations."

"Fair enough." Rosie took a sip of wine. "Are you okay?"

"Fine. Are the kids okay?"

"Fine. So is my mother."

"Good."

Her post-Earthquake bungalow seemed bigger now that Grace was married, and Tommy was in college. The fog

NEVER PLEAD GUILTY   149

covered the house, and a cool breeze was coming in through the open window. I still expect to see the lights on in Grace and Tommy's bedrooms.

"You didn't sound like your usual jovial self on the phone," she said.

"Just busy." My head throbbed. "How did the meeting with your campaign team go?"

"It's challenging to run against somebody who is bankrolled by a billionaire. The polling looks good. It will all come down to turnout."

"Your opponent isn't going to catch up."

"You never want to get complacent in politics or in court. This is going to be my last campaign, Mike. I've never lost one. I don't like to lose."

Neither do I.

Her expression turned thoughtful. "Are you good to go in the morning?"

"Yes."

"Do you have enough to get to reasonable doubt?"

"You keep asking me that question."

"It's my job."

I answered her honestly. "I'm not wildly optimistic. Our statistics may take a hit."

"You'll find a way."

"I hope it doesn't adversely impact the election."

"It won't." She asked me (yet again) about our narrative.

"The usual recipe. The main storyline is that the prosecution can't prove its case beyond a reasonable doubt. We'll sprinkle in the argument that Freddie didn't have the requisite time or knowledge of Moriarty to have acted with premeditation. We'll add rush to judgment, shaky evidence, and somebody else did it."

"You've ruled out self-defense or diminished capacity?"

"Yes. If we want to use either of those defenses, we would have to admit that Freddie killed Moriarty. He says that he didn't."

Her eyes sparkled. "Did he?"

"He says that he didn't," I repeated. "We'll do the usual defense-attorney dance to muddy the waters. We'll challenge the prosecution's witnesses. We'll argue that chain of custody was breached. We'll put on our own blood spatter, fingerprint, and DNA experts. If that doesn't seem to be working, we'll try to foist the blame on somebody else."

"Evidence?"

"Nothing solid."

"You can only use the evidence that you have, Mike. And if it isn't enough?"

"We'll put Freddie on the stand and issue a strong denial. It might be enough to get one juror to reasonable doubt."

"Maybe Pete will come up with something. How is Freddie holding up?"

"Not great. At times, I think he's ready to fight. Other times, I think he just wants it to be over."

"And Nady?"

"If I ever get into trouble, I would call her second. I would call you first."

"Good answer." She reached over and clasped my hand. "Is your heart working properly?"

"Perfect."

She flashed the million-watt smile that gets my heart pounding. "Do you have enough energy to do our usual pregame ritual?"

I grinned. "I think so."

For almost thirty years, Rosie and I have spent the night before trials in bed. She says that it helps us focus.

Her smile broadened. "It's nice to know that there are a few things that ChatGPT can't replace."

29

"ALL RISE"

At nine-fifteen on an overcast Monday morning, Nady and I kept our heads down as we lugged our laptops, trial bags, and exhibits past a handful of reporters who were waiting for us on the steps of the Hall of Justice.

"Mr. Daley? Is your client going to cut a deal?"

"Ms. Nikonova? Have you found any other witnesses?"

"Mr. Daley? Does the Public Defender believe that an acquittal for Freddie Alvarez will ensure a victory for her in the election in November?"

I stopped, turned around, and offered the platitude that defense attorneys recite before the start of every trial. "We are pleased to have the opportunity to defend our client in court. We are confident that Freddie will be exonerated."

The reporters shifted to our media-savvy DA, who was heading up the steps. Vanessa Turner was flanked by a couple of ADAs and her ever-present press secretary. She was running for re-election, so she was looking for a little free airtime. Catherine O'Neal wasn't on the ballot, so she had entered the building without talking to the press.

Turner looked into the cameras and spoke in an appropriately somber tone. "The evidence against Freddie Alvarez is overwhelming. My administration prosecutes criminals to the fullest extent of the law. We cannot jeopardize the rights of law-abiding citizens by allowing the unhoused to engage in senseless violence on our streets."

She touted her alleged success at reducing crime. In San Francisco politics, perception and spin are often more important than reality.

As Turner played to the cameras, Nady and I slipped inside the Hall.

"All rise," the bailiff intoned.

Judge McDaniel's courtroom smelled of mold as two deputies escorted Freddie to the defense table. Freshly shaved and wearing the charcoal suit and striped tie that I had picked out for him from the donated clothes closet at the PD's Office, he appeared jumpy.

I whispered, "I need you to stay calm and look the jurors in the eye."

He nodded, but I wasn't sure that he was listening.

I looked around the airless room. Freddie had no rooting section. There were no members of Moriarty's family in the gallery, either. His parents were deceased, his ex-wives had no desire to be here, and his children were estranged and lived out of town. O'Neal stood at the prosecution table along with a junior prosecutor and Inspector Wong. As the lead homicide inspector, Wong was the only witness allowed in court before her testimony.

The gallery was half-full. Interest in Freddie's case had waned in the year that he had been in jail. In a display of institutional support, Turner was in the front row behind O'Neal. I figured that she would stay through the start of jury selection.

Rosie stood behind me. She usually showed up for the start of major trials in a display of solidarity. She exchanged greetings with Roosevelt Johnson, who was standing next to her. He was wearing his customary suit and tie. I like having Pete sit in the gallery because he has good instincts for jury selection, but he was on our witness list. More importantly, he was busy trying to find additional witnesses.

Jerry Edwards stood by himself in the third row. He stared at his spiral notebook and made no attempt to interact with two reporters from the local TV stations. In a sign of the times,

I recognized two influencers who would post updates on TikTok and Instagram. Nady told me that they're making six figures. The cable news networks didn't deem our case juicy enough to cover. As always, the courtroom junkies, retirees, law students, and homeless people took their regular spots in the gallery. Only one person wore a mask—a homeless guy named Marvin who showed up in court almost every day.

Here we go.

A standing fan pushed the heavy air as Judge McDaniel emerged from her chambers, surveyed her domain, and strode to her leather chair. She turned on her computer and glanced at her docket. "Please be seated."

She wouldn't touch her gavel.

She addressed the bailiff. "We are in session and on the record. Please call our case."

"The People versus Frederick Alvarez. The charge is first-degree murder."

"Counsel will state their names for the record."

"Catherine O'Neal and Edward George for the People."

"Michael Daley and Nadezhda Nikonova for the defense."

"Thank you." The judge cleared her throat. "Pursuant to updated City Covid policy, I am no longer required to ask you to wear a face covering, but you may do so if you wish. I would ask attorneys and witnesses to remove your masks when you address the court. I will allow potential and seated jurors to wear masks if they desire, but I will not require them to do so. Any questions or last-minute issues?"

Silence.

"Let's pick a jury."

Prosecutors and defense lawyers disagree about almost everything, but everybody acknowledges that trials are frequently won and lost at jury selection. The tedious process is the most important and least scientific part of trial work. Big-time jury consultants charge well-heeled clients hundreds of thousands of dollars to analyze questionnaires, prepare demographic studies, dissect body language, and, supposedly, pick the perfect panel. I have always been skeptical, but I have seen cases where jury consultants have had a major impact. In Freddie's case, it was an unaffordable luxury, so Nady and I would have to rely on intuition.

Conventional wisdom says that defense lawyers should choose jurors who are attentive, thoughtful, and, most importantly, susceptible to persuasion. The oversimplified version of this trope suggests that we should try to pick idiots. I'm as cynical as the next guy, but I've never fully bought into it, and I have found that most jurors take their responsibilities seriously. I prioritize people who appear likely to listen carefully, keep an open mind, and follow the jury instructions. Freddie's case would require the jurors to do an analysis of the concept of reasonable doubt. As a result, I was inclined to seat a few people with college degrees. You never know if you've chosen wisely until the trial is over.

Under Judge McDaniel's skillful supervision, we selected twelve jurors and four alternates by eleven o'clock the following morning. Those who hadn't come up with a convincing sob story were seated in the box, feigning nonchalance, eyes revealing nervousness. In a sign that the Covid era was finally behind us, nobody wore a mask. All were focused—for now.

Including alternates, our lineup was evenly divided with eight women and eight men. We had two African Americans, two Latinas, and one Filipino. Six jurors had college degrees. Three worked for tech firms, two worked for the City, one was a postal clerk, one was a supervisor at the Hertz counter at SFO, one was a lawyer with a big firm downtown, one was a grammar school principal, and the rest were retirees. I was hoping that the lawyer would take a leadership role. The woman from Hertz was my sleeper pick for jury foreperson.

Judge McDaniel thanked the jurors for their service. Then she read the standard instructions which she could have recited by heart. "Do not discuss this case with anyone or among yourselves until deliberations begin. Do not do any research on your own or as a group. You may take notes, but do not use a dictionary or other reference materials, investigate the facts or law, conduct experiments, or visit the scene of the events to be described at this trial. Do not look at anything involving this case in the press, on TV, or online."

She added the now-standard admonition that was unnecessary when I started as a Deputy Public Defender. "Do not post anything on Facebook, Twitter, Instagram, Snapchat, WhatsApp, TikTok, or other social media. If you tweet or text, it will cost you."

A couple of jurors nodded.

The judge looked at O'Neal. "Do you wish to make an opening statement?"

She wasn't required to do so, but she wasn't going to decline the invitation.

"Yes, Your Honor." She stood, buttoned the jacket of her charcoal pantsuit, strode to the lectern, opened her laptop, and addressed the jury. "My name is Catherine O'Neal. I am an Assistant District Attorney and a felony prosecutor. I have been a DA for ten years. I am grateful for your service to our community, and I appreciate your time and attention."

Freddie tensed.

O'Neal activated the flat-screen TV and showed a glossy photo of a smiling Moriarty along with his first ex-wife and two children, none of whom were in court. The picture was taken thirty years ago. The happy family posed in front of the Sleeping Beauty Castle at Disneyland.

She cleared her throat. "Frank Moriarty was a successful attorney, valued mentor, generous philanthropist, and loyal friend. He was a loving father and grandfather."

Who cheated on the ex-wife in the photo and two others. The smiling children hadn't spoken to him in years. He barely knew his grandchildren.

O'Neal was still talking. "Frank Moriarty was sixty-six years old when the defendant hit him on the head with a rusty steel rod and murdered him in cold blood in his driveway."

I could have objected on the grounds that O'Neal hadn't proved that Moriarty was murdered, but it's bad form to interrupt early in an opening, and it probably wouldn't have had any impact on the jury.

O'Neal pushed out a melodramatic sigh. "Frank's death is an unspeakable tragedy."

I whispered to Freddie, "She's going to point at you. Look her right in the eye when she does."

O'Neal pointed at Freddie—just the way every prosecutor is taught. "The defendant, Freddie Alvarez, is sitting at the defense table."

Freddie stared right back at her.

O'Neal lowered her arm. "Frank Moriarty lived in a beautiful house in the Marina across the street from the Palace of Fine Arts. On September fifth of last year, he found the defendant smoking heroin in his driveway. He attempted to rob Frank. Then Frank asked him to leave. The defendant refused and became angry. He grabbed a rusty piece of rebar and hit Frank on the back of the head. The Medical Examiner concluded that Frank died instantly."

She was following the conventional playbook. She would always refer to Moriarty by name to humanize him. The jurors didn't know that he had cheated on his wives, ignored his kids, got thrown out of a prestigious law firm, and fought incessantly with his neighbors. Likewise, O'Neal would never mention Freddie's name to dehumanize him. To the jurors, he would always be "the defendant." It may seem trivial, but every detail counts.

O'Neal continued. "Frank's children, grandchildren, friends, and neighbors are devastated. We cannot bring him back, but we can bring his murderer to justice."

I interrupted her to let the jurors know that I was paying attention. "Objection to the term 'murderer.' My client is innocent until proven otherwise."

"Sustained. The jury will disregard the use of the term 'murderer.'"

Sure, they will.

O'Neal plowed ahead. "Frank was a highly acclaimed lawyer who spent his career fighting for the little guy."

Especially himself.

"A neighbor found the defendant—a homeless heroin addict—passed out on Frank's driveway. There was a rusty steel rod on the ground next to him. The rust on the rod matched rust on the defendant's gloves. The blood on the rod matched Frank's. The Medical Examiner determined that Frank died of a blow to the head. The facts are not in dispute."

At trial, every fact is in dispute.

O'Neal spent ten minutes walking the jurors through the crime scene, the discovery of the rebar, and the Medical Examiner's analysis. The jurors were locked in.

Freddie leaned over and whispered, "Can you stop this?"

No. "It'll be our turn shortly."

O'Neal shot a disdainful glance my way, then she faced the jury. "Mr. Daley is going to try to convince you that the defendant didn't attack Frank. Or he'll claim that the defendant acted in self-defense, even though there is no evidence that he did. Or perhaps he'll try to persuade you that it was just happenstance that the defendant was found on Frank's driveway next to a dead body and a bloody steel rod. Or maybe he'll suggest that Frank's death was an accident. Mr. Daley's job is to distract you. That's why I ask you to evaluate the evidence carefully."

O'Neal returned to the lectern. "You are going to hear a lot about the legal concept of 'reasonable doubt.' But common sense is just as critical. It's your job to evaluate the evidence, deliberate carefully, and, most important, use your common sense. I am confident that you will do so. I promise to provide more than enough evidence for you to find beyond a reasonable doubt that the defendant is guilty of murdering Frank Moriarty."

She returned to the prosecution table and sat down.

Judge McDaniel looked my way. "Opening statement, Mr. Daley?"

"Yes, Your Honor." I could have deferred until after O'Neal had completed the prosecution's case, but I wanted to connect with the jurors right away.

I walked to the lectern and placed a single notecard in front of me. "My name is Michael Daley. I am the co-head of the Felony Division of the Public Defender's Office. Freddie Alvarez has been wrongly accused of a crime that he did not commit. It's your job to correct this error and see that justice is served."

I moved closer to the jurors. "Freddie is a San Francisco native and a military veteran. He's a good man who caught some bad breaks. When he was healthy, he was a productive member of society who served his country, worked hard, paid his taxes, and played by the rules. He is honest. He is kind. And he is resilient.

"Freddie doesn't want me to make excuses for him, but I want you to understand why he was living in a tent in the park next to the Palace of Fine Arts on the morning that Frank Moriarty died. He had a bad knee from an IED in Kabul. He suffered from physical and emotional stress when he returned from his military service. He became addicted to alcohol and drugs. He entered treatment programs several times, but he always relapsed. He ran out of money and spiraled into homelessness. He ended up living in several homeless encampments. On the night that Mr. Moriarty died, Freddie had purchased a bottle of vodka at the Walgreens on Lombard Street. He was making his way back to his tent when he stopped to rest in the construction zone in front of Mr. Moriarty's house. Shortly thereafter, Freddie passed out. He was awakened at six o'clock the following morning when a neighbor discovered Freddie sleeping close to Mr. Moriarty's body. The neighbor called the police, who took Freddie in for questioning. Freddie was cooperative. Notwithstanding the fact that he said that he did not kill Mr. Moriarty, the police arrested him.

"Freddie does not deny that he woke up in Mr. Moriarty's driveway. However, he did not kill Mr. Moriarty. He had no reason to attack him, and he didn't have the physical ability to do so. A frail heroin addict and alcoholic with a bad knee did not have the strength to attack a bigger man."

The jurors were listening, but I couldn't tell if they were buying what I was selling.

"The Medical Examiner concluded that Mr. Moriarty died of a crushed skull. However, the purported evidence that Freddie hit Mr. Moriarty is shaky. Ms. O'Neal alleges that Freddie attacked Mr. Moriarty at close quarters. Yet the forensic technicians did not find Mr. Moriarty's blood on Freddie's gloves, person, or clothing. How is that possible?"

I took a deep breath. "Ms. O'Neal noted that Mr. Moriarty was a successful attorney. However, she also left out some important facts. Mr. Moriarty went through three acrimonious divorces and was estranged from his children. He was fired from a prominent law firm because of his combative nature. He was on terrible terms with his neighbors, whom he sued multiple times. He was especially hostile to the homeless people in the Marina. We will provide evidence that several people other than Freddie were in the immediate vicinity on the morning that Mr. Moriarty died. It is possible, even likely, that one of them killed Mr. Moriarty."

O'Neal spoke up. "Move to strike, Your Honor. This is beyond the scope of what is appropriate for an opening."

Yes, it is.

The judge addressed the jury. "I am going to sustain Ms. O'Neal's objection. An opening statement should not be treated as fact. It merely constitutes a road map of what the anticipated evidence will show. Please disregard what Mr. Daley just said."

As if they're going to forget what they just heard.

I lowered my voice. "Ms. O'Neal and I agree on one thing: Frank Moriarty's death is a tragedy. On the other hand, it would compound the tragedy to convict an innocent man of a crime that he did not commit."

"Objection," O'Neal said. "Argumentative."

"Overruled."

I kept my voice even. "The law requires Ms. O'Neal to prove her case beyond a reasonable doubt, a very high standard. Freddie doesn't have to prove his innocence. Nor is he required to put on a defense. Ms. O'Neal asked you to use common sense. So do I. I would also ask you to keep an open mind. Bottom line: Ms. O'Neal will not be able to prove her case beyond a reasonable doubt. As a result, you cannot convict Freddie of murder."

There was no reaction from the jurors as I walked back to the defense table.

The judge spoke to O'Neal. "Please call your first witness, Ms. O'Neal."

"The People call Mr. Henry Keller."

30

"HE WAS DIFFICULT AT TIMES"

O'Neal stood at the lectern. "Please state your name and occupation for the record."

"Henry Keller. I have ownership interests in a portfolio of office buildings, commercial space, and multifamily housing properties worth more than a billion dollars."

I'm impressed.

In his double-breasted Italian suit, powder-blue shirt, and polka dot necktie with a matching pocket square, Keller evoked confidence, authority, and, above all, money. Well, other people's money. Most of the funding for the investments he boasted about came from his well-heeled investors and lenders. His hair was dyed a half-shade darker than when I saw him earlier in the week. I guess he figured that it made him look more sincere. In court, he took on the persona of an avuncular grandfather who would swap jokes with his pals while playing cards and drinking single-malt scotch at the Pacific Union Club. In real life, he would fight his lenders to the death over a tenth of a point on a loan.

O'Neal's tone was conversational. "Could you please tell us where you were at approximately six AM on Tuesday, September fifth, of last year?"

"In my driveway. I was taking out the trash." Keller pivoted toward the jury and flashed a phony smile. "I forgot to do it the night before."

O'Neal asked for permission to approach Keller, which Judge McDaniel granted. She stopped a few feet from the box and pointed at the flat-screen, which showed a Google Maps aerial photo of his house and Moriarty's. "Would you please identify your house?"

"Yes." Keller walked over to the TV and pointed at his house. "3410 Baker Street." He confirmed that Moriarty lived next door.

"You knew Mr. Moriarty?"

"Yes. Frank and I were neighbors for many years."

"Could you please show us Mr. Moriarty's driveway?"

Keller pointed at the driveway of the house next door to his. "Frank was having his driveway replaced. It was covered in gravel and rebar at the time."

"Did you see Mr. Moriarty in his driveway on September fifth of last year?"

"Yes." Keller's expression turned somber. "Sadly, he was deceased."

Not yet. "Move to strike," I said. "With respect, Mr. Keller is not a doctor. It is therefore beyond the scope of his knowledge as to whether Mr. Moriarty was deceased."

Judge McDaniel nodded. "The jury will disregard Mr. Keller's last statement."

Not for long.

O'Neal asked Keller if Moriarty was moving.

"No. He had a substantial wound in the back of his head."

"Did it appear that somebody had hit him with a blunt instrument?"

"Objection. Calls for speculation."

"Overruled."

"Yes," Keller said. "I checked for a pulse. As far as I could tell, there was none."

"Did it appear to you that Mr. Moriarty was dead?"

"Yes."

O'Neal had put the first points on the board. In a murder case, you need a decedent. She pointed at the TV again. "Could you please show us where you found the body?"

"At the red 'X' in the driveway."

O'Neal was conducting a by-the-book direct exam. She was asking Keller precise questions, and he was responding with short answers.

"Did you see anyone else in the driveway?"

"Yes." Keller pointed at Freddie. "The defendant. He was lying unconscious about a yard from Frank's body. I tried to talk to him, but he didn't answer."

"Did you notice anything else?"

"There was a rusty steel rod next to his right hand. I think it was rebar."

"Did you touch it?"

"No. I called 9-1-1. The police and EMTs arrived within ten minutes. I gave my initial statement to Sergeant David Dito. I gave a more detailed statement to Inspector Melinda Wong later the same day."

O'Neal moved back to the lectern. "Did Mr. Moriarty ever have any previous contact with the defendant?"

"Objection," I said. "This is outside the scope of Mr. Keller's knowledge."

"No, it isn't," O'Neal said. "Mr. Keller has direct personal knowledge of contact between Mr. Moriarty and the defendant."

"Overruled."

Keller sat up taller. "A few nights before Frank was killed, I saw him arguing with the defendant. Frank was upset that the defendant was smoking heroin in his driveway. He ordered the defendant to leave. After a brief argument in which the defendant threatened Frank, the defendant left."

Freddie's neck turned red. He leaned over and whispered to me. "He's lying."

"We'll deal with it."

The judge looked my way. "Please instruct your client not to speak unless I invite him to do so."

"Yes, Your Honor." I leaned over and whispered in Freddie's ear. "Please, Freddie."

O'Neal had what she needed. "No further questions."

"Cross-exam, Mr. Daley?"

You bet. "Yes, Your Honor. May we approach the witness?"

"You may."

I buttoned my suit jacket and headed to the front of the box. "Mr. Keller, you knew the decedent for many years, didn't you?"

O'Neal stood up as if she was thinking about objecting but reconsidered. It was a legitimate question, and, on cross, you're allowed to lead the witness.

"Yes," Keller said.

"You didn't always get along, did you?"

"He was difficult at times."

"You and Mr. Moriarty had a contentious relationship involving multiple lawsuits, didn't you?"

"Objection. Mr. Daley's question is about a subject that wasn't addressed on direct."

She was right. You aren't allowed to ask questions on cross-exam about matters that were not discussed during direct.

"Sustained."

One more time. "You and Mr. Moriarty didn't like each other, did you?"

"Objection."

"Sustained. You know better, Mr. Daley."

Yes, I do. We'll get back to this when we present our defense. I inched closer to Keller. "You didn't see any activity in Mr. Moriarty's driveway prior to the time that you found his body, did you?"

"No."

"You therefore don't know how or when Mr. Moriarty and Freddie found their way to the driveway, do you?"

"No."

"It's possible that Mr. Moriarty was already dead by the time that Freddie arrived and passed out, isn't it?"

"I suppose."

"You have no personal knowledge of how or when Mr. Moriarty died, do you?"

"It looked like your client hit him in the head with a piece of rebar."

"But you didn't see my client hit him, did you?"

"No."

Good. "You also claimed that you saw and heard my client arguing with Mr. Moriarty at some point before Mr. Moriarty died, right?"

"I did."

"When exactly did that happen?"

"I don't recall the exact date."

"A week before Mr. Moriarty died? A month? A year?"

"A few days."

"Did you talk to Mr. Moriarty about it?"

"No."

"That's because your relationship with Mr. Moriarty had deteriorated to the point that you were communicating only through your lawyers, right?"

"Objection. Relevance."

"Your Honor," I said, "Mr. Keller's relationship to the decedent is relevant to the matters at hand."

"Overruled."

Keller invoked a dismissive tone. "I didn't talk to Frank about it. And yes, on those rare occasions that he and I needed to communicate, we did so through our lawyers."

"That's because you detested him, right?"

"Objection."

"Sustained."

Fine. I moved closer to Keller. "When did this alleged conversation take place?"

"I believe it was around two AM."

"Do you know what the alleged argument was about?"

"Frank was upset that your client was smoking heroin in his driveway. It wasn't the first time. Frank told him to get off his property. Your client refused to leave."

"You were sleeping inside your house when this was happening?"

"Yes."

"They woke you up?"

"Yes."

"Did you go outside to see what was going on?"

"No."

"Did you look out the window?"

"Yes."

"Was it dark?"

"Of course."

"Foggy? Cold?"

"It was San Francisco weather."

"It probably means that your windows were closed."

"Probably."

I pointed at Freddie. "But you're absolutely sure that you saw my client arguing with Mr. Moriarty in the middle of the night?"

"Yes."

"What was he wearing?"

"A windbreaker, I believe."

"What color?"

"I don't recall. It was dark."

"How long was his hair?"

"I don't recall."

"Was he clean-shaven or wearing a beard?"

"I don't recall."

"You don't recall much of anything, do you?"

"Objection. Argumentative."

"Withdrawn." I took a step back. "How old are you, Mr. Keller?"

"Objection. Relevance."

"Your Honor," I said, "Mr. Keller is purporting to describe a conversation that he personally observed. As a result, his age, health, vision, and hearing are very relevant."

"Overruled."

"Sixty-six," Keller said.

"You're wearing eyeglasses today. Is that for near-sightedness or far-sightedness?"

"Near-sightedness."

"So you have difficulty seeing things that are far away without your glasses?"

"That's what near-sightedness is, Mr. Daley."

Here goes. "Were you wearing your glasses when you allegedly saw this argument in your neighbor's driveway in the middle of the night?"

"Yes."

"You're absolutely sure?"

The telltale hesitation. "Absolutely."

"Absolutely," I repeated, sarcastic. "You weren't wearing your glasses, were you?"

"Yes, I was. I keep them next to my bed. I always put them on as soon as I wake up."

"Come on, Mr. Keller."

"Objection."

"Sustained. Move on, Mr. Daley."

"Mr. Keller," I said, "I notice that you are wearing hearing aids today."

"I am. Is there something wrong with that?"

"Absolutely not." I faked a smile. "Some of my colleagues think that I should get them, too. You said that you were asleep right before you allegedly heard this argument?"

"Yes."

"Were you wearing your hearing aids?"

"I believe so."

"You leave them in when you go to sleep?"

"Sometimes."

"Which means that sometimes you don't," I said. "Did you put them on when you got out of bed?"

"I don't recall."

"Sounds like you weren't wearing them."

"I believe that I was."

"But you aren't absolutely sure?"

"I don't recall."

"I think you do."

"Objection."

"Sustained."

I stayed focused on Keller. "Are you absolutely sure that you put on your hearing aids and your glasses when you got up to find out what was going on outside?"

"Objection. Asked and answered."

"Asked, but not answered," I said.

"Overruled. Please answer the question," the judge said.

He shrugged. "I don't recall."

"That's because this entire episode never happened, right? And even if Mr. Moriarty did, in fact, yell at a homeless person in the middle of the night, given your issues with your hearing aids and your glasses, it's possible that Mr. Moriarty with arguing with a different homeless person in the driveway, correct?"

"No."

"You can't possibly know that for sure."

"Objection. Mr. Daley is testifying."

Yes, I am.

"Sustained."

One more time. "Let's be honest, Mr. Keller. You have no idea if my client was there, do you?"

"I believe that he was."

"You were able to make this determination in the middle of the night while you weren't wearing your glasses or your hearing aids?"

"Objection. Asked and answered."

"Sustained."

I exhaled heavily. "And since you weren't wearing your hearing aids, you have no idea what was said, do you?"

"I couldn't hear every word clearly, but I got the gist of it. Frank ordered your client to leave his property. Your client refused."

"If it happened at all, you would acknowledge that it could have been somebody else—perhaps another homeless person, right?"

Keller's voice was adamant. "It was your client. Frank knew who he was. He called him by name: Freddie."

"Isn't it possible that he could have been addressing somebody else with a similar-sounding name such as Eddie or Teddy?"

"No."

"Would it change your answer if I could demonstrate to you that there was a person named Eddie in the immediate vicinity that morning?"

Another hesitation. "No."

"You're absolutely sure even though you weren't wearing your hearing aids?"

"Yes."

"Are you aware of the penalties for perjury, Mr. Keller?"

"Objection."

"Sustained."

"No further questions, Your Honor."

O'Neal passed on re-direct.

The judge looked at the clock above the door. "It's almost noon. This would be a good time to recess for lunch."

31

"CAN HE JUST SIT THERE AND LIE?"

Freddie was agitated as I sat in the holding tank down the hall from Judge McDaniel's courtroom. "Keller was lying," he insisted. "I never met Moriarty. I never talked to him. I never smoked in his driveway until the night that he died. I sure as hell didn't argue with him a few days before."

"We discredited his testimony on cross," I said.

"I'm not so sure."

"The jurors were paying attention."

"That doesn't mean that they agreed with you."

True. "Can anybody corroborate your story?"

"Of course not. There's no way to prove I wasn't there."

"Is it possible that he confused you with somebody else?"

"Of course." His tone turned acerbic. "Guys like Keller think all homeless people look alike."

That's probably true.

He lowered his voice. "Put me on the stand to testify that this phantom argument never took place. The jury will believe me."

"We'll make that decision later in the trial."

"We should make the decision now."

I kept my voice even. "It's early, Freddie. We'll go after Keller again during our defense. In the meantime, I need you to remain calm and stay the course."

"Fine."

Nady pushed a turkey sandwich across the table to Freddie. "Eat something."

"I'm not hungry."

"You need to keep up your strength."

"What difference does it make if guys like Keller can just make stuff up?"

"We'll deal with it, Freddie. Things are never as bad as they seem at first."

"We're getting killed."

I spoke up again. "The prosecution always has the upper hand at the beginning of a trial."

"Then you guys had better start fighting back."

"We already are."

32

"IT'S THE DEFENDANT"

Trial resumed at two PM. O'Neal stood at the lectern and spoke in a respectful voice. "Do you live around the corner from Frank Moriarty's house?"

Shreya Patel's demeanor was professional. "Yes."

"Do you have a security camera mounted above your garage door which points toward the street?"

"Yes."

O'Neal introduced Patel's security video into evidence. She ran it for the jury at regular speed, then in slow motion, then regular speed again. She stopped it at twelve-thirty AM.

"Could you please confirm that this image was taken by your security camera at 12:30 AM on September fifth of last year?"

"Yes."

"Do you recognize the person who passed in front of your house?"

"Yes." Patel glanced at Freddie. "It's the defendant."

O'Neal ran a little more of the video and stopped it again. "This image was taken by the same camera at twelve-thirty-nine that morning?"

"Correct."

"Do you recognize the person in the video?"

"Yes. It's my neighbor, Frank Moriarty."

"How long would it have taken Mr. Moriarty and the defendant to have walked around the corner to Mr. Moriarty's house?"

"About thirty seconds."

"So it's likely that the defendant was already at Frank's house when Frank walked around the corner?"

"Objection," I said. "Calls for speculation."

"Sustained."

O'Neal had what she needed. "No further questions."

"Cross-exam, Mr. Daley?"

"Yes, Your Honor." The judge granted my request to approach the box. "Ms. Patel, the video shows your driveway, the street in front of your house, and the house across the street, right?"

"Right."

"It doesn't show Mr. Moriarty's house, does it?"

"No."

"You were asleep when Mr. Moriarty and my client walked by your house?"

"Yes."

"So you didn't see anything that happened in front of Mr. Moriarty's house, did you?"

"No."

"And you have no personal knowledge as to the circumstances surrounding Mr. Moriarty's death, do you?"

"No."

Time to try to plant a few seeds with the jury. "You and Mr. Moriarty had an acrimonious relationship, didn't you?"

"Objection," O'Neal said. "Once again, Mr. Daley knows better than to ask questions on cross-exam regarding matters that were not addressed on direct."

Yes, I do.

"Sustained."

I was still looking at Patel. "You were angry at Mr. Moriarty because his contractors arrived early every morning and repeatedly woke up your daughter, weren't you?"

"Objection."

"Sustained."

"You and Mr. Moriarty dated for a short time which ended badly, didn't it?"

O'Neal's voice rose. "Objection. This wasn't addressed on direct exam. Moreover, it lacks foundation and is irrelevant to these proceedings."

Correct, correct, and correct.

"Sustained." Judge McDaniel rolled her eyes. "If you wish to pursue these lines of questioning, Mr. Daley, you'll have to do so when you present your defense."

"Yes, Your Honor. No further questions."

Sergeant David Dito sat in the box, uniform pressed, star polished, manner professional. He wouldn't touch the cup of water that he had poured for himself. Strong witnesses never drink because it makes them look nervous.

He spoke deliberately as O'Neal led him through a crisp summary of his CV. "I have been a sworn officer since 2014." He confirmed that he had started his career at Mission Station, and then he worked at Taraval, Central, and Park Stations. "I moved to Northern Station about five years ago."

"Were you on duty on the morning of Tuesday, September fifth, of last year?"

"I was." Dito said that he had worked a double shift on Labor Day. "My partner and I were preparing to log out when we got a call from 9-1-1 dispatch at six AM. Mr. Henry Keller had discovered an unresponsive individual in the driveway of the house next door to his. A second man was also unconscious but breathing. I answered the call and requested police backup and a medical unit. At six-oh-five, I checked out a police unit and drove to the scene. I arrived at six-twelve. I was the first officer at the scene."

"You met Mr. Keller in the driveway?"

"I did. He said that the decedent was a man named Frank Moriarty, who was his next-door neighbor. He directed me to Mr. Moriarty's body."

"Move to strike," I said. "Officer Dito is not qualified to determine whether Mr. Moriarty was deceased at the time."

Judge McDaniel looked at Dito. "Could you please clarify your answer?"

"Yes, Your Honor. Mr. Moriarty was unconscious when I arrived. As far as I could tell, he wasn't breathing. There was a substantial wound on the back of his skull. His shirt had blood stains. Mr. Keller had attempted to revive Mr. Moriarty, but he couldn't get a pulse. I administered CPR, but I was unsuccessful. The EMTs arrived two minutes later. Unfortunately, Mr. Moriarty never regained consciousness. He was pronounced dead at the scene by the EMTs who were in real-time contact with an emergency room physician at San Francisco General."

It was solid testimony from a veteran cop.

"Did you question Mr. Keller?"

"Yes. I conducted a preliminary interview after the EMTs arrived. Inspector Melinda Wong took a more detailed statement later the same day."

"Did you see anybody else in the vicinity?"

"Yes." Dito pointed at Freddie. "The defendant was unconscious and lying down on the driveway about a yard from the victim's body. Mr. Keller had woken him up briefly, but he passed out again. I woke him up a second time and determined that he was unarmed and not threatening. I helped him sit up, and I asked the EMTs to assist him."

"Did the defendant say anything to you?"

"He told me that he was coming down from a heroin high. He had also consumed a bottle of vodka. I found drug paraphernalia and an empty bottle within his reach."

"How would you describe his demeanor?"

"Disoriented. I tried to question him, but he was incoherent. I instructed two of my backup officers to accompany the defendant and the EMTs to San Francisco General. My colleagues were able to obtain identifying information from him at that time. He was discharged from San Francisco General and transported to the intake center at County Jail #2, where Inspector Wong conducted further questioning and placed him under arrest. The DA filed murder charges on Wednesday, September sixth."

O'Neal led Dito through a concise description of how he secured the scene and organized a search for witnesses. Then she walked over to the evidence cart and picked up a clear plastic evidence bag containing the rusty steel rod.

She introduced it into evidence and handed it to Dito. "Can you identify this item?"

"Yes. I found this steel rod on the ground next to the defendant's right hand. It appeared that there was blood on it."

"Do you know where this rod came from?"

"I have no personal knowledge, but the driveway was being replaced and there were several similar rods lying on the ground in the gravel."

"It was later determined that the rust on this rod matched rust on the defendant's gloves, wasn't it?"

"Objection," I said. "Calls for a conclusion beyond Officer Dito's knowledge and expertise."

"Sustained."

O'Neal pushed forward. "It was also determined that the victim's blood was on this rod, right?"

"Objection. Also outside Officer Dito's expertise."

"Sustained."

It would be another short-lived victory. O'Neal would undoubtedly call a forensics expert to confirm that the rust on the rod matched the rust on Freddie's gloves. Likewise, a DNA expert would confirm that it was Moriarty's blood.

"No further questions," O'Neal said.

"Cross-exam, Mr. Daley?"

"Yes, Your Honor." I walked to the front of the box and pointed at the rod, which Dito was still holding. "Did Mr. Keller see my client strike Mr. Moriarty with that rod?"

"No."

"Did you?"

"Of course not, Mr. Daley. I wasn't there."

"Did you find any witnesses who did?"

"No."

"So, you don't know what happened to Mr. Moriarty, do you?"

"I have no personal knowledge."

"Did you consider the possibility that somebody other than my client hit Mr. Moriarty?"

"We consider everybody as a potential suspect until we rule them out."

Good answer. "Did you consider the possibility that Mr. Moriarty attacked my client? And that Freddie grabbed this rod to protect himself?"

"We consider all possibilities, Mr. Daley. We found no evidence that he did."

"Bottom line, you have no direct knowledge of how Mr. Moriarty died, do you?"

"No, Mr. Daley."

"No further questions."

O'Neal spent the next twenty minutes laying the foundation. The lead EMT confirmed that Moriarty had no pulse when he arrived. Efforts to resuscitate him were unsuccessful. Moriarty was pronounced dead at the scene at six-thirty-five AM. A crime scene technician testified that there were no working surveillance cameras showing Moriarty's driveway.

I objected to O'Neal's questions from time to time, but there were few items that I could legitimately dispute. On cross, I got each witness to confirm that they had no personal knowledge as to how Moriarty had died. More important, they admitted that they had no knowledge of Freddie's involvement in Moriarty's death. It wasn't going to get the charges dropped, but it inched us a little closer to creating some doubt in the jurors' minds.

Having checked off the boxes regarding the discovery of the body and the securing of the scene, O'Neal turned to the next order of business: cause of death. "The People call Dr. Joy Siu."

Dr. Siu strode to the front of the court, was sworn in, and took her place in the box. She tapped the microphone, nodded at the jury, and looked straight at O'Neal.

"What is your occupation?" O'Neal asked.

Siu adjusted the collar of her pressed white coat. "I have been the Chief Medical Examiner of the City and County of San Francisco for eleven years. Before that, I was a tenured professor and Chair of the PhD program in anatomic pathology at UCSF."

There was nothing to be gained by letting her recite her resume into the record. "Your Honor, we will stipulate that Dr. Siu is a recognized authority in her field."

"Thank you, Mr. Daley."

O'Neal introduced the autopsy report into evidence and presented it to Siu as if it was the Rosetta Stone. "You performed the autopsy of Mr. Frank Moriarty on Wednesday, September sixth, of last year, and you prepared this report?"

"I did."

"Were you able to determine the cause of death?"

"I was." Siu pretended to glance at her report. "Massive brain trauma and a fractured skull from an overpowering blow to the back of the head inflicted by a rusty steel rod."

"How soon did he die?"

"Almost instantaneously."

"Any chance of survival?"

"Unlikely."

"Were you able to determine time of death?"

"Based upon a video sighting of the decedent at twelve-thirty-nine AM along with an analysis of undigested food in his stomach and the usual markers such as rigor mortis and body temperature, I concluded that Mr. Moriarty died sometime between twelve-forty and four AM."

"No further questions."

"Cross-exam, Mr. Daley?"

I wasn't going to score any points with the jury by questioning Siu's conclusion. "No, Your Honor."

"Please call your next witness, Ms. O'Neal."

"The People call Lieutenant Kathleen Jacobsen of the San Francisco Police Department."

O'Neal was building her case one block at a time. Jacobsen is SFPD's highly regarded forensic evidence expert.

33

"RUST IS RUST"

O'Neal's next witness sat in the box, manner professional, expression stoic. "My name is Lieutenant Kathleen Jacobsen. I have been an evidence technician for the San Francisco Police Department for thirty-six years."

O'Neal spoke from the lectern. "It's good to see you again, Lieutenant."

"Thank you, Ms. O'Neal."

Judge McDaniel nodded at Jacobsen. The two veterans of the justice system have crossed paths countless times, and they respect each other. I stipulated to Jacobsen's expertise. The no-nonsense dean of SFPD's evidence gurus is in her mid-sixties. Her badge was displayed in the breast pocket of the jacket. Her makeup was subtle, her salt-and-pepper hair styled in a low-maintenance layered cut. The daughter of an IBM engineer grew up in Atherton. She turned down a tennis scholarship from Stanford to play water polo and study criminal justice at USC, where she graduated summa cum laude. She earned a Master's from Cal in forensic science and joined SFPD. One of the first lesbians to work her way up the ranks, she has a stellar reputation on forensic evidentiary matters, with specialties in fingerprints and blood spatter. Her wife, Jill, is a retired San Francisco firefighter.

O'Neal stayed at the lectern. "On Tuesday, September fifth, of last year, were you called to the scene of an apparent homicide in front of the home of Mr. Frank Moriarty?"

"Yes." She said that she arrived at seven-fifty-seven AM. "Mr. Moriarty had been pronounced dead at the scene at six-thirty-five AM."

"Who else was there?"

She pointed at the prosecution table. "Inspector Melinda Wong had taken charge. Sergeant David Dito was the first officer at the scene. They had secured the vicinity in accordance with standard procedure. Sergeant Dito had assembled a team to canvass for witnesses."

O'Neal put a photo of the scene on the flat-screen. "Could you please describe what you saw?"

"Of course." Jacobsen walked over to the TV and used a Cross pen to point at a red "X." "The decedent's neighbor, Mr. Henry Keller, discovered the body here on the driveway. Attempts by the EMTs to resuscitate the victim were unsuccessful." She pointed at a blue "X" close to the location of Moriarty's body. "The defendant was found here. As you can see, he was within a few feet of the body." Jacobsen pointed at a yellow "X." "Sergeant Dito found a rusty steel rod that would have been used as rebar in connection with the repaving of the driveway."

Freddie leaned over and whispered, "Can you do anything?"

Not yet. "Soon."

O'Neal walked to the evidence cart, picked up the rod, and gave it to Jacobsen. "Did you find any fingerprints on this rod?"

"It is impossible to lift identifiable fingerprints from a rusty steel rod."

"Did you find any blood?"

"I did." Jacobsen sat up taller. "DNA tests confirmed that the blood matched the blood of the victim, Frank Moriarty."

I spoke up in a subdued voice. "With respect, Your Honor, I must move to strike Lieutenant Jacobsen's testimony. I stipulated to her expertise on forensics, not DNA."

"Agreed, Mr. Daley. The jury will disregard Lieutenant Jacobsen's testimony regarding DNA evidence."

O'Neal didn't argue. It was a legitimate objection. More importantly for her, it would be another temporary victory for me. Her next witness would likely be her DNA expert.

O'Neal walked over to the evidence cart and picked up Freddie's gloves, which were enclosed in a clear evidence bag. She handed them to Jacobsen. "When the defendant was taken in for questioning, he was wearing these gloves, wasn't he?"

"Yes. The defendant surrendered them to Inspector Wong voluntarily."

"Did you find anything on the gloves?"

"Rust."

"Did you compare the rust on the gloves to the rust on the steel rod?"

"I did. In my professional opinion, the rust matched."

"No further questions."

"Cross-exam, Mr. Daley?"

"Yes, Your Honor." I moved to the front of the box. "Lieutenant Jacobsen, you're an expert on blood spatter, right?"

"Right."

"So you must have studied the blood spatter at the scene, right?"

"Right. Unfortunately, because the scene was covered in gravel and dust, it was difficult to analyze the extent of the spatter, which was limited to a two-foot circular area near the decedent's head."

"Did you find any blood on my client's gloves, hands, clothing, or person?"

"No."

"Ms. O'Neal claims that my client struck the decedent with this rod, which means the attack would have been at very close range, right?"

"Correct."

"And it was the type of wound that would have led to substantial bleeding, which would presumably have resulted in a significant blood spatter, wouldn't it?"

"Not necessarily, Mr. Daley. Especially if Mr. Moriarty had turned and was moving away from the defendant."

"How is it possible that you found none of Mr. Moriarty's blood on my client's gloves, clothing, or person?"

"As I said, I believe that the decedent was moving away from the defendant when he was struck."

I shook my head melodramatically. "Right."

"Move to strike," O'Neal said.

"The jury will disregard Mr. Daley's last statement."

I kept my eyes on Jacobsen. "You testified that this rod was covered with rust, right?"

"Right."

"And you found traces of rust on my client's gloves?"

"Correct."

"And you believe that the rust on his gloves matched the rust on the steel rod?"

"Yes."

"How many steel rods did you find in the driveway?"

Jacobsen paused. "About a dozen."

"Were they all the same?"

"I believe so."

"Every one of them was covered in rust, right?"

"Right."

"Rust is rust, isn't it?"

"I don't understand your question."

"The rust on one steel rod is the same as the rust on all of the others, right?"

"If they're made of the same steel."

"Did you test each of the rods to determine whether they were made of the same steel?"

"No, but it appeared to me that they were of the same type."

"How do you know that the rust on my client's gloves came from the particular steel rod that was nearest his hand?"

"The rust matched."

"It also matched a dozen other steel rods on the same driveway. I'm asking you once again, how can you be sure that the rust on Freddie's glove came from the rod that had traces of Frank Moriarty's blood?"

"Because that rod was found within inches of your client's hand."

"But you just admitted that there were a dozen other identical rods on the driveway, right?"

"Right."

"You would therefore acknowledge that my client could have handled another piece of steel on that driveway or even at some other time and place that would have left identical traces of rust on his gloves, right?"

"Anything is possible, Mr. Daley. But it seems highly unlikely to me."

Me, too. "But it's possible, right?"

"Anything is possible," she repeated.

"No further questions."

The wiry man with the pale complexion, widow's peak, rimless spectacles, and dour demeanor hunched in the box. "My name is George Romero. I am a supervising lab technician in the Forensic Services Division of SFPD's Criminalistics Lab. I have held that position for eighteen years. Before that, I was an assistant lab technician for twelve years."

O'Neal was standing in front of him. "What is your area of expertise?"

"DNA evidence."

Romero is a dreary but competent little drone who has spent three decades working in a windowless bunker in the basement of the Hall of Justice. The native of Bernal Heights has a chemistry degree from State, a meticulous manner, and an inquisitive mind. He isn't charismatic or engaging, but he has a knack for explaining complex scientific concepts in easy-to-understand sound bites. If Lieutenant Jacobsen is the DA's point person on fingerprints, Romero is the go-to guy on DNA.

O'Neal led him through his CV. Then she held up the steel rod as if it was the Holy Grail. "You're familiar with this piece of rebar, Mr. Romero?"

"Yes. It was found at the scene of the murder of Frank Moriarty."

Come on. "Move to strike the term 'murder,'" I said.

Judge McDaniel rolled her eyes. "So ordered. You know better, Mr. Romero."

"I'm sorry, Your Honor."

O'Neal pretended that she hadn't heard the exchange. "Mr. Romero, you found blood on this bar, didn't you?"

"Yes."

"Did you analyze it for DNA?"

"Yes."

O'Neal led Romero through a concise explanation of the tests that he had performed. Romero's rehearsed presentation included just enough technical jargon to lend an air of gravitas but was accessible enough to keep the jurors' interest. Most important, it was short.

O'Neal asked Romero if he had obtained a DNA sample from Moriarty.

"Yes. We had samples of his hair, fingernails, skin, and blood from his autopsy."

"Did the DNA from the blood on this bar match Mr. Moriarty's DNA?"

Romero waited a beat in a ham-handed attempt to build suspense. "It did."

This comes as no surprise.

O'Neal put the ball on the tee for him. "What did you conclude?"

"This bar was used to strike the fatal blow to Mr. Moriarty's head."

And that's that.

"No further questions," O'Neal said.

"Cross-exam, Mr. Daley?"

"Yes, Your Honor." I walked to the front of the box. "Mr. Romero, did you find DNA on this bar from anybody other than the decedent?"

"Objection," O'Neal said. "Mr. Daley is raising an issue not addressed on direct."

Here goes. "Your Honor, Ms. O'Neal asked Mr. Romero to discuss matters relating to DNA tests that he performed on evidence collected at the scene of Mr. Moriarty's death. She opened the door. I should be allowed to explore the scope of Mr. Romero's investigation."

O'Neal fired back. "Mr. Daley can address these issues during the defense case."

True.

Judge McDaniel opted for expediency. "I'm going to overrule the objection and give you a little leeway, Mr. Daley. If you start straying too far from the matters at hand, I will stop you and insist that you'll need to address those issues during your defense."

Fine. "Thank you, Your Honor." I turned back to Romero. "Did you find anybody else's DNA on the bar?"

Romero paused. "I found traces of DNA that did not match the decedent's."

"Were you able to identify this person?"

"No."

"And it wasn't Freddie Alvarez's DNA, was it?"

"No."

"Somebody else must have touched this steel rod, right?"

"It appears to be the case."

"Did you consider the possibility that the unidentified individual killed Frank Moriarty?"

"I found no evidence, Mr. Daley."

"But it's possible, right?"

"Anything is possible."

Was that so hard? "Are you aware that Ms. O'Neal believes that my client struck Mr. Moriarty with this bar? And that it opened a substantial wound?"

"Yes."

"Such a wound would have generated a significant blood spatter, right?"

"Objection. This is outside Mr. Romero's area of expertise."

"Sustained."

I didn't react. "Were you asked to test my client's skin, gloves, or clothing for Mr. Moriarty's blood?"

"Yes."

"Did you find any DNA that matched Mr. Moriarty's?"

Romero darted an uncomfortable glance at O'Neal. "No."

"How is that possible, Mr. Romero? Especially if my client supposedly hit Mr. Moriarty in the back of the head in close quarters and opened a substantial bloody wound?"

"Objection," O'Neal said. "Mr. Romero is an expert on DNA, not blood spatter."

"Sustained."

"Did you consider the possibility that somebody else hit Mr. Moriarty?" I asked.

"Objection. Speculation."

"Your Honor," I said, "I am simply asking if he considered any alternate suspects."

"Overruled."

Romero fidgeted. "I found no DNA evidence that somebody other than the defendant hit the decedent."

"Because you didn't look? Or Inspector Wong and the DA didn't ask you to look?"

"Move to strike."

"Withdrawn. No further questions, Your Honor."

"Re-direct, Ms. O'Neal?"

"No, Your Honor."

"Please call your next witness."

"The People call Inspector Melinda Wong."

34

"THE EVIDENCE POINTED AT HIM"

O'Neal stood at the lectern at three-forty-five on Wednesday afternoon, expression somber, voice deliberate. "Could you please show us exactly where Sergeant Dito found the rusty steel rod that was covered in Frank Moriarty's blood?"

"Of course." A confident Inspector Wong stood next to the flat-screen and pointed at the yellow "X" on an enlarged photo of Moriarty's driveway. "Here."

"And the spot where the neighbor, Henry Keller, found Frank's body?"

Wong pointed at a red "X." "Here."

"And the defendant?"

"He was passed out here at the blue 'X.'" Wong noted that the rebar was between Freddie's right hand and Moriarty's body.

"How far was the steel rod from the defendant's hand?"

"One foot."

"And how far was Mr. Moriarty's body from the rod?"

"Less than two feet."

"Less than two feet," O'Neal repeated. "Was anybody else in the vicinity when Mr. Keller found the body?"

"According to Mr. Keller, no."

Judge McDaniel's courtroom was filled with an intense silence. The twelve jurors and four alternates were focused on Wong. She and O'Neal were executing a textbook direct exam. Their carefully-rehearsed presentation was concise and convincing. I objected frequently, emphatically, and, for the most part, inconsequentially.

Wong returned to the box and described how she had secured the scene and supervised the collection of evidence in accordance with SFPD's best practices. She assured the jurors that there had been no lapses in the chain of custody. She said that Sergeant Dito had taken statements from everybody in the immediate vicinity, although there were no witnesses to Moriarty's death. O'Neal built her case block by block. Instead of reading casebooks on evidence, the professors from the local law schools should have brought their students to Judge McDaniel's court.

O'Neal was still at the lectern. "Could you please describe the defendant's demeanor when you first encountered him?"

"He was disoriented and combative. I suspected that he was coming down from an alcohol or drug high."

"Move to strike," I said. "Foundation. If Ms. O'Neal wishes to argue that my client was drunk or high, she should introduce evidence of alcohol or drug tests taken at the time."

O'Neal shrugged. "I was simply asking for Inspector Wong's observations, not a medical diagnosis."

"Overruled."

It probably doesn't matter.

Wong added, "The defendant did not deny the fact that he had consumed drugs and alcohol on the morning that he killed Frank Moriarty."

Nice try. "Move to strike. A non-denial is not the same as an admission. In addition, Inspector Wong offered a conclusion that is not supported by the evidence. It's up to the jury to decide whether my client killed the decedent."

"The jury will disregard Inspector Wong's last statement."

Sure, they will. Either way, O'Neal made her point.

O'Neal continued to work methodically. "Did the defendant offer any explanation as to what happened to Mr. Moriarty?"

"Objection," I said. "The defendant was under no obligation to answer Inspector Wong's questions, and no negative inference should be suggested to the jury if he refused to do so."

"Sustained."

"Did he offer any explanation as to how a rusty steel rod with Mr. Moriarty's blood on it found its way to a spot between the defendant's and Mr. Moriarty's body?"

"Objection. Same.

"Sustained."

"Inspector, based upon the evidence at the scene and your interviews with the defendant and others, could you please summarize your conclusion as to what happened in Mr. Moriarty's driveway on the morning of September fifth of last year?"

"Yes, Ms. O'Neal." Wong turned and spoke directly to the jury. "The defendant, a homeless person with a history of animosity toward Frank Moriarty, came to Mr. Moriarty's driveway and attempted to rob him. Mr. Moriarty confronted the defendant for trespassing and smoking heroin on his property. The defendant picked up a rusty steel rod from the construction area on the driveway and hit Mr. Moriarty on the head, crushing his skull and killing him instantly. Mr. Moriarty's blood was found on the rod. Traces of rust matching rust on the bar were found on the defendant's gloves. After killing Mr. Moriarty, the defendant passed out from a combination of alcohol and drugs. Mr. Henry Keller, a neighbor, found Mr. Moriarty's body along with the steel rod and the defendant the following morning."

"You believe that the defendant caused Mr. Moriarty's death?"

"Yes. Mr. Keller provided evidence that the defendant had a verbal confrontation with Mr. Moriarty a few days before he killed Mr. Moriarty. I believe that the defendant sought out Mr. Moriarty because of the prior confrontation. But for the fact that the defendant bludgeoned him with a steel rod, Frank Moriarty would be alive today."

"No further questions." O'Neal nodded at the jury, closed her laptop, and walked to the prosecution table.

"Cross-exam, Mr. Daley?"

"Yes, Your Honor." I walked over to the evidence cart, picked up the rebar, and handed it to Wong. "You didn't find my client's fingerprints on this steel rod, did you?"

"No."

"Or his blood?"

"No."

"Or his DNA?"

"No."

"So you have no direct evidence connecting him to this rod, do you?"

"It was within inches of the defendant."

"It doesn't mean that Freddie used it to bludgeon Mr. Moriarty."

"It's obvious to me."

"Not to me."

"Objection."

"Withdrawn. You were here when Lieutenant Jacobsen testified that it is virtually impossible to distinguish the rust from one piece of steel to the next, right?"

"Right."

"She noted that it was therefore impossible to determine whether the rust on my client's gloves came from this rod or another piece of steel, didn't she?"

"She said that the rust on this bar was consistent with the rust on the defendant's gloves."

"And every other piece of rusty steel on Mr. Moriarty's driveway, right?"

"That's theoretically possible, but this bar was within inches of your client's hand."

"That doesn't prove that he touched it."

"Objection. Argumentative."

"Overruled."

Wong answered in a dismissive voice. "It seems highly likely to me."

"Then perhaps we'll have to agree to disagree."

"Objection. There wasn't a question there."

"Sustained."

I inched closer to the box. "Your DNA expert didn't find my client's fingerprints, blood, or DNA on Mr. Moriarty's clothing, did he?"

"No."

"Likewise, he didn't find Mr. Moriarty's fingerprints, blood, or DNA on my client's gloves, person, or clothing, did he?"

"No."

"Doesn't it seem unusual to you that an alleged blow of this type at close range did not cause any blood or DNA to be spattered onto my client's hands?"

"No."

"You also heard Mr. Romero testify that he found DNA on this rod from at least one person other than Mr. Moriarty and my client, right?"

"Right."

"Did you consider the possibility that the unidentified individual killed Mr. Moriarty?"

"I found no evidence, Mr. Daley."

It's your story and you're sticking to it. "My client is homeless and in bad physical condition. He has trouble walking and was addicted to heroin. Given his physical limitations, do you really think he could have attacked a much larger man like Mr. Moriarty with such power?"

"The evidence pointed at him."

"You keep mentioning that the rusty steel rod was found next to my client's right hand. Do you believe that my client used his right hand to hit Mr. Moriarty?"

"It seems likely."

"Are you aware that my client is left-handed?"

"Yes."

"Does it strike you as odd that my client would have used his off-hand to grab a heavy steel bar and hit Mr. Moriarty?"

"It is what it is, Mr. Daley."

"Perhaps it isn't what you think it is, Inspector."

"Objection. Argumentative."

"Sustained."

"You also suggested that Mr. Henry Keller heard my client arguing with the decedent a few nights before he died, didn't you?"

"Yes."

"Yet as we pointed out earlier, Mr. Keller's purported identification of my client was not convincing because it was in the middle of the night and he wasn't wearing his glasses or hearing aids, right?"

"I disagree with your characterization of Mr. Keller's testimony, which I found to be very credible."

"I didn't."

"Objection."

"Withdrawn. You have also suggested that Freddie tried to rob Mr. Moriarty, didn't you?"

"Yes."

"Yet you didn't find Mr. Moriarty's wallet or other belongings in Freddie's possession, did you?"

"No."

"How did you possibly conclude that he attempted to rob Mr. Moriarty?"

"Because of their history."

"Which was based on tenuous testimony by Mr. Keller."

"I disagree."

I feigned exasperation. "Let's be honest, Inspector. You just assumed that my client attacked Mr. Moriarty, didn't you?"

"No."

"Come on, Inspector."

"Look at the evidence, Mr. Daley."

"I did. Did you?"

"Objection."

"Withdrawn," I said. "The fact remains that you don't know what happened, do you?"

"The evidence pointed at him," she repeated.

"By the time you talked to him, you had already decided that Freddie was guilty, right?"

"Objection. Argumentative."

"Sustained."

"You didn't seriously consider any other suspects, did you?"

"Objection. Argumentative."

"Sustained."

"For example," I said, "Mr. Moriarty and his neighbor, Mr. Keller, had a long-running feud that resulted in multiple lawsuits. Did you consider the possibility that Mr. Keller became so upset that he finally snapped and killed Mr. Moriarty?"

"Objection. Calls for speculation. Moreover, Mr. Daley is asking Inspector Wong about matters that were not addressed during direct exam."

"Sustained."

We'll talk about additional potential suspects when we get to our defense.

I hammered Wong on the collection of the evidence and the lack of a direct physical connection between Freddie and Moriarty, but she remained resolute. The jury was paying attention, but I saw no signs that I was convincing them.

After twenty minutes, I turned to the judge. "No further questions, Your Honor." I made my way back to the defense table.

"Re-direct, Ms. O'Neal?"

"No, Your Honor. The prosecution rests."

The judge looked my way. "I am going to adjourn for the day."

No surprise. O'Neal had timed her presentation to conclude at the end of the day so that the jurors would have an opportunity to think about it overnight.

The judge added, "Mr. Daley, do you wish to make a motion before we recess?"

"Yes, Your Honor. The defense moves for a directed acquittal under Penal Code Section 1181.1. We request that the charges against Mr. Alvarez be dropped as a matter of law because there is insufficient evidence to find him guilty beyond a reasonable doubt."

"Denied."

No surprise there, either.

She added, "We will resume at ten o'clock tomorrow morning when you should be prepared to start the defense case."

35

"YOU TRY YOUR CASE WITH THE EVIDENCE THAT YOU HAVE"

Nady looked up from her laptop. "Are we still putting our blood spatter expert up first?"

"Yes," I said.

"Should we change the order of our witnesses?"

I looked at the list on the flat-screen. "No."

At nine-fifteen on Tuesday night, Nady, Dazzle, and I were sitting in the conference room at the PD's Office and refining our defense presentation. Terrence "The Terminator" was at his cubicle down the hall. Rosie was in her office. She had just returned from a campaign meeting. The remaining offices were empty except for a couple of attorneys who were also preparing for trial tomorrow. Luna was sleeping in the corner.

Nady asked if I had heard from Pete.

"Yes," I said. "He just checked in with Jack at his motel. He's had somebody watching him all day. He hasn't left his room."

"Any sign of Jill?"

"Not yet."

Dazzle studied the list. "Should we put Keller up earlier?"

I thought about it for a moment. "I think we should stick to the script. We'll do forensics and experts first. If the jury is buying what we're selling, we might be able to stop there. If not, we'll put up Patel and Keller to establish that they had issues with Moriarty. More important, we'll get them to confirm that Moriarty had big issues with the homeless."

Dazzle grinned. "Are you planning to accuse them of murder?"

"I may suggest it. It will also tee up testimony from Eddie Reynolds. I definitely plan to accuse him of murder. If the jury still isn't buying, we'll put up Jack and accuse him of murder, too."

Dazzle's expression turned serious. "Seems like a stretch."

It is.

We spent another hour fine-tuning our narrative. We would challenge every piece of evidence introduced by the prosecution and try to convince the jury that the DA didn't prove her case beyond a reasonable doubt. We would also try to rebut Wong's testimony that there were no other viable suspects. Admittedly, our presentation wasn't going to be profoundly creative or earth-shatteringly original. When you have nothing else, you stick with what Rosie calls the "nuts and bolts" of criminal defense work. In essence, it means that you try to throw enough mud into the gears of the justice system to gum up the DA's case.

Dazzle took off her reading glasses. "What if it isn't enough?"

We're in serious trouble. "You try your case with the evidence that you have, not the evidence that you wish you had."

36

"HE WOULD HAVE BEEN COVERED IN BLOOD"

I stood at the lectern at ten o'clock the following morning. "Please state your name for the record."

"Dr. Lloyd Russell."

"You're a medical doctor?"

"I have a PhD in criminology. My area of expertise is blood spatter."

I have known Lloyd for decades. Of the hundreds of expert witnesses that I've examined over the years, he's in my personal Hall of Fame. He knows his stuff. He's great in court. He's a straight shooter of unquestionable integrity. Because of our relationship, he doesn't charge me. On top of it all, he's one of the nicest guys on Planet Earth.

"Water?" I asked.

"No, thank you, Mr. Daley."

Lloyd was my criminology professor at Cal. At eighty-eight, the relentlessly upbeat academic has a cherubic face, dancing blue eyes, and a trim gray goatee. Though he had moved to emeritus status, he still teaches a wildly popular graduate seminar every spring. His credentials are impeccable: BS from Harvard, Master's from Stanford, and PhD from Cal. The champion bridge player, scratch golfer, and expert skier always shows up in court in a corduroy jacket with elbow patches, a checkered shirt, and a polka dot tie to bolster his academic bona fides. Outside of court, he wears top-of-the-line Italian suits.

O'Neal stopped me just as I started walking Lloyd through his CV. "Your Honor," she said, "we will stipulate that Dr. Russell is an expert on blood spatter."

Good call, Catherine.

Judge McDaniel was pleased. "Thank you, Ms. O'Neal." She sat in the same row at the symphony as Lloyd and Joni Russell.

I moved to the front of the box and handed the autopsy report to Lloyd. "You reviewed this document?"

"I did."

"Do you agree with Dr. Siu's conclusion as to cause of death?"

"I have no reason to question her findings. She's an excellent pathologist."

"You noted that Dr. Siu identified the cause of death as a blow to the back of the decedent's head with a steel rod?"

He flipped to the last page and pretended to study it. "Yes, Mr. Daley."

I returned to the lectern. "Have you ever been asked to analyze a similar wound?"

"Unfortunately, yes. I have studied several similar cases. As you might expect, the scenes were quite gruesome."

"Would such a wound have generated a substantial spatter?"

"Yes." He stroked his beard. "There are countless blood vessels in the human skull. The nature of the wound would almost certainly have caused blood to fly in a projectile manner that would have resulted in droplets covering an area of several square feet."

"Would you therefore have expected to see a lot of blood in the immediate area of the decedent's body?"

"Yes."

Perfect. "You reviewed the crime scene photos?"

"I did."

"You observed that my client was found unconscious on the ground close to the decedent's body, right?"

"Right."

"You're aware that my client has been accused of bludgeoning the decedent to death with a steel rod from the construction site where the body was found?"

"Yes."

"The steel rod was approximately four feet long, right?"

"Right."

"If that's the case, it means that the person who hit Mr. Moriarty would have been within two feet of him when he hit him, right?"

"Probably closer."

"Given the close quarters, is it your expert opinion that the person who bludgeoned the decedent would have gotten a lot of blood on his hands and clothing?"

"Absolutely."

I pointed at a photo of the crime scene on the flat-screen. "You've seen this?"

"Yes, Mr. Daley. It was taken in the decedent's driveway shortly after his body was removed." He noted the chalk outline and the yellow markers.

"Could you please show us the blood stains on the ground?"

"Of course." He walked over to the TV and removed the wire-rimmed glasses that he always brought to court—even though his eyesight was twenty-twenty—and used them to gesture. "It's a little hard to see because the driveway was being repaved and there was a lot of dust. There are droplets of blood underneath and surrounding Mr. Moriarty's head." He made a slightly larger circle. "There are also droplets within two feet of his head, which indicates that they projected a little farther, which is not uncommon for wounds of this type."

I gave Lloyd a moment to return to the box. "Dr. Russell, in your expert opinion, how likely is it that Mr. Moriarty's blood would have been found on the gloves, skin, and/or clothing of the person who hit him?"

"I can't give you an exact percentage, but it's very likely."

"Ballpark? Fifty percent? Seventy-five percent? Ninety percent?"

He went through his full repertoire of scholarly gestures to give the impression that he was deep in thought, even though he knew the question was coming. He took off his glasses. He played with the elbow patch on his jacket. He stroked his goatee. Finally, he turned and spoke directly to the jury. "Ninety-nine percent."

"Ninety-nine percent," I repeated. "You would have expected to find the decedent's blood on my client's gloves, skin, and/or clothing?"

"Yes. He would have been covered in blood."

I walked over to the evidence cart and picked up a copy of Inspector Wong's report, which O'Neal had introduced into evidence during Wong's testimony. I brought it over to the box and handed it to Lloyd. "You reviewed this report?"

"I did."

"Was there any mention of Mr. Moriarty's blood on my client's gloves, skin, or clothing?"

"No."

"Did that surprise you?"

"Yes. In my opinion, it is highly likely that the decedent's blood would have been found on the defendant's gloves, skin, and/or clothing."

"No further questions."

"Cross-exam, Ms. O'Neal?"

"Yes, Your Honor." She stood at the prosecution table. "Dr. Russell, it's possible that the defendant might have avoided a projectile of blood when he hit Mr. Moriarty, isn't it?"

"Anything is possible, Ms. O'Neal."

"For example, if the defendant had hit Mr. Moriarty while Mr. Moriarty was trying to run away, the blood might not have spattered toward the defendant, right?"

Lloyd closed his eyes and shook his head. "Highly unlikely."

"And even the most sensitive equipment can't always find traces of blood on a person's skin or clothing, right?"

Lloyd kept his voice even. "Like I said, anything is possible—,"

O'Neal cut him off. "Thank you, Dr. Russell."

"Your Honor," I said, "Dr. Russell had not finished his answer."

"Anything you'd like to add, Dr. Russell?"

"Yes, Your Honor. The equipment available to law enforcement nowadays is state-of-the-art and very sensitive. As a result, I believe that Ms. O'Neal's suggestion that no traces of blood would have been found is highly unlikely, if not impossible."

"Any further questions, Ms. O'Neal?"

You should sit down now.

"One more item, Your Honor." She turned to Lloyd. "You've known Mr. Daley for a long time, haven't you?"

"Almost forty years. He was my student at Cal."

"You would therefore be inclined to help him, wouldn't you?"

"I would never let my personal relationships color my professional judgment."

Excellent answer.

"How much is Mr. Daley paying you to appear today?"

I was hoping you would ask.

"Nothing," Lloyd said. "I have reached the point in my career where I don't need the money, and I am more interested in justice."

You should have sat down a couple of minutes ago, Catherine.

"No further questions, Your Honor."

"Re-direct, Mr. Daley?"

"No, Your Honor."

"I was just handed a note that requires me to call a brief recess to review a document. Please be ready to call your next witness in ten minutes."

"He was good," Freddie said, eyes a little brighter.

"He's a gem," I replied.

"Is it enough?"

Not even close. "Not yet."

We were sitting at the defense table awaiting the judge's return. The door in the back of the courtroom opened, and two unexpected visitors made their way down the center aisle and took seats next to Roosevelt. Nick "The Dick" and his great-granddaughter, Nicki, took turns shaking hands with Roosevelt.

Nick turned and spoke to me. "Nice to see you, Mike."

"Thanks for coming out to watch the show."

"I wouldn't miss it. I heard that things aren't going so well."

"We're just starting our defense."

Nick's eyes danced. "Sounds like you're going to have to impress the jury with a little razzle-dazzle."

"That's the idea, Nick."

"Indeed it is. Who's up next?"

"Our fingerprint expert."

37

"FORENSIC EVIDENCE"

The slender man with the jet-black hair, trim mustache, and extended bags under his eyes spoke deliberately. "My name is Sridar Iyengar. I recently retired after thirty years at the San Mateo County Crime Lab. I am now a private consultant."

I stood at the lectern. "What is your area of expertise?"

"Forensic evidence with a specialty in fingerprints."

The gallery was half-empty at ten-fifteen on Tuesday morning. Several of the regulars had headed across the street for coffee. I was grateful that Nick "The Dick" and Roosevelt were still in their seats.

I led Sridar through his resume. He explained that he's a native of San Francisco whose parents were born in India and moved to the Bay Area to be closer to his grandfather, a researcher at UCSF. "I earned my Bachelor's in criminology from San Francisco State and spent my entire career at the San Mateo County Crime Lab."

O'Neal spoke from her seat. "We will stipulate as to Mr. Iyengar's expertise in forensics."

Good decision. Sridar is, in fact, one of California's foremost authorities on fingerprints and forensic evidence. He is also my former neighbor, longtime friend, and one of the most meticulous guys I've ever known. His mom and dad operated an Indian restaurant a few doors from Dunleavy's, which became an unlikely hit among the neighborhood's Irish, Italian, and, later, Chinese families. His scholarly demeanor and engaging manner make him an ideal expert witness, and I have recommended him to several defense attorneys. His post-retirement side hustle has turned into a lucrative second career.

"Have you read the forensic evidence report prepared by Lieutenant Kathleen Jacobsen of the San Francisco Police Department?" I asked.

"I have."

"Do you have any reason to question its contents?"

"No. Lieutenant Jacobsen is an excellent technician with a superb reputation."

I walked over to the evidence cart, picked up the steel rod, and handed it to Sridar. "You're familiar with this object?"

"Yes, Mr. Daley. It is the steel rod that was allegedly used to administer a fatal blow to the back of Frank Moriarty's head."

"You had a chance to examine it?"

"I did, although I was not allowed to remove it from the plastic evidence bag."

"You noticed that it is covered in rust?"

"Yes."

"You are aware that traces of rust were found on the gloves of my client, Freddie Alvarez?"

"Yes."

"Did the rust on his glove match the rust on this rod?"

Sridar's mustache twitched. "There were several identical rods at the construction site in front of the decedent's house. Moreover, the steel used in this type of rebar is very common, as is the rust associated therewith. It is therefore impossible to state with any certainty whether the rust on Mr. Alvarez's gloves came from this rod or from another source of rusty steel."

I glanced at the jurors, who were listening intently to the diminutive man with the twinkling eyes and the soft-spoken, but authoritative voice.

"Did you examine the rod for fingerprints?" I asked.

"I did not. As I said, I was not permitted to open the evidence bag."

"Did the report indicate whether my client's fingerprints were found on this rod?"

"According to the report, no fingerprints were found on this rod."

"Other than the coincidence that the rust on this rod happened to be similar to the rust found on my client's gloves, you found no forensic evidence that directly places this rod in his hand, did you?"

"Objection. Leading."

True. "I'll rephrase. Other than the rust—which you've said could have come from virtually any piece of rusty steel—did you find any forensic evidence placing this particular steel rod in my client's hand on the night of September fifth of last year?"

"No."

It's the best that I can do. "Mr. Iyengar, were you able to determine the weight of this rod?"

"Yes. Rebar of this type weighs approximately 0.668 pounds per foot. Since this rod is approximately four feet in length, I estimate that it weighs approximately 2.672 pounds."

"You're aware that Freddie Alvarez has a bad leg from an injury that he incurred while he was in the military, right?"

"Yes. I understand that it makes it difficult for him to walk at times. It also impacts his balance."

"Given Mr. Alvarez's physical limitations and the weight of this bar, did it strike you as unlikely that he would have been able to maintain his balance while he was allegedly striking the decedent, a much bigger man?"

"Objection. Mr. Iyengar is an expert on fingerprints. He is not a doctor. Nor is he an expert on balance."

"Sustained."

I had made my point to the jury. "Mr. Iyengar," I continued, "how is it possible that a man of limited physical means with a bad leg and balance issues who was high on heroin and drunk on vodka could have struck somebody with a heavy object?"

"Objection. Speculation." O'Neal feigned exasperation. "Mr. Daley posed a hypothetical without a shred of evidence to support it."

Yes, I did.

"Sustained." Judge McDaniel's voice showed a hint of impatience. "Anything else for this witness, Mr. Daley?"

"No, Your Honor."

"Cross-exam, Ms. O'Neal?"

"No, Your Honor."

"Please call your next witness, Mr. Daley."

"The defense calls Dr. Carla Jimenez."

Nady moved to the lectern. We decided to let the jurors hear a fresh voice for our next exercise in misdirection.

"What is your occupation?" she asked.

Dr. Carla Jimenez adjusted the sleeve of her Hermès blouse and spoke with understated authority. "I am a senior forensic DNA Analyst at the Serological Research Institute in Richmond, California. I have worked at SERI for twenty-four years."

"Are you a medical doctor?"

"PhD. I earned my Bachelor's in chemistry and biological science from San Francisco State, and a Master's and then a PhD in forensic science from UC Davis. My area of expertise is forensic serology and forensic DNA. I have testified in hundreds of cases in state and federal courts nationwide as well as in federal and military courts."

You're very good at your job.

Carla was our go-to DNA expert. Rosie's classmate at Mercy High School had graduated second in her class, worked her way through State, and was accepted into UCLA Medical School. She deferred her admission to work in a research lab in the Department of Forensic Science at UC Davis, where her professor offered her a scholarship to earn a Master's and then a PhD. She went to work at SERI, the pre-eminent DNA lab in Northern California. She was testifying *pro bono* as a favor to Rosie and a promise that we would buy her dinner at Chez Panisse in Berkeley.

Nady moved closer to the box. "You have received many citations for your work over the years, haven't you?"

"I am a Fellow of the American Board of Criminalistics in Forensic Biology with subspecialties in Forensic Biochemistry and Forensic Molecular Biology. I am also a member of the California Association of Criminalists, the Northwest Association of Forensic Scientists, the California Association of Crime Laboratory Directors, and the Association of Forensic Quality Assurance Managers."

O'Neal spoke from her seat. "We will stipulate that Dr. Jimenez is an expert in the fields of forensic serology and DNA."

What took you so long?

Nady walked to the evidence cart, picked up an official-looking document, introduced it into evidence, and handed it to Carla. "You're familiar with this report?"

"Yes. It is a DNA analysis of blood samples obtained from the steel rod found next to the body of Frank Moriarty on September fifth of last year. It was prepared by Mr. George Romero of the Forensic Services Division of the San Francisco Police Department's Criminalistics Laboratory."

"Do you believe that it was prepared in accordance with highest industry standards?"

"I do. Mr. Romero has an excellent reputation."

"Mr. Romero concluded that Mr. Moriarty's DNA was on the rod?"

"Yes. He made that determination based upon a sample of Mr. Moriarty's blood."

"We provided you with a DNA sample from our client, Freddie Alvarez, didn't we?"

"Yes."

"Did the DNA found on this rod match Mr. Alvarez's DNA?"

"No."

"Did the report indicate whether there was DNA from anyone other than the decedent on this rod?"

"Yes, it did. At least one other person handled the rod."

"Were you able to identify that person?"

"I was not. I submitted the information to the various national databases used by law enforcement throughout the country, including the Combined DNA Index System known as CODIS. There were no matches."

"Did the report mention whether Mr. Romero performed a DNA analysis of Freddie Alvarez's gloves, skin, or clothing?"

"Yes, it did. The report said that Mr. Romero performed a DNA test on Mr. Alvarez's gloves and clothing."

"Did Mr. Romero find any traces of the decedent's DNA?"

"He did not."

Nady was pleased. "You are aware that the Medical Examiner determined that Mr. Moriarty died as a result of a blow to the back of the head from a steel rod?"

"Yes."

"Such a blow would have caused substantial blood spatter, right?"

"Objection. Dr. Jimenez is an expert on DNA, not blood spatter."

"Sustained."

Nady ignored the objection. "Would you therefore have expected to see evidence of the decedent's DNA on my client's gloves, skin, or clothing?"

"Objection. Same basis."

"Sustained."

Nady tried once more. "But Mr. Romero found no such evidence, right?"

"Objection. Asked and answered."

"Sustained."

"Did it strike you as unusual that the decedent's blood was not found on my client's gloves, skin, or clothing?"

"Objection," O'Neal said. "Speculation."

"Sustained."

"No further questions." Nady returned to the defense table, triumphant in the fact that she had made her points by asking impermissible questions which Carla didn't have a chance to answer.

"Cross-exam, Ms. O'Neal?"

"No, Your Honor."

"Please call your next witness, Ms. Nikonova."

Nady looked my way as if to say, "It's time to start pointing fingers." "The defense calls Ms. Shreya Patel."

38

"HE WASN'T ALWAYS EASY TO BE AROUND"

I stood in front of the box. "I would remind you that you are still under oath."

Shreya Patel nodded dismissively. She struck me as someone who could dominate a boardroom full of men without raising her voice. "Thank you, Mr. Daley."

"You're a venture capitalist?"

"Correct. My undergrad degree was in biochemistry at Princeton. I earned a Master's, PhD, and MBA from Stanford. I started my career at Genentech. I worked at a couple of startups, and then I moved into venture capital. I worked at Kleiner Perkins and Andreessen Horowitz before I formed my own firm."

"Your firm was one of the early investors in Uber, wasn't it?"

"Yes."

"You must have made a lot of money."

She feigned modesty. "I did."

I looked over at the jury. I got the impression that the retirees weren't impressed.

"You testified earlier that you live around the corner from Frank Moriarty's house?"

"Correct."

"You knew him?"

"Not well." She said that they exchanged greetings when they saw each other.

"Were those conversations pleasant?"

"For the most part."

"But he could be difficult?"

"At times. He wasn't always easy to be around."

"I understand that he had a temper."

"He did."

"Was he ever angry toward you?"

"Yes."

"Could you please explain the circumstances?"

Her expression indicated that she didn't want to provide details. "Over the years, he had a lot of work done on his house. He gutted and rebuilt the interior, added a rooftop deck, and repaved his driveway. It was very noisy and disruptive for his neighbors."

A couple of jurors nodded. It is a universal rule of life that every remodel project takes longer than expected and costs more than anticipated.

I kept my voice modulated. "You said that he got angry at you?"

"During the construction of his deck, his contractor's crew started work at seven o'clock every morning. I am a single mother of a twelve-year-old daughter. The noise woke up my daughter. I asked Mr. Moriarty to instruct his contractor to start later. He told me that he was within his legal rights to have his contractor start work at seven, and that was how he planned to proceed."

Not very neighborly. "You're aware that Mr. Moriarty died on September fifth of last year?"

"Yes."

"Did you provide a statement to the police?"

"Yes. I told them that I didn't see anything, and I didn't know what happened."

"You didn't see my client kill Mr. Moriarty, did you?"

"No, Mr. Daley."

"You also provided security videos to the police from the morning that Mr. Moriarty died, didn't you?"

"Yes." She confirmed that the video showed Freddie walking by her house at twelve-thirty AM. Moriarty walked by at twelve-thirty-nine.

"There was also a person in the driveway across the street, wasn't there?"

"Possibly. It was difficult to see him—if he was there."

"And a homeless couple walked by your house?"

"Correct."

"Did you consider the possibility that one of those individuals may have been involved in Mr. Moriarty's death?"

"Objection. Ms. Patel is not a member of law enforcement, and she was not involved in the investigation of Mr. Moriarty's death."

"I'm not asking for an expert opinion," I said. "I'm simply asking her to describe what she saw in the video that she provided to the police."

"Overruled."

Patel shrugged. "I have no idea, Mr. Daley."

"Perhaps we should take another look at the video."

I ran the video on the flat-screen. I stopped it when Reynolds appeared. Patel said that she didn't know who he was. Likewise, she said that she didn't know Jack and Jill. The jurors were paying attention, but her denials were adamant and appeared convincing.

I turned off the TV and moved in front of the box. "You also had a personal relationship with Mr. Moriarty, didn't you?"

"Objection. Relevance."

"Your Honor," I said, "Ms. Patel lived around the corner from the decedent and knew him reasonably well. Her relationship with Mr. Moriarty is relevant."

"I'll allow it for now."

Patel flashed an icy glare at Nick Hanson. "Mr. Moriarty and I went out a couple of times. It wasn't serious, and I decided not to pursue it."

"So, you knew him a little better than just saying hello over the fence, right?"

"It wasn't serious," she repeated.

"Was he angry or abusive toward you?"

"He was a perfect gentleman."

The judge spoke up again. "Let's move on, Mr. Daley."

"Yes, Your Honor." Nady and I had considered the possibility of accusing Patel of being a jilted lover who killed Moriarty in a fit of rage, but it didn't seem likely that the jury would buy it. Moreover, we had no evidence to support the contention.

I moved back to the lectern. "When we talked a few days ago, you mentioned that Mr. Moriarty didn't like the homeless people in the neighborhood."

"Objection. That was a statement, not a question."

"I'll rephrase," I said. "Ms. Patel, did you tell me that Mr. Moriarty didn't like the homeless people who occasionally slept on the streets of the Marina?"

"I did."

"Why was he so angry?"

"You would have been frustrated if a homeless person was smoking heroin in your driveway."

True.

"In addition," she continued, "there were several instances where Mr. Moriarty's cars were vandalized. He called the police, but they never did anything about it."

"He became hostile toward the homeless, didn't he?"

"I saw him order them to leave his property on several occasions. I would have done the same thing."

"Did he ever become physical?"

"Not that I saw."

"Given his hostile nature and his temper, it wouldn't have surprised you if he did, right?"

"Objection. Calls for speculation."

"Your Honor," I said, "I'm simply asking Ms. Patel to comment upon her observations of her neighbor, not to read his mind."

"Overruled."

Patel shrugged. "I suppose that I wouldn't have been surprised, but I really don't know, Mr. Daley."

Not as much as I was hoping for, but it may help a little. "We understand that he used to threaten homeless people with a baseball bat."

"I saw him take a bat outside once. I never saw him use it."

"What's the worst thing that you ever saw him do to a homeless person?"

Patel considered her answer. "After his car was vandalized, Frank started carrying a can of pepper spray. I saw him use it on homeless people on a few occasions."

This was news. "Did the homeless people threaten or otherwise provoke Mr. Moriarty?"

"Not that I saw."

"He just sprayed them for no apparent reason?"

"I don't know what he was thinking, Mr. Daley."

"That must have been very painful."

"I wouldn't know, Mr. Daley. I have never been pepper-sprayed."

Thankfully, neither have I. "Is it possible that Mr. Moriarty may have pepper-sprayed one or more of the homeless people who were in the vicinity on the morning that he died? And is it possible that one of them fought back and hit Mr. Moriarty in self-defense?"

"Objection. Speculation. Mr. Daley hasn't offered a shred of evidence in support of any of these wild accusations."

No, I haven't. I'm just throwing spaghetti at the wall to see if anything sticks.

"Sustained."

I feigned contrition, but I didn't apologize. Long ago, Rosie taught me that you never apologize to a judge unless she's about to throw you in jail.

I spoke to the judge. "May I take a moment to confer with Ms. Nikonova?"

"Make it quick, Mr. Daley."

I walked over to Nady and asked her if there was any mention of a can of pepper spray in the crime scene inventory.

"No," she said. She confirmed that there wasn't a baseball bat at the scene, either.

I walked back to the front of the box. "Mr. Moriarty also got into it with some of your neighbors, didn't he?"

"So I've heard."

"He was openly hostile to Mr. Henry Keller, who lived next door to him, wasn't he?"

"He and Henry had a long history of litigation."

"Mr. Moriarty was even more hostile to Mr. Keller than he was to you, wasn't he?"

"Objection. This is outside the scope of Ms. Patel's knowledge."

Yes, it is.

"Sustained."

"No further questions," I said.

"Cross-exam, Ms. O'Neal?"

"No, Your Honor."

"Please call your next witness, Mr. Daley."

Time to fling a little more spaghetti. "The defense calls Mr. Henry Keller."

39

"WE HAD A FEW DISAGREMENTS"

"Nice to see you again, Mr. Keller," I lied.

He responded in kind. "Nice to see you again, Mr. Daley."

The supremely confident billionaire sat in the box, arms folded, demeanor impatient. He didn't fill his water cup. His expression suggested that I was wasting his time.

I stood in front of the box. "You testified earlier that you lived next door to Frank Moriarty, and you found his body on the morning of September fifth of last year?"

"Correct."

"That must have been very upsetting for you."

"It was."

"You and Mr. Moriarty had an acrimonious relationship over the years, didn't you?"

"We had a few disagreements."

"Which led to multiple lawsuits, right?"

"It wasn't my choice. Frank was an excellent lawyer. It should come as no surprise to another fine lawyer like yourself that he was litigious."

I ignored the backhanded dig. "You didn't like him, did you?"

"It was never personal."

It's always personal. I moved within two feet of the box. "We have heard testimony that Mr. Moriarty didn't like homeless people, and that he threatened them with a baseball bat on several occasions. Did you ever see him do that?"

"Once or twice. I never saw him hit anybody."

"Did he ever threaten you with a bat?"

"Of course not."

"You testified earlier about an alleged argument between Mr. Moriarty and my client that took place a few days before Mr. Moriarty died. Did Mr. Moriarty threaten my client with a baseball bat?"

"I don't recall."

"You allegedly remembered many details from that conversation even though you weren't wearing your hearing aids or glasses, but you can't recall whether Mr. Moriarty had his Louisville Slugger with him?"

"Objection. Asked and answered."

"Sustained."

"Even if he didn't threaten my client with the bat, did he have the bat in his possession when this alleged argument took place?"

"Objection. Asked and answered."

"Asked," I said, "but not answered. Mr. Keller purports to have remembered many details about an argument that he could barely see or hear. Surely, he must remember whether Mr. Moriarty was carrying his bat."

"Overruled."

I didn't think the judge would give me that one.

"I don't recall," Keller said.

"We've also heard testimony that he was in the habit of carrying pepper spray to use on homeless people. Did you ever see him do so?"

Keller waited a beat. "Once or twice."

"Did he pepper-spray the man you believed was my client when they allegedly argued a few days before Mr. Moriarty died?"

"Not that I recall."

"You don't recall much of anything about this phantom conversation, do you? In fact, it sounds very likely to me that it never happened at all."

"Objection. Mr. Daley is testifying again."

"Sustained. Anything else for this witness, Mr. Daley?"

I glanced at Nady, who nodded. "Just a couple more questions, Your Honor." I moved closer to Keller. "You really disliked Mr. Moriarty, didn't you?"

"It wasn't personal."

"He sued you a dozen times, didn't he?"

"Yes."

"One of his lawsuits caused you to delay the construction of your rooftop deck for almost ten years, didn't it?"

"It was several years," Keller acknowledged.

"You must have been pretty upset about the cost and the delay."

"Litigation is expensive and time-consuming, Mr. Daley."

"It finally reached the point where you and Mr. Moriarty stopped talking to each other, didn't it?"

"It seemed like a good solution."

"You started communicating through your lawyers, right?"

"It also seemed like a good solution."

I moved right in front of Keller. "You finally had enough, didn't you?"

"I was tired of the acrimony."

"And on the morning that Mr. Moriarty died, you saw him in his driveway, didn't you?"

"No."

"And he insulted you again, didn't he?"

"No."

"And he threatened you, didn't he?"

"Objection to this line of questioning," O'Neal said. "Mr. Daley has provided no evidence that this alleged conversation ever took place."

That's because it probably didn't. "Your Honor," I said, "the only person still alive who can describe this conversation is Mr. Keller."

"I'm going to overrule the objection. Please answer the question, Mr. Keller."

Keller folded his arms and spoke in a petulant tone. "Mr. Daley is dreaming. This conversation never took place."

I don't care. "He finally said something to you that was too much, didn't he?"

"No."

"And you grabbed a piece of rebar and you hit him, didn't you?"

"No."

"And you dropped the rebar next to my client to give the impression that he had killed Mr. Moriarty, didn't you?"

"No."

"Maybe you did it in self-defense. Maybe he said something so insulting that you finally snapped. Maybe he came after you with a baseball bat or a can of pepper spray. You'll feel much better if you tell the truth, Mr. Keller."

"You're living in a fantasy world, Mr. Daley. I did not kill Frank Moriarty. I didn't see him on the morning that he died."

"Until you conveniently found his body."

"Objection."

"Sustained."

"No further questions."

"Cross-exam, Ms. O'Neal?"

"No, Your Honor."

"Please call your next witness, Mr. Daley."

"The defense calls Eddie Reynolds."

40

"YOU PANICKED"

I stood at the lectern and spoke in a modulated voice. "Where are you from?"

Eddie Reynolds took a sip of water and shifted uneasily in the box. "Daly City."

"Westmoor High?"

"Jefferson."

"Fine school. What is your occupation?"

He adjusted the sleeve of the gray sport jacket that his lawyer—who was sitting in the gallery—had brought for him to wear in court. "I am currently between jobs."

"What was your last job?"

"I worked for a moving company."

"How long ago was that?"

"About three years. It was hard finding work during Covid."

I asked Judge McDaniel for permission to approach the witness, which she granted. I moved to the front of the box. "Where do you live?" I asked Reynolds.

"San Francisco."

"Where in San Francisco?"

"In the building across the parking lot."

"You're incarcerated in County Jail #2, aren't you?"

"Yes."

"For what crimes?"

"Objection," O'Neal said. "Mr. Daley is well-aware that the criminal record of the witness has no bearing on this case."

"Your Honor," I said, "Ms. O'Neal is well-aware that this witness was seen in a security video around the corner from Frank Moriarty's house shortly before he died. His background is relevant to these proceedings."

O'Neal's voice became louder. "There is no evidence that Mr. Reynolds was anywhere near Mr. Moriarty's house on the morning that he died."

"He was in the security video provided by Ms. Patel."

"Inspector Wong and I viewed that video. There is no conclusive evidence that Mr. Reynolds is the person in the video."

"That's a question of fact for the jury to decide."

Judge McDaniel tapped her microphone. "I am going to overrule the objection and ask the witness to answer the question."

Reynolds cleared his throat. "Auto theft. Breaking and entering. Selling stolen goods."

That covers most of it. "How much longer will you be incarcerated?"

He looked at his lawyer. "Nine hundred and twelve days."

Only two and a half years to go. "Among other things, you were convicted of breaking into several garages in the Marina, weren't you?"

"Yes."

"One of those garages was in a house belonging to Frank Moriarty, wasn't it?"

"I don't recall."

"You were also convicted of stealing several cars in the Marina."

"I entered into a plea bargain."

Fine. "Mr. Moriarty was killed in the early morning of September fifth of last year. You were at his house that morning, weren't you?"

"No."

I was a bit surprised that his lawyer didn't tell him to take the Fifth. Then again, it probably meant that Reynolds was prepared to deny any involvement in Moriarty's death.

I walked back to the lectern, punched a button on my laptop, and activated the flat-screen. "Let me refresh your memory."

I pulled up the security video from Patel's house. "This video was taken by a security camera at a house located around the corner from Mr. Moriarty's at approximately twelve-thirty-five AM." I ran fifteen seconds of the video at regular speed and then in slow motion. I froze the video when Reynolds appeared. "This frame shows a person crouching behind a car in the driveway across the street."

Reynolds squinted at the screen. "I'll take your word for it."

"That's you, Mr. Reynolds, isn't it?"

Reynolds looked at the screen. "No, it isn't."

I pointed at the Oakland A's cap that he was wearing in the video. "Two days later, you were arrested for breaking into another garage. You were wearing the same A's cap, weren't you?"

"I don't recall."

"When you were arrested, the inventory of your personal items included an A's cap, didn't it?"

"I don't recall."

I moved to the front of the box. "What were you doing around the corner from Mr. Moriarty's house at twelve-thirty AM?"

"I wasn't there."

"You were looking for a garage or a car to break into, weren't you?"

"No."

"Come on, Mr. Reynolds. You'll feel better if you start telling the truth."

"Objection."

"Sustained."

"You saw Mr. Moriarty walk by, and you followed him home, didn't you?"

"No."

"You tried to rob him, didn't you? And he resisted, didn't he?"

"No."

"Or maybe he threated you with a baseball bat or pepper spray, didn't he?"

"No."

"And you grabbed a rusty steel rod from the construction area in his driveway, and you hit him, didn't you?"

"Objection," O'Neal said. "There isn't a shred of evidence supporting Mr. Daley's wild and unsubstantiated accusations."

"Your Honor," I said, "Mr. Reynolds was spotted less than a hundred feet from Mr. Moriarty's house a few minutes before Mr. Moriarty returned home. Mr. Reynolds should explain what he was doing there."

Judge McDaniel considered her options. "The issue of whether it is Mr. Reynolds in the video is a factual question for the jury to decide. The objection is therefore overruled, and the witness will answer the question."

Reynolds shook his head with feigned disdain. "I wasn't there. I did not kill Moriarty."

I inched closer to Reynolds. "Mr. Moriarty yelled at you, didn't he?"

"No."

"And he threatened you with a baseball bat, didn't he?"

"No."

"And he pepper-sprayed you, didn't he?"

"No."

"And you got angry, didn't you? And you defended yourself, didn't you?"

"No."

"Your eyes were burning, and you panicked. You did what any of us would have done in the circumstances. You wanted to protect yourself, so you grabbed a steel rod from the construction site, and you hit him, didn't you?"

"No, I did not."

"Yes, you did."

"Objection. There wasn't a question there. And even if there was, the witness has already answered, and there isn't a shred of evidence in support of Mr. Daley's unsubstantiated claims."

All true. "The witness is lying," I said.

The judge's voice was stern. "That's for the jury to decide, Mr. Daley. The objection is sustained. Any further questions?"

"No, Your Honor."

"Cross-exam, Ms. O'Neal?"

"Just one question, Your Honor." She spoke from the prosecution table. "Mr. Reynolds, did you kill Frank Moriarty?"

"No."

"No further questions, Your Honor."

Judge McDaniel looked at her watch. "It's almost noon, so I am going to adjourn until two o'clock. Mr. Daley, who do you plan to call as your next witness?"

"Jack Allen."

Freddie's voice filled with resignation as he picked at his turkey sandwich. "Now what?"

"We'll put Jack on the stand and go after him," I said.

"Do you have any hard evidence connecting him to Moriarty?"

"Other than the fact that he was around the corner from Moriarty's house, no."

The air was heavy in the holding tank down the hall from Judge McDaniel's courtroom. My suit jacket was drenched in perspiration. My head throbbed. I hadn't touched my unwrapped tuna sandwich or unopened bottle of water.

Freddie frowned. "You really think that's going to work?"

"We don't need to prove that Jack killed him. We just need to persuade one juror that there is reasonable doubt as to whether you did."

"That's lawyerly BS."

Yes, it is. "That's how the system works."

"And if that isn't enough?"

I exchanged a glance with Nady, then I turned back to Freddie. "We'll put Inspector Wong back on the stand and go after her. If it isn't enough, we need you to be ready to testify."

He didn't hesitate. "I will."

Good. My phone vibrated. Pete's name appeared on the display.

I answered immediately. "Where are you?"

"Sitting in my car outside Jack's motel room."

"I need you to bring him to court to testify when we resume at two o'clock."

"I can't, Mick." He cleared his throat. "He's dead."

What the hell? "What happened?"

"The police and the EMTs think he took some Percocet pills spiked with fentanyl. He OD'd."

My head felt like somebody had hit me with a two-by-four.

"You still there?" Pete asked.

"Yes. You told me that you searched his room and his belongings when you checked him in."

"I did. He had a bottle of Percocet to help with the pain in his shoulder. They looked legit to me. It turns out that they were fake pills spiked with fentanyl."

My stomach churned. "Did you find his body?"

"No. The housekeeper did."

Good. "Cooperate with the police."

"Of course, Mick."

"And find Jill."

"Working on it." He ended the call.

I put my phone on the table. I took a deep breath and spoke to Freddie. "Jack's dead. He got some pain pills spiked with fentanyl. He OD'd in his motel."

Freddie stared at me in disbelief before he fired off a string of expletives. "I'm screwed."

"Not necessarily. We can throw Jack under the bus, and he won't be available to defend himself."

"How?"

"We stick to the plan and call our next witness: Inspector Wong. We'll try to get her to implicate Jack or Reynolds."

"Do you think it will work?"

Hard to say. "At the moment, we have no better options."

41

"WE FOUND NO EVIDENCE"

It was sunny outside at two o'clock on Wednesday afternoon, but nobody inside Judge McDaniel's courtroom was thinking about the weather. The regulars had returned to their seats in the gallery, but their presence was irrelevant to us. We were playing to an audience of the twelve jurors and four alternates in the jury box.

I stood in front of the stand, eyes locked onto Wong's. "You interviewed my client on September fifth of last year?"

"Yes. He was unconscious when the first officer arrived at the scene, so I spoke to him later in the afternoon after he was taken to San Francisco General for medical attention."

"Was he cooperative?"

"He wasn't hostile, but he was disoriented from drugs and alcohol."

"He answered your questions?"

"For the most part."

"Did he attempt to run?"

"No." Wong cleared her throat. "He wouldn't have gotten anywhere very quickly, Mr. Daley. He has a bad knee."

"How long have you been a homicide inspector?"

"Eight years."

"How long were you a police officer before you became an inspector?"

"Fourteen years."

"How many homicides have you investigated over that time?"

"I don't recall."

"Ballpark estimate. A dozen? Two dozen? Fifty?"

"About two dozen."

"You've interviewed hundreds of suspects?"

"Yes."

"Did any of them try to run after you caught them?"

"Some."

"You probably took that as a likely sign of their guilt, didn't you?"

"Sometimes."

"If you had killed Frank Moriarty, would you have tried to run?"

"Objection. Calls for speculation."

"Sustained."

"Do you really think Freddie would have talked to you if he had killed Frank Moriarty?"

"Objection. Argumentative."

"Sustained."

I was still looking at Wong. "Did Freddie ask for a lawyer?"

"Not until I placed him under arrest."

"Did that strike you as odd?"

"Not really."

"If he was guilty, don't you think he would have asked to speak to an attorney?"

"Objection. Inspector Wong isn't a mind reader."

"Sustained."

"Inspector, you heard testimony from Dr. Joy Siu that Mr. Moriarty died of a blow to the head. Did you find any of his blood on my client's gloves, person, or clothing?"

"We found Mr. Moriarty's blood on a rusty steel rod near the body. The rod was inches from your client's right hand. We found rust on your client's gloves. The rust matched the rust on the rod. The evidence of your client's guilt is overwhelming."

I turned to the judge. "Would you please instruct the witness to answer my question?"

"Please, Inspector."

Wong rolled her eyes. "We did not find Mr. Moriarty's blood on the defendant's gloves, person, or clothing."

Thank you. "Did it strike you as odd given the fact that you are alleging that my client struck Mr. Moriarty at close range?"

"Not necessarily."

"You were here when our blood spatter expert testified that my client's clothing would have been covered in blood if he had attacked Mr. Moriarty at close range, right?"

"Our expert disagreed with yours."

"Did you consider the possibility that your expert was wrong?"

"We found Lieutenant Jacobsen's analysis to be very persuasive."

"You rushed to judgment."

"The evidence is overwhelming."

"Especially when you didn't consider any other potential suspects."

"Objection. Argumentative."

"Sustained."

I moved closer to the box. "Mr. Moriarty's family, colleagues, friends, and neighbors told you that Mr. Moriarty had a bad temper, didn't they?"

"Yes."

"Several of his neighbors had long-running feuds with Mr. Moriarty, didn't they?"

"I would call them differences of opinion."

"Differences of opinion generally don't result in multiple lawsuits, do they?"

"Objection. Argumentative."

"Sustained."

"For example," I said, "Ms. Shreya Patel complained to Mr. Moriarty about the noise from a lengthy construction project at his house, didn't she?"

"Yes."

"Ms. Patel testified that she was very upset because the noise was waking up her daughter. When she complained to Mr. Moriarty, he refused to do anything about it, right?"

"Right."

"Did you consider the possibility that she may have lost her temper and attacked Mr. Moriarty?"

Wong kept her tone even. "We found no evidence suggesting that anyone other than your client was involved with Mr. Moriarty's death."

"That's because you jumped to the conclusion that he's guilty."

"Objection. Argumentative."

"Withdrawn. We also heard testimony from Mr. Moriarty's neighbor, Henry Keller, about multiple lawsuits that Mr. Moriarty filed against him involving disputes over noise, dust, property lines, etc., didn't we?"

"Mr. Moriarty was a lawyer. He was litigious."

"Given the years of animosity between Mr. Keller and Mr. Moriarty, did you consider the possibility that Mr. Keller may have been involved in Mr. Moriarty's death?"

"Other than the fact that Mr. Keller took out his garbage on the morning of September fifth of last year and found Mr. Moriarty's body, we found no evidence that he had any involvement in Mr. Moriarty's death."

"Mr. Keller also claimed that he heard Mr. Moriarty arguing with my client a few days before Mr. Moriarty's death, right?"

"Right."

"Mr. Keller made the unsubstantiated claim even though he was inside his house, and he wasn't wearing his glasses or hearing aids."

"We found Mr. Keller to be credible."

"In other words, you chose to believe him, but not my client?"

"Correct."

"That's because Mr. Keller's far-fetched version of the story fit within your pre-established theory of the case, didn't it? And it gave you a plausible-sounding motive for my client to have killed Mr. Moriarty, didn't it?"

"Objection. Argumentative."

"Sustained."

I spent the next five minutes trying to get Wong to acknowledge that it was possible that Keller killed Moriarty, but she didn't give an inch. In fairness, I didn't have any physical evidence connecting Keller to Moriarty's death. I glanced at the jury and surmised that my attempt to paint Keller as a murderer wasn't winning any points, so I decided to pivot.

I walked back to the lectern and activated the TV. "Ms. Patel provided you with video taken by her security camera on the morning of September fifth of last year, didn't she?"

"Yes."

I ran it at regular speed and then in slow motion. "We previously noted that my client walked by Ms. Patel's house at twelve-thirty AM, and Mr. Moriarty walked by her house at twelve-thirty-nine AM, right?"

"Correct."

I reran the video and stopped it at twelve-thirty-five. "You can also see a man named Eddie Reynolds in the driveway across the street from Ms. Patel's house, can't you?"

She stared at the TV. "It appears that there may have been a person in the driveway whom we could not positively identify."

"Would you agree that it looked a lot like Mr. Reynolds?"

"I can't say."

"Were you able to rule out the possibility that it was Mr. Reynolds?"

"As I said, we were unable to positively identify the man in the video."

"Did you question Mr. Reynolds after we pointed out that he was in the video?"

"Yes. He denied that he was the person in the video."

"You believed him even though Mr. Reynolds was convicted of breaking into several houses and cars in the Marina and other parts of town shortly thereafter?"

"Yes."

"The man in the video was wearing an A's cap. When Mr. Reynolds was arrested a few days later, he was also in possession of an A's cap, wasn't he?"

"So it appears."

"It's your contention that this was just a coincidence?"

"We found no evidence connecting Mr. Reynolds to Mr. Morarity's death."

"Did you consider the possibility that he followed Mr. Moriarty home and tried to rob him? And that he possibly killed him?"

"We were unable to positively identify Mr. Reynolds in the video, and we found no evidence placing him at the scene of Mr. Moriarty's death."

"Given the fact that we have documented video evidence that Mr. Reynolds was within a few feet of Mr. Moriarty's house on the morning of September fifth of last year, why didn't you even consider the possibility that he was involved in Mr. Moriarty's death?"

"I disagree with your premise, Mr. Daley. We have no documented proof that Mr. Reynolds was the man in the video."

"That's because you had already decided that my client was guilty."

"Objection. Argumentative."

"Sustained."

I moved right in front of Wong. "We heard testimony from Ms. Patel and Mr. Keller that Mr. Moriarty had a serious problem with the homeless people in the Marina, right?"

"Yes."

"In fact, Mr. Moriarty threatened them with a baseball bat and sprayed them with pepper spray, didn't he?"

"According to the witnesses."

"The security video from Ms. Patel's house also showed two homeless people identified as Jack Allen and Jill Harris walking toward Mr. Moriarty's house at twelve-forty-five that same morning, didn't it?"

"Yes. We found them and we questioned them. They said that they did not see Mr. Moriarty that morning. We found no evidence that Mr. Allen or Ms. Harris were at the scene or involved in Mr. Moriarty's death."

"You took their word for it, too?"

"We found no evidence that they were lying."

"Yet when my client told you that he did not kill Mr. Moriarty, you chose not to believe him."

Wong feigned exasperation. "Mr. Keller found your client passed out near Mr. Moriarty's body. The murder weapon was next to him. There was rust from the murder weapon on his gloves. It wasn't difficult to make the connection."

"That's because you had already decided that my client was guilty."

"That's not true, Mr. Daley. We consider everybody to be a potential suspect until we can rule them out."

"How did you possibly rule out Mr. Reynolds or Jack and Jill?"

"We found no evidence connecting them to Mr. Moriarty's death."

"That's certainly convenient for your narrative, isn't it?"

"Objection. Argumentative." O'Neal's tone turned caustic. "It seems that Mr. Daley is prepared to accuse every resident of San Francisco of Mr. Moriarty's murder."

I might.

"The objection is sustained. Any further questions for this witness, Mr. Daley?"

"No, Your Honor."

O'Neal declined cross-exam.

The judge looked my way. "Do you plan to call any additional witnesses, Mr. Daley?"

"I would like to request a brief recess to consult with our client."

Nady and I were walking down the corridor toward the holding tank to meet Freddie when Roosevelt stopped us.

"Interesting trial," he understated. He removed the toothpick from the corner of his mouth. "Got anything else?"

"Not sure," I said.

"Are you going to put Freddie on the stand?"

"We haven't decided."

We stood in silence as a few lawyers, cops, and spectators shuffled by us. Roosevelt's eyes kept moving. Even though he retired a long time ago, he didn't miss anything.

I lowered my voice. "Is it enough?"

The corner of his mouth turned up slightly. "I learned a long time ago not to predict how a jury will rule."

Fair enough. "What is your gut telling you?"

"You still have some work to do to get to reasonable doubt."

"Would you put Freddie on the stand to issue a denial?"

He chuckled. "I don't give legal advice to lawyers."

"I'm just asking for your opinion."

He removed his glasses, cleaned them with a cloth, and put them back on. "Probably."

"Thanks." I looked at Nady. "Let's go talk to Freddie."

Freddie's mood was somber when Nady and I entered the consultation room. "It isn't enough," he said.

Maybe not. "How would you feel about testifying in your own defense?"

His eyes lit up. "I'm in."

"Good. We've practiced your testimony a dozen times. Answer only the questions that we ask. Keep your answers short and don't volunteer anything, especially during cross-exam. O'Neal is going to go after you."

"I'm ready."

I turned to Nady. "I think it might play better to the jury if you handle Freddie's direct exam."

"I'd love to."

42

"NO, MA'AM"

"How old are you?" Nady asked.

Freddie gulped down his second cup of water. "Thirty."

Nady had positioned herself in front of the box where Freddie could speak directly to the jury while she blocked his view of O'Neal. The jurors leaned forward. The gallery was silent. Rosie had entered Judge McDaniel's courtroom without fanfare and taken a seat in the back row. Roosevelt remained stoic. Nick "The Dick" appeared bemused. Jerry Edwards scribbled furiously in his notebook.

"Are you a native of San Francisco?" Nady asked.

"Yes." Freddie adjusted the striped tie that I had given to him. "Born and raised in the Mission. Graduate of Sacred Heart. I was an altar boy at St. Peter's Parish."

Nice answer. Just the way we practiced.

Nady's voice was calm. "Where were you living on the night of September fourth of last year?"

"In a tent next to the lagoon at the Palace of Fine Arts." Another sip of water. "I lost my job and my apartment after I got hooked on alcohol and heroin."

"Did the City ever offer you housing and services?"

"A couple of times. I tried really hard, Ms. Nikonova, but I couldn't get straight."

Nady shot a glance at the retired teacher in the second row of the jury, then she turned back to Freddie. "Prior to this case, were you ever arrested?"

"A couple of times for shoplifting."

"Have you ever hurt anybody?"

"No, ma'am."

So far, so good. Nady looked my way, and I touched my right ear. It was the signal to get down to business and get Freddie off the stand ASAP.

She turned back to Freddie. "Where were you at approximately twelve-thirty AM on Tuesday, September fifth, of last year?"

"I bought a bottle of vodka at Walgreens at Lombard and Divisadero. I walked up Divisadero to North Point, then I turned left and headed toward the Palace of Fine Arts."

"Did you consume any of the vodka along the way?"

"All of it." Freddie said that he stopped to rest in a construction zone in a driveway in front of a house located at the corner of Baker and North Point. "I have a bad knee, so I sat down next to the Dumpster and took a hit of smack."

"That's heroin?"

"Yes."

"The house belonged to the decedent, Frank Moriarty?"

"So I've been told."

"Was anybody else there?"

"No."

"What happened next?"

"I passed out."

"Did you see Mr. Moriarty?"

"No, ma'am."

"Did he talk to you?"

"No, ma'am."

"Did he threaten you or hit you?"

"No, ma'am."

"Did you pick up a steel rod and hit him?"

"No, ma'am."

"You're sure?"

"Yes, ma'am."

"Is it possible that you don't remember what happened?"

"No, ma'am." Freddie's voice became resolute. "I would have remembered if I had hit somebody, Ms. Nikonova."

"What is the next thing that you remember?"

"One of the neighbors woke me up in the morning. Mr. Moriarty's body was on the driveway near me. He was dead."

Nady lowered her voice. "Did you kill Mr. Moriarty?"

Freddie sat up taller. "No, ma'am. I did not."

"No further questions, Your Honor."

"Cross-exam, Ms. O'Neal?"

"Yes, Your Honor. May we approach the witness?"

"You may."

My heart beat faster. *Keep your answers short, Freddie.*

O'Neal marched to the front of the courtroom and planted herself directly in front of Freddie. "More water?" she asked.

"Yes, please." Freddie poured himself another cup and gulped it down.

O'Neal spoke in a rapid staccato. "You've admitted that you were at Frank Moriarty's house in the early morning of September fifth of last year?"

"Yes, ma'am."

"You saw Mr. Moriarty?"

"No, ma'am."

"You had met him before, right?"

"No, ma'am."

"He yelled at you the previous time that you saw him, didn't he?"

"No, ma'am. I never met him."

"And he yelled at you on the morning of September fifth, didn't he?"

"No, ma'am."

"I think he did."

"Objection," Nady said. "There wasn't a question."

"Sustained."

O'Neal spoke to Freddie as if they were the only people in court. "You tried to rob him, didn't you?"

"No, ma'am."

"You picked up a rusty steel rod from the construction area on his driveway, didn't you?"

"No, ma'am."

"Your gloves were covered in rust, Mr. Alvarez."

"I must have gotten rust on my gloves when I sat down in the driveway."

"I think you got rust on your gloves when you picked up a rusty steel rod and used it to hit Frank Moriarty."

"Objection. There wasn't a question."

"Sustained."

Stay the course, Freddie.

O'Neal's tone turned sharper. "When Inspector Wong interviewed you about your prior interactions with Mr. Moriarty, you told her that you had never met him, right?"

Freddie hesitated. "Right."

"That was a lie, wasn't it?"

"No, ma'am."

"You lied to her then, and you're lying to us now, aren't you?"

"Objection. Asked and answered."

"Sustained."

O'Neal moved within a foot of Freddie. "You killed Frank Moriarty, didn't you?"

"No, ma'am."

"You just lied again, didn't you?"

"No, ma'am."

"You'll feel better if you tell the truth, Mr. Alvarez."

"Objection," Nady said. "Argumentative."

"Sustained."

O'Neal was right in Freddie's face. "You killed him, didn't you? And now you're lying about it, aren't you?"

"Objection. Asked and answered. Argumentative."

"Sustained. Any more questions for this witness?"

"No, Your Honor."

"Re-direct, Ms. Nikonova?"

"No questions, Your Honor."

"The witness is excused. Do you wish to call any additional witnesses, Mr. Daley?"

"One moment, Your Honor." I turned and whispered to Nady, "Is it enough?"

"It will have to be. We don't have anybody else."

I looked up at Rosie, who discreetly held up a hand as if to say, "You did everything that you could."

The door in the back of the courtroom opened, and Pete made his way inside. He walked to the gate separating the gallery from the defense and prosecution tables and nodded.

I turned back to the judge. "Your Honor, I would like to request a moment to confer with our investigator."

"Fine, Mr. Daley."

I walked over to Pete, who leaned over the rail and whispered to me. "I found Jill in a homeless shelter. I sent one of my operatives to stay with her."

"Have you talked to her?"

"Briefly."

"Will she testify?"

"I think so."

I turned back to the judge. "We will be calling one more witness. Her name is Jill Harris. She's already on our witness list."

O'Neal spoke from her seat. "We haven't had an opportunity to prepare for this witness, Your Honor."

"You've had over a year," I snapped. "She just became available. She has critical information." *Well, I hope so.*

Judge McDaniel drummed her hands on the bench. "I want to see counsel in chambers."

43

"THIS IS HIGHLY IRREGULAR"

O'Neal's voice filled with faux indignation as she sat in the chair opposite Judge McDaniel's desk. "This is highly irregular."

"She's on our witness list," I said. "She's been there for weeks."

"We haven't been given an opportunity to interview her before her testimony."

Neither have we. "We just found her."

"Have you spoken to her?" the judge asked.

"Our investigator has. He has assured me that the witness has relevant information."

O'Neal let out a derisive laugh. "The investigator is Mr. Daley's brother."

"He's a licensed PI," I said. "He's very reliable."

"He'll say whatever you ask him to say."

"No, he won't." *Yes, he will.* "Besides, I'm not planning to put him on the stand."

"He's on your witness list, too. You'll call him if your phantom last-minute witness doesn't agree to testify."

Possibly. "I have no intention of doing so."

Judge McDaniel remained silent as O'Neal and I sniped at each other. Things got more heated as we blew off steam. Inevitably it turned personal.

O'Neal's tone was accusatory when she spoke to the judge. "Mr. Daley is creating chaos at the last minute to set up a demand for a mistrial."

The thought has crossed my mind. "No, I'm not."

"Yes, you are."

Judge McDaniel cut to the chase. "I'm not going to grant a motion for a mistrial, Mr. Daley."

I don't expect you to do so. "I have no intention of making such a motion," I lied.

"That's exactly what he's planning to do," O'Neal said. "Even after you deny his motion and the defendant is convicted, he's going to use this as another issue on appeal."

I'm not going to rule it out.

Judge McDaniel frowned. "Mr. Daley is free to file an appeal on whatever grounds he chooses." She turned my way and added, "No matter how baseless his claims are."

Well played. "Your Honor, this witness and her partner walked by the scene of the crime around the time that Mr. Moriarty died. We believe that she saw what happened. That information is relevant and has probative value. Her testimony is essential."

O'Neal fired back. "Mr. Daley's office has been investigating this case for more than a year. They should have located this witness long ago. We found no evidence suggesting that she or her partner were involved in Frank Moriarty's murder. This is nothing more than a Hail Mary Pass."

You may be right. "She has information that is important to finding the truth."

"You have no idea if she's lying."

"Why on earth would she lie?"

"To protect herself."

"If you believe that she committed murder, you should charge her. At the very least, you'll have the opportunity to question her on cross-exam."

Judge McDaniel let us go at it for another five minutes before she ruled. "I believe that this witness has relevant information that the jury should hear. I am going to allow her to testify."

O'Neal feigned exasperation. "But Your Honor—,"

"I've ruled, Ms. O'Neal. We will hear testimony from Jill Harris first thing tomorrow morning."

"Thank you, Your Honor," I said.

She wasn't finished. "Given the unusual circumstances, Mr. Daley, I plan to give Ms. O'Neal a great deal of latitude. Understood?"

"Yes, Your Honor."

The judge pointed at the door. "I'll see you in the morning."

44

"HOW DID YOU FIND HER?"

Rosie was seated behind her desk at six-thirty that same night. "How did you find her?" she asked Pete.

He was standing in his usual spot next to the window. "I put out the word that we were looking for her. She checked into a homeless shelter in the Tenderloin a couple of weeks ago. I know a guy who works there. He recognized her photo."

"You have sources everywhere."

Nady and I were sitting in the chairs opposite Rosie's desk. Dazzle was at the conference table. Terrence "The Terminator" was at his cubicle outside the open door. The PD's Office was quiet.

Pete, Nady, and I had just returned from a brief meeting with Jill. One of Pete's operatives was now sitting in the lobby of the shelter. Pete would camp out in front of the building overnight. Jill told us that she had been drug-free for three weeks—a huge triumph. She confirmed that she had been with Jack on the morning that Moriarty died. She agreed to testify, and she said that she knew what had happened in front of Moriarty's house. We pressed her, but she wouldn't provide details.

Dazzle looked up from her laptop. "Do you think she'll be a strong witness?"

"Hard to say," I said. "She talked to us for just a few minutes because she was late for a counseling session. She used to be a teacher, so she's smart. She's well-spoken, and I think she'll connect with the jury. On the other hand, some of the law-and-order jurors may be less sympathetic to a woman who was hooked on crack for the last three years."

Rosie looked at Pete. "What do you think?"

"She's willing to testify. That's good."

"Not if she implicates our client."

"She said that she wouldn't."

"Do you trust her?"

"We talked to her for less than five minutes. I have no idea."

Rosie spoke to me. "You don't know what she's going to say. That violates every rule of direct exam."

"I know." *You're never supposed to ask a question in court unless you already know the answer.*

She gave me a knowing look. "You're prepared to put her on the stand and roll the dice?"

"At the moment, I don't think we have enough to get the jury to reasonable doubt."

She looked at Nady. "What do you think?"

"It's a risk worth taking."

Rosie turned back to Pete. "How would you approach it?"

It might seem curious that Rosie asked a non-lawyer for advice on trial strategy. Then again, Pete has testified in hundreds of cases in his capacity as a cop and more recently as a PI. He has an uncanny sense of what plays well to a jury. Rosie calls him the "jury whisperer."

He played with the sleeve of his bomber jacket. "It's going to be a finesse game. You'll need to build trust with Jill before you ask her about what happened on the night that Moriarty died."

"Probably right," Rosie said. She looked my way. "You or Nady?"

"Nady has a better bedside manner than I do—especially with a female witness."

"Agreed." She turned to Nady. "Are you up for it?"

"Absolutely."

45

"I DIDN'T THINK ANYBODY WOULD BELIEVE ME"

Nady stood a respectful distance from the box. "Please state your name."

"Jillian Harris. I prefer to be called Jill."

Judge McDaniel's courtroom was sweltering at ten o'clock the next morning. It seemed fitting that our trial was coming to a head on Halloween.

Jill tugged at the sleeve of the plain white blouse. She was thirty-two, but her world-weary demeanor and sad brown eyes made her look at least fifty. Her ebony skin had a yellowish cast, and her hair was cut short—more salt than pepper. She wore no makeup or jewelry. She spoke in a raspy smoker's whisper. Her careful word choices hinted at her former life as a teacher.

"Are you from the City?" Nady asked.

"The Fillmore. I graduated from Galileo High School and San Francisco State." She said that her father was a high school social studies teacher who had died when she was in kindergarten. Her mother worked at the Safeway on Webster. "I got my degree in sociology from State and then my teaching credential. I taught third grade at Rosa Parks Elementary School on O'Farrell for three years."

"Why did you decide to become a teacher?"

"I come from a family of teachers. I thought that I could make a difference." In response to Nady's gentle questioning, Jill confirmed that she once lived in a studio apartment on McAllister, attended First Union Missionary Baptist Church in the Fillmore, and played softball at the Kimbell Playground.

"Did you like being a teacher?" Nady asked.

"I loved it."

"When did you leave teaching?"

"June of 2020."

"Why?"

"I got a bad case of Covid at the end of the school year. I was in the hospital for two weeks, and I almost died. Around the same time, I broke up with my boyfriend. I started taking antidepressants, then I got hooked on Percocet after I had ankle surgery. I took a leave of absence from my teaching job, and I never went back. By the end of 2020, I was out of money, and I couldn't get off the painkillers. I couch surfed with friends for a few months, then I ended up living in my car. Eventually, I had to live on the street."

Nady's tone was somber. "You lived on the street for almost four years?"

"Yes."

"I understand that you recently moved into a shelter."

"I did. A social worker got me into a room and a treatment program. I've done this twice before. I'm hoping the third time is the charm."

"I wish you the very best, Ms. Harris."

"Thank you, Ms. Nikonova."

Judge McDaniel's courtroom was stone-cold silent. If a teacher could end up on the street, so could any of us. Rosie says that there's a fine line between those of us who have roofs over our heads, and those who don't.

Nady inched closer to the box. "You had a companion for part of the time that you lived on the street, didn't you?"

"Yes. His name was Jack Allen. I was told that he recently passed away." Jill said that Jack grew up in Vallejo. He enlisted in the Army after high school and served in Afghanistan. He came home with PTSD. After his discharge, he worked as a mechanic for a couple of years, but he started drinking. Then he started doing drugs. Eventually, he became addicted to heroin. "Jack was a hero. He tried to make the demons go away, but he couldn't."

"Where did you meet him?" Nady asked.

"In the Haight. He was living in Golden Gate Park. I was living in the Panhandle. I was walking down Haight Street one night when I saw somebody hassling Jack. I yelled at the guy, and he ran away. Jack and I started talking. Then we talked some more. We started looking out for each other."

"Was he your boyfriend?"

"Not exactly. We were more than friends, but we weren't romantically involved."

"Did you live together?"

"Sometimes. He was difficult to be around when he was taking heroin."

"When was the last time you saw him?"

"About six months ago. His addiction was out of control. I couldn't be around him anymore."

"Were you with Jack late at night on September fourth, and early in the morning of September fifth of last year?"

"Yes. We were living in the Presidio near the Lombard Gate."

Nady went back to the lectern and activated the flat-screen from her laptop. The security video from Patel's house appeared on the TV. Nady ran a portion of the video and stopped it. "That's you and Jack walking west on North Point Street at twelve-forty-five AM on Tuesday, September fifth, of last year, isn't it?"

"Yes."

"It's around the corner from the house of the decedent, Frank Moriarty, right?"

"Right."

"Did you and Jack walk by Mr. Moriarty's house?"

"Yes."

"Had you ever met Mr. Moriarty?"

"A couple of times."

"Did he ever give you any trouble?"

"Yes. He had a big problem with unhoused people."

Nady gave her an inquisitive look. "What sort of a problem?"

"He hated us."

"Move to strike," O'Neal said. "With respect, Ms. Harris is not qualified to comment upon Mr. Moriarty's state of mind."

Nady kept her tone modulated. "I did not ask Ms. Harris to read the decedent's mind, Your Honor. I simply asked for her observations as to how Mr. Moriarty treated her."

"Overruled."

Nady turned back to Jill. "How did he express his hatred toward you?"

Jill's lips turned down. "He told us to get off his property. He swore at us. He threatened us with a baseball bat. On one occasion, he pepper-sprayed us."

"How did that feel?"

"It burned like hell. I think it caused permanent damage to my eyes."

"Do you know if Mr. Moriarty ever sprayed other homeless people?"

"Yes. A couple of our acquaintances said that he did. Jack and I tried to avoid him."

Nady remained a couple of feet from the box. "Did you see Mr. Moriarty when you walked by his house on the morning of September fifth?"

A hesitation. "Yes."

"What was he doing?"

Jill pointed at Freddie. "He was pointing a can of pepper spray at the defendant. It was crazy because there was no reason to spray him. Freddie was passed out in Moriarty's driveway."

"Did Freddie attempt to defend himself?"

"He couldn't. He was just lying there and moaning."

"Did Freddie attack Mr. Moriarty?"

"No."

"What happened next?"

She took a deep breath. "I told Moriarty to leave Freddie alone. He got mad and pointed his pepper spray at me. Jack stepped in front of me and tried to protect me. Then Moriarty pepper-sprayed Jack."

"How did he respond?"

"Jack was in a lot of pain, and he tried to defend himself—and me. He was flailing when he picked up a piece of rebar and swung it at Moriarty. I don't know if Jack could see what he was doing because of the pepper spray. He may have swung blindly. Moriarty turned and tried to avoid it, but Jack got him in the back of the head. Moriarty dropped to the ground near Freddie."

Nady gave the jury a moment to digest Jill's answer. "Just to be clear, Jack struck Mr. Moriarty with a rusty steel rod?"

"He acted in self-defense, and he was trying to protect me."

"Were you okay?"

"Just a little shaken up."

"And Jack?"

"He was in a lot of pain. He was really angry at Moriarty."

Nady moved back to the lectern. "What happened to the steel rod?"

"Jack dropped it on the ground between Moriarty and Freddie."

"What did you and Jack do next?"

"We ran."

"Did you report this to the police?"

"I was afraid to." Jill's gravelly voice was somber. "I was a homeless African American woman and crack addict. I didn't think anybody would believe me."

"Why did you come forward now?"

"Jack is dead. I don't think Freddie should be blamed for a crime that he didn't commit."

"Thank you for coming forward, Jill. I wish you the very best."

"You're welcome, Ms. Nikonova."

"No further questions for this witness, Your Honor."

"Cross-exam, Ms. O'Neal?"

"Yes, Your Honor." O'Neal spoke from the lectern. "You and Mr. Allen had been drinking and taking drugs that night?"

"Yes."

"It is therefore possible that your recollection might be a little cloudy, right?"

Jill's voice was firm. "I remember what happened, Ms. O'Neal. If somebody tried to pepper-spray you, you would have remembered, too."

Good answer.

O'Neal feigned skepticism. "That's curious, Ms. Harris. The police reports did not mention finding a can of pepper spray at the scene. There was no pepper spray, was there?"

"Yes, there was."

"No, there wasn't."

"Move to strike," Nady said. "Ms. O'Neal is testifying."

Judge McDaniel made the call. "The jury will disregard Ms. O'Neal's last statement."

O'Neal moved closer to the box. "What happened to the pepper spray, Ms. Harris?"

"Jack took it."

O'Neal stopped cold. "Why?"

"For protection against crazy people like Moriarty."

O'Neal grimaced. "No further questions, Your Honor."

Sometimes lawyers ask one more question than they should. And sometimes you get help from unexpected sources.

"Re-direct, Ms. Nikonova?"

Stay seated, Nady.

"No, Your Honor."

"The witness is excused."

Jill walked up the center aisle and out the door with her head held high.

Judge McDaniel spoke to Nady. "Any additional witnesses, Ms. Nikonova?"

"No, Your Honor. The defense rests."

She turned to O'Neal. "Anything more from you before we get to closing arguments?"

"No, Your Honor."

"Ms. Nikonova?"

I turned to Nady and whispered, "Make the motion."

She stood and spoke from the defense table. "Your Honor, given Ms. Harris's testimony, the defense moves that the charges against the defendant be dismissed as a matter of law."

"On what grounds?"

"Lack of evidence against the defendant, and evidence that it was Mr. Allen, and not our client, who killed Mr. Moriarty."

"I want to see everybody in chambers—now."

46

"WHAT POSSIBLE MOTIVE WOULD SHE HAVE TO LIE?"

Judge McDaniel hung her black robe on the hook on the back of the door to her chambers. She sat down at her desk and motioned O'Neal, Nady, and me to take our places in the chairs on the opposite side.

She addressed O'Neal first. "Interesting testimony, eh, Catherine?"

"Yes, Your Honor."

The judge's Alabama drawl became more pronounced. "Your case is looking shaky."

"We remain very confident, Your Honor."

"We are not." Betsy's tone turned pointed. "Your case is on life support."

It is not in O'Neal's nature to capitulate. "At the very least, you have to give it to the jury."

"You really want me to do that?"

You might want to take the hint, Catherine.

O'Neal kept her tone respectful. "It's the jury's job to decide whether Jill Harris was telling the truth, Your Honor."

"Not if I'm convinced that her testimony means that you haven't proven your case beyond a reasonable doubt."

"At a minimum, we will need time to look for witnesses who can verify her testimony."

"You've had more than a year to do so."

"You have to let me talk to her to decide whether she was telling the truth."

"I don't have to do anything."

I finally spoke up. "What possible motive would she have to lie?"

O'Neal glared at me. "Maybe she's trying to protect herself from a murder charge."

"You don't have a shred of evidence that she killed Moriarty."

"She admitted that she was there. She could have hit Moriarty."

"You can't prove it beyond a reasonable doubt."

"Not yet."

"You just admitted that there is reasonable doubt about Freddie."

"No, I didn't."

"Yes, you did."

The judge spoke to O'Neal. "I found Ms. Harris's testimony to be compelling. If she is telling the truth, she has cast serious doubt upon your case against Freddie Alvarez. If you want to charge her with a crime, that's your prerogative. If you elect to do so, it casts even more doubt on your case."

O'Neal didn't fluster. "I am now considering a potential charge of obstruction of justice."

"That's up to you."

"Your Honor," I said, "Jill is entitled to a lawyer."

"Agreed. Is the Public Defender's Office willing to represent her?"

"Absolutely."

"That creates a conflict of interest for the Public Defender's Office," O'Neal said. "Mr. Daley cannot represent Mr. Alvarez and Ms. Harris."

"There is no conflict if you dismiss the charges against Freddie," I said to the judge.

Judge McDaniel nodded. "I'm still thinking about it. In the meantime, I will request an attorney for Ms. Harris from our conflict panel just in case one is needed."

Perhaps you could think a little faster.

O'Neal tried again. "Before you make a decision, Your Honor, fundamental fairness dictates that I should be given an opportunity to question Ms. Harris."

"You had that opportunity in court," I snapped. "She has no obligation to talk to you."

"I'll issue her a subpoena."

"You can compel her to testify in court, but you can't make her talk to you outside." I added, gratuitously, "As her attorney, I will advise her not to do so."

"You aren't her attorney yet."

"I am now." *Well, sort of.* "I am putting you on notice in front of Judge McDaniel that I have accepted Ms. Harris as a client. You have no legal basis to prevent me from talking to her. Whether she's willing to talk to me is up to her. She is, of course, free to choose other counsel."

"Ask your new 'client' if she'll talk to me voluntarily."

"Only if you agree to grant her immunity."

"No."

"Then I will advise her not to do so."

"You have a legal obligation to convey my request."

"I will, but I will not recommend that she talk to you. If she chooses to disregard my advice and talk to you anyway, it will be with the understanding that I will be present in my capacity as her attorney—assuming that she wants me to be there."

"Fine."

Judge McDaniel leaned back in her chair. "I'm going to hold off on making a decision on the defense motion to dismiss the charges. I am also going to adjourn our court session until tomorrow at ten AM. Let me know where we stand by the end of the day."

At four-thirty on Thursday afternoon, Rosie walked into my office, took a seat next to Nady, and smiled. "Jerry Edwards called to say that he thinks the judge is going to dismiss the charges against Freddie."

"Jerry is a fine journalist," I said, "but he isn't a lawyer. He's never been very good at prognosticating the results of legal matters."

Her smile disappeared. "Is O'Neal going to charge Jill with obstruction?"

"She's thinking about it."

"Are we representing Jill?"

"For now."

"That creates a conflict of interest."

"Only if Betsy rules against our motion to dismiss the charges against Freddie. In an abundance of caution, I informed Jill that she may need to retain separate counsel. If she can't afford it, we'll ask the Attorney General's Office to step in and find somebody to represent her."

"Did Jill agree to talk to O'Neal?"

"Absolutely not. Nady and I explained the potential downside to her. She agreed that it wouldn't be in her best interests."

"Good. Where does this leave us?"

"O'Neal is talking to her boss about whether she will contest our motion to drop the charges against Freddie. They're also trying to decide whether to file charges against Jill."

"When do you expect to hear back from her?"

I glanced at my watch. "Any minute now."

Terrence "The Terminator" appeared at my door. "I have Catherine O'Neal on line one."

"Put her through, T." I looked over at Nady. "You want to listen in?"

"Absolutely."

I pointed at Rosie. "You?"

"Wouldn't miss it for the world."

47

"WE FOUND HER TO BE CREDIBLE"

I activated my speakerphone. "Michael Daley speaking."

"It's Catherine O'Neal. I'm here with the DA."

"Nady is here with me. So is the Public Defender."

Our DA spoke up. "Hello, Rosie."

Rosie's voice filled with sugar. "Hello, Vanessa."

"I hear you're going to win re-election in a few weeks."

"I hear the same thing about you."

"Sounds like we'll be enjoying each other's company for another four years."

Rosie rolled her eyes. "Looking forward to it."

Notwithstanding the phony pleasantries, it was no secret that Rosie and Turner couldn't stand each other.

"How can we help you?" I asked.

O'Neal spoke up again. "Vanessa and I had a few minutes to discuss Jill Harris's testimony from earlier today." She cleared her throat. "We found her to be credible."

Good. And?

O'Neal hesitated. "We have therefore decided to dismiss the charges against Freddie Alvarez."

Ta da! Nady smiled broadly. True to form, Rosie's reaction was subdued.

"Thank you, Catherine," I said. "I trust that you will inform Judge McDaniel?"

"I will."

Excellent. "I think we got the correct result."

"Right."

I sense that you are somewhat less than ecstatic. "Are you planning to file charges against Jill?"

Turner answered. "I have asked Catherine to conduct a full investigation of Ms. Harris's involvement in this matter. We will make a decision in due course."

"Our office will be representing her unless she decides to hire private counsel. I must therefore ask you not to talk to her unless I am present."

"Duly noted."

There is no chance in hell that I will ever let her talk to you. "We are going to head over to give Freddie the good news."

"We'll be in touch."

"Thank you."

I ended the call, waited a beat, and gave Nady and Rosie high-fives. Then I called Pete to give him the news. He acted as if he expected it. A moment later, Dazzle and Terrence joined the celebration. When you're a Public Defender, the victories don't come very often, so you savor them.

We celebrated for a full five minutes before I accompanied Nady back to her office. Luna woke up to greet us, and I gave her a victory treat.

"You just made her very happy," Nady said.

"She's easy to please." I gave Nady an appreciative nod. "You did an excellent job on this case."

"Thank you." She grabbed her coat. "Let's go see Freddie."

48

"JUSTICE WAS SERVED"

Freddie's voice was filled with relief. "Thanks for everything."

"You're welcome," I said.

He turned to Nady. "Thank you, too."

"Justice was served, Freddie."

"No Pete tonight?"

"He's working on a new case," I said. "Something about a cheating wife in Silicon Valley."

"Does he ever sleep?"

"Not much."

"You'll thank him for me?"

"I will."

He was sitting on the sagging double bed in a musty room on the ground floor of the Folsom Street Inn, a one-star motel a couple of blocks north of the Hall of Justice. The PD's Office has a deal with the Folsom to provide short-term rentals for our clients after they're released from jail. The accommodations are what you might expect from an establishment shoehorned between a gas station and a check-cashing service. The mattresses are old, the furniture worn, the bathroom dated. The building vibrates from the vehicles barreling down the elevated I-80 Freeway across the street.

"How long can I stay here?" Freddie asked.

"It's supposed to be three nights, but I got you a week," I said. "Sorry about the noise."

"It was worse when I lived under the freeway."

I'll bet. "I've asked one of our transition people to come over and see you tomorrow. She'll bring you some clothes and other necessities. She'll set you up with a social worker and help you start the process of finding temporary housing, counseling, and services. She can refer you to a rehab program if you need it."

"Thanks."

I eyed him. "Do you think you can stay clean?"

"I'm going to try."

Nady spoke up. "You can do it, Freddie."

"I'm going to try," he repeated.

"Is there anybody we can call?" I asked.

"I don't think so. I talked to my mother. We're going to get together and see if we can start trying to work things out."

"It's a start."

"Baby steps." His expression turned thoughtful. "I learned a few things over the last year. First, stay clean. Second, if you ever get into trouble, find a couple of smart lawyers. And third, never plead guilty."

"Good advice," I said.

Nady and I wished Freddie well. We left him in the cramped room that smelled of disinfectant and dust.

As Nady and I were walking under the freeway toward the PD's Office, I turned to her and asked, "Do you think he's going to stay clean?"

"Hard to say. He's going to try."

Dazzle was sitting at her cubicle when Nady and I returned. Most of our colleagues had gone home. It was Halloween, and they wanted to take their kids trick-or-treating.

"You working at the club tonight?" I asked her.

"I'm taking the night off. Halloween is crazy."

"Is Terrence around?"

"He went home early." She pointed at the open door to Rosie's office. "The boss wants to see both of you."

It never ends.

We headed into Rosie's office, where she smiled broadly. "Congratulations on Freddie's case. You got an excellent result, and it will look nice on our statistics. I just got a call from our esteemed District Attorney. She and Catherine O'Neal have decided not to file charges against Jill."

"Admirable restraint," I observed. "I guess we won't be representing Jill after all."

Nady grinned. "Tuesday is Election Day. The DA would have filed charges already if she thought it would help her win re-election."

Rosie's eyes twinkled. "You're getting as cynical as Mike."

"I learned from the best."

Rosie looked my way. "Did you get any feedback from the jurors?"

"I ran into the woman who worked at Hertz. She said that the jury hadn't started deliberations yet, so she couldn't speak for everybody. She thought that her fellow jurors were impressed by Freddie's testimony. She wouldn't have voted to convict him for murder, but she might have voted to convict for manslaughter if we hadn't put Jill on the stand."

"It's good that Pete found her." Rosie pointed at the door. "I want both of you to go home. Luna has had a busy week, and I need Mike to hand out candy."

"I'll give you a ride home," I said.

Rosie shook her head. "Politics doesn't stop for trick-or-treating, Mike. I have a campaign dinner at the Italian Athletic Club. Tuesday is Election Day."

49

"TO BIG JOHN"

"What'll it be, lad?" I asked, using my best fake Irish brogue.

Joey's blue eyes danced as he stood in unfamiliar territory on the customer side of the bar at Dunleavy's. "That's my line."

I pointed at the photo of Big John on the wall behind me. "Your grandfather taught it to me before you were born."

His jowls wiggled as he smiled. "You don't work here anymore."

"I do tonight. You get the night off."

His grin widened. "Guinness, please."

"Coming right up." I pointed at Tommy, who was standing next to me. "Would you mind pouring a pint for your cousin?"

"Coming right up," he repeated.

At twenty-two, Tommy was now half a head taller than I was, and his broad shoulders reflected the time he spent in the weight room when he was the starting quarterback at Redwood High School in Larkspur. His hair was a shade darker than mine, and his charismatic smile was almost identical to his namesake, my older brother, Tommy, who was a star quarterback at St. Ignatius and Cal before we lost him in Vietnam.

Joey grinned at him. "You need to work on your brogue, lad."

Tommy returned his smile. "I'll go on YouTube tonight and search for 'fake brogues for working at an Irish pub in San Francisco.'"

"Very resourceful, Tommy."

"Thanks, Joey."

Dunleavy's was packed for Joey and Margarita's engagement party on Saturday, November ninth. Almost two hundred people filled the main bar, the back room, the sidewalk in front, and the patio in the back. Tommy and I were holding down the bar. Pete was in the kitchen churning out fish and chips. Terrence "The Terminator" and Dazzle were chatting with guests near the door. Nady and Max were somewhere on the patio. Luna took the night off. A mariachi band led by one of Margarita's cousins shared the mike in the back room with a heavy metal band fronted by one of Joey's classmates at State. Margarita's family was even larger than the Daley/Fernandez clan, and everybody seemed to be getting along.

Tommy poured a pint and slid it across the bar to Joey. "How old were you when you started tending bar here?"

"Twelve. Grandpa liked to start them young." Joey pointed at me. "How old were you when you poured your first Guinness?"

"Fourteen. I was tall and very advanced for my age."

"Nobody reported it?" Tommy asked.

"Big John's regulars included all of the assistant police chiefs." I turned back to Joey. "Have you and Margarita set a date?"

"Springtime at St. Peter's. She doesn't want a big wedding, but we'll need enough space to fit our immediate families."

"You will recall that my parents were married at St. Peter's. So were Rosie and I. And Grace and Chuck."

His smile broadened. "You also had your engagement party here."

"Big John insisted, and we couldn't talk him out of it."

"Did you ever win an argument with him?"

"Nope. You?"

"Seriously? Not a chance."

Rosie pushed her way through the crowd and joined us at the bar. "I need a sherry for Mama, an old fashioned for Margarita's grandmother, coffee for Roosevelt, Guinness for Nady and Max, and club sodas for Rolanda and Zach and Grace and Chuck."

Tommy grinned. "Coming right up, Mom."

Rosie shook her head. "Another generation of Daleys tending bar at Dunleavy's. Big John would have been proud." She turned to Joey. "Congratulations to you and Margarita."

"Thank you. Is your mom okay?"

"She's fine. She's dancing in the back room with Margarita's grandmother. Between the two of them, they have three artificial knees and two new hips. I hope I'll be as active as they are when I'm eighty-seven. I deputized Grace and Chuck to keep an eye on them. Roosevelt is also standing guard. I don't want to make a trip to the emergency room tonight."

"They'll be fine. It's nice that they get along so well."

"Mama invited Margarita's grandmother to join her mah-jongg group."

"That's a big honor. How does she feel about playing with a group who consume cannabis during their games?"

"She's bringing edibles tomorrow night."

"Sounds like a good fit. Congratulations on winning the election. The criminals of San Francisco are in good hands for another four years."

"Thank you. It was a little closer than I had hoped."

"It was a landslide." Joey pointed at me. "The Co-Head of the Felony Division and Ms. Nikonova got a good result for Freddie Alvarez."

"Mike and Nady are good lawyers."

"I take it this means that you're going to let Mike keep his job?"

"That's the plan for now."

"If you change your mind, he can always come back and tend bar for me." Joey turned to me. "How did you figure out that Jack Allen killed Moriarty?"

"I didn't. I played a hunch."

"You don't believe in hunches."

"I do when I have no better options. It was a Hail Mary pass, and we got lucky. Sometimes they work, most of the time they don't. If Pete hadn't found Jill, we probably would have gotten a less satisfying result."

"Where is Freddie?"

"We got him a room in a halfway house near the Hall of Justice. It has food, services, and counseling. He seems ready to accept help and try to stay clean."

"What are the odds?"

"I'd say fifty-fifty."

He looked over at Rosie. "Are you still planning to turn the PD's Office over to Rolanda and Nady at the end of your term?"

She grinned. "We aren't allowed to say that aloud, Joey." Then she nodded.

We chatted for a few more minutes before Tommy came back with a tray filled with drinks. Rosie lifted it effortlessly and prepared to make her way to the back room.

"You're good," Joey said. "I didn't expect the Public Defender to wait tables."

"I waited tables at the Roosevelt Tamale Parlor when I was in college."

"You haven't lost your touch. If you ever want to get back into the hospitality business, there will always be a place for you here at Dunleavy's."

"I'll talk to you in four years." Rosie headed to the back room.

Joey held up his pint. "Thanks for throwing us a nice party."

"You're welcome, Joey." I looked around the homey bar that Joey's grandfather had run for six decades. I saw the children and grandchildren of people who had attended the engagement party for Rosie and me almost three decades ago. I thought of my mom and dad. I could still see my dad sitting at the back table with Roosevelt, a Guinness in front of him, a cigarette in his hand. The faces were familiar, although many were second- and third-generation versions. I remembered Big John's German shepherd, Lucky, who greeted guests at the door for fourteen years. When some of the regulars had a little too much to drink, Lucky made sure that they got home.

I looked up again at the photo of a smiling Big John that was taken when he still had a full head of red hair. As always, there was a cigarette in his mouth and a pint of Guinness in his hand. He was younger in that photo than Joey is today. The resemblance was striking.

"You should visit with your guests," I said to Joey.

"I will."

I raised my Guinness. So did Joey. We looked at Big John's photo and touched our mugs.

"To Big John," I said.

"To Big John."

"I'M JUST LIKE HER"

"Margarita and Joey make a lovely couple," Rosie said.

I smiled. "Yes, they do."

We were sitting on her back porch and sipping Pride Mountain Cab Franc at eleven-forty-five on Saturday night. The fog had rolled in, but the winds were calm. The embers were glowing in the firepit. A lamp in the window of the house behind Rosie's provided a little illumination.

Rosie's expression turned wistful. "It reminded me of our engagement party."

"Me, too. Joey was tending bar that night. He was a kid."

"Big John kept an eye on him."

"He kept an eye on all of us." I reached over and squeezed her hand. "We've had some really nice times at Dunleavy's."

"And in a lot of other places, too."

"True. Did everybody make it home safe and sound?"

"Yes. Tommy is going to join us at church on Sunday. Mama promised to take us for burgers at the St. Francis Fountain afterward. Grace and Chuck are going to Napa for the weekend. They need a little time off."

"They work too hard."

"So do we."

Maybe we do. "Are you thinking of slowing down?"

"In four years. Are you in?"

"Absolutely."

"Good. Mama was pestering Grace again about another great-grandchild."

"You can't stop her. Grace and Chuck will get around to it when they're ready."

"Mama isn't patient."

"Neither are you."

Her eyes gleamed. "I know."

I took another sip of wine. "She was a demon on the dance floor tonight. I wish I had her energy."

"So do I. It's nice that she gets along so well with Margarita's grandmother."

"Did your mom really offer her a spot in the mah-jongg group?"

"Yes." Her grin broadened. "Margarita's cousin runs a high-end dispensary in Palo Alto that's wildly popular among some of the bigwigs in Silicon Valley."

"Any names I might recognize?"

"Yes."

"Can you share them?"

"No." She flashed a conspiratorial grin. "When we first met, did you ever think that we would be admonishing our octogenarian parents to be responsible about their marijuana use?"

"It wasn't on my bingo card," I said. "Your mom is still a pistol."

"I know."

"She's just like you."

"No, Mike. I'm just like her. So is Grace. And Rolanda. When she gets older, I'll bet you that Rolanda's daughter will be, too. And when Grace and Chuck have kids, they'll be like Mama, too."

Probably true. "And Tommy?"

Rosie's eyes lit up. "He's just like you."

"Is that a bad thing?"

"No, Mike. It's a very good thing." She arched an eyebrow. "Mama gave me some edibles. Are you interested?"

"Not tonight, Rosie."

"You just got an acquittal for Freddie. I won the election. We should celebrate a little."

"I'll stick to wine."

She took a sip of Cab Franc. "Do you think that Catherine O'Neal would have charged Jack with murder if he was still alive?"

"Probably. At the very least, she would have charged him with manslaughter. After all, he did kill Moriarty."

"How would you have defended him?"

"I would have argued that he acted in self-defense. Either way, it isn't our problem. We'll have plenty of new cases waiting for us when we get back to the office on Monday."

"You and Nady did a nice job on short notice. So did Pete. Do you think we should hire him to work for us?"

"I've asked him many times. He likes being on his own. Some people are better suited to being lone rangers."

"I suppose. You should take a few days off."

"Too busy."

"At the very least, you should walk the steps with Zvi tomorrow."

"I will. What about you? You won the election. You should take some time off, too."

"Too busy. I have a lot of work to catch up on now that the campaign is over."

"You should go to spin class in the morning."

She grinned. "I'm signed up for Attila's class in the morning."

Excellent. "Congratulations on vanquishing your latest challenger."

"Thank you. That we did. Four more years?"

"Four more years," I repeated.

She finished her wine. "I promised Rolanda that we would take her kids to the park after we get back from lunch with Mama tomorrow."

"I'd like that."

"We should do more of that, too." She turned serious. "Do you think it's time for you and Wilma and Betty to move over here? You already spend most nights here."

It's tempting. "We've talked about this, Rosie. I think it would be better to keep the apartment for the times when we need a little space. Besides, Wilma and Betty like having their own place."

"You'll think about it?"

"I will."

She picked up her wine glass and stood up. "It's getting cold. We should go inside."

"Right behind you. Do you want to watch a movie?"

"I had something else in mind that would require a little more energy." She arched an eyebrow. "If you aren't too tired."

"I can make myself available."

"Good to hear." She grabbed my hand, pulled me close, and kissed me. "After all these years, I still love you, Mike."

"I love you, too, Rosie."

A Note to the Reader

San Francisco is a city of wonderful neighborhoods, and the Marina is one of my favorites. In 1915, it was the site of the Panama Pacific International Exposition, a World's Fair that was purportedly to celebrate the opening of the Panama Canal but was widely seen as an opportunity for San Francisco to show its recovery from the 1906 Earthquake. After the fair, the area transformed into a working-class neighborhood between Fort Mason and the Presidio (the Golden Gate Bridge wasn't completed until 1937). Perhaps its most famous residents were Joe DiMaggio and Marilyn Monroe, who lived at 2150 Beach Street, two blocks from the Palace of Fine Arts (the last remaining building from the fair). Over the decades, the sunny neighborhood in the shadow of the bridge gentrified into an affluent enclave.

As for the plotline (it helps if you have one of those, too), I'm always looking for opportunities to put people in situations where they are out of place or uncomfortable. It is no secret that San Francisco has a substantial homeless population, so I decided that Mike and Rosie would represent a heroin-addicted homeless man accused of murdering a hotshot lawyer in front of his mansion in the Marina. I figured that if I wrote a story about murder, drugs, homelessness, infidelity, grudges, dishonesty, and money, there would be something for everybody! And since a San Francisco story should always involve food, I decided to do scenes at iconic locations such as Caffe Trieste, Original Joe's, Mel's Drive-In, and the Balboa Café. Writing books always makes me hungry.

I couldn't write a Mike Daley story without an appearance by the ageless Nick "The Dick" Hanson, the nonagenarian private investigator, mystery writer, real estate tycoon, TV star, and bon vivant. The only thing Nick hasn't done yet is appear on Dancing With The Stars. Hmm, maybe that could be a future crossover opportunity.

I like spending time with Mike and Rosie, and I hope that you do, too. I hope you enjoyed **NEVER PLEAD GUILTY**. If you like my stories, please consider posting an honest review on Amazon or Goodreads. Your words matter and are a great guide to help my stories find future readers.

If you would like to chat, please feel free to e-mail me at sheldon@sheldonsiegel.com. We lawyers don't get a lot of fan mail, but it's always nice to hear from my readers. Please bear with me if I don't respond immediately. I answer all of my e-mail myself, so sometimes it takes a little extra time.

Many people have asked to know more about Mike and Rosie's early history. As a thank you to my readers, I wrote **FIRST TRIAL,** a short story describing how they met years ago when they were just starting out at the P.D.'s Office. I've included the first chapter below and the full story on my website (www.sheldonsiegel.com).

Also on the website, you can read more about how I came to write my stories, excerpts and behind-the-scenes from the other Mike & Rosie novels and a few other goodies! Let's stay connected. Thanks for reading my story!

Regards,
Sheldon

Acknowledgements

On the twenty-fifth anniversary of the release of my first novel, Special Circumstances, it seems appropriate to note once again that I am extraordinarily fortunate to have a very supportive and generous "board of advisors" who graciously provide their time and expertise to help me write these stories. It's also a reminder that we should be thankful for all of the nice people who pass through our lives over the years. Once again, I have a lot of thank yous!

Thanks to my beautiful wife, Linda, who reads my manuscripts, designs the covers, is my online marketing guru, and takes care of all things technological. I couldn't imagine trying to navigate the publishing world without you.

Thanks to our son, Alan, for your endless support, editorial suggestions, and thoughtful observations. I will look forward to seeing your first novel on the shelves in bookstores in the near future.

Thanks to our son, Stephen, and our daughter-in-law, Lauren, for being kind, generous, and immensely talented people.

Thanks to my teachers, Katherine Forrest and Michael Nava, who encouraged me to finish my first book. Thanks to the Every Other Thursday Night Writers Group: Bonnie DeClark, Meg Stiefvater, Anne Maczulak, Liz Hartka, Janet Wallace, and Priscilla Royal. Thanks to Bill and Elaine Petrocelli, Kathryn Petrocelli, Karen West, and Luisa Smith at Book Passage.

A huge thanks to Jane Gorsi for your excellent editing skills.

Big thanks to Linda Hall for your excellent editing skills, too.

Much thanks to Vilaska Nguyen of the San Francisco Public Defender's Office for your thoughtful comments and terrific support. If you ever get into serious trouble, he's your guy.

Thanks to Joan Lubamersky for providing the invaluable "Lubamersky Comments" for the seventeenth time. Nobody knows more about San Francisco than you do.

Thanks to Tim Campbell for your stellar narration of the audio version of this book (and many others in the series). You are the voice of Mike Daley, and you bring these stories to life!

Thanks to my friends and former colleagues at Sheppard, Mullin, Richter & Hampton (and your spouses and significant others). I can't mention everybody, but I'd like to note those of you with whom I worked the longest: Randy and Mary Short, Chris and Debbie Neils, Joan Story and Robert Kidd, Donna Andrews, Phil and Wendy Atkins-Pattenson, Julie and Jim Ebert, Geri Freeman and David Nickerson, Bill and Barbara Manierre, Betsy McDaniel, Ron and Rita Ryland, Bob Stumpf, Mike Wilmar, Mathilde Kapuano, Susan Sabath, Guy Halgren, Ed Graziani, Julie Penney, Christa Carter, Doug Bacon, Lorna Tanner, Larry Braun, Nady Nikonova, and Joy Siu.

Thanks to Jerry and Dena Wald, Gary and Marla Goldstein, Ron and Betsy Rooth, Jay Flaherty, Lloyd and Joni Russell, Rich and Leslie Kramer, Debbie and Seth Tanenbaum, Jill Hutchinson and Chuck Odenthal, Tom Bearrows and Holly Hirst, Julie Hart, Burt Rosenberg, Ted George, Phil, Diane, and David Dito, Char Saper, Flo and Dan Hoffenberg, Roberta Berg and Stan Roodman, Lori Gilbert, Paul Sanner, Stewart Baird, Mike Raddie, Peter and Cathy Busch, Steve Murphy, Gary and Debbie Fields, Bob Dugoni, and John Lescroart.

Sadly, we recently had to say goodbye to the marvelous Bonnie DeClark, who was a charter member of the Every Other Thursday Night Writers Group. Thank you for your kindness and support for so many years.

Thanks to Tim and Kandi Durst, and Bob and Cheryl Easter, at the University of Illinois. Thanks to Kathleen Vanden Heuvel, Bob and Leslie Berring, Jesse Choper, and Mel Eisenberg at Berkeley Law.

Thanks to the incomparable Zvi Danenberg, who motivates me to walk the Larkspur steps.

Thanks as always to Ben, Michelle, and Andy Siegel, Margie and Joe Benak, Joe, Jan, and Julia Garber, Scott, Michelle, Kim, and Sophie Harris, Stephanie, Stanley, Will, and Sam Coventry, Cathy, Richard, and Matthew Falco, Sofia Arnell, Oliver and Elliot Falco, and Julie Harris and Matthew, Aiden, and Ari Stewart.

A huge thanks once again to our mothers, Charlotte Siegel (1928-2016) and Jan Harris (1934-2018), whom we miss every day.

Excerpt from FIRST TRIAL

Readers have asked to know more about Mike and Rosie's early history. As a thank you to all of you, I wrote this short story about how Mike & Rosie met years ago as they were just starting out at the P.D.'s Office. Here's the first chapter and you can download the full story (for FREE) at: www.sheldonsiegel.com. Enjoy!

1
"DO EXACTLY WHAT I DO"

The woman with the striking cobalt eyes walked up to me and stopped abruptly. "Are you the new file clerk?"

"Uh, no." My lungs filled with the stale air in the musty file room of the San Francisco Public Defender's Office on the third floor of the Stalinesque Hall of Justice on Bryant Street. "I'm the new lawyer."

The corner of her mouth turned up. "The priest?"

"Ex-priest."

"I thought you'd be older."

"I was a priest for only three years."

"You understand that we aren't in the business of saving souls here, right?"

"Right."

Her full lips transformed into a radiant smile as she extended a hand. "Rosie Fernandez."

"Mike Daley."

"You haven't been working here for six months, have you?"

"This is my second day."

"Welcome aboard. You passed the bar, right?"

"Right."

"That's expected."

I met Rosita Carmela Fernandez on the Wednesday after Thanksgiving in 1983. The Summer of Love was a fading memory, and we were five years removed from the Jonestown massacre and the assassinations of Mayor George Moscone and Supervisor Harvey Milk. Dianne Feinstein became the mayor and was governing with a steady hand in Room 200 at City Hall. The biggest movie of the year was *Return of the Jedi*, and the highest-rated TV show was *M*A*S*H*. People still communicated by phone and U.S. mail because e-mail wouldn't become widespread for another decade. We listened to music on LPs and cassettes, but CD players were starting to gain traction. It was still unclear whether VHS or Beta would be the predominant video platform. The Internet was a localized technology used for academic purposes on a few college campuses. Amazon and Google wouldn't be formed for another decade. Mark Zuckerberg hadn't been born.

Rosie's hoop-style earrings sparkled as she leaned against the metal bookcases crammed with dusty case files for long-forgotten defendants. "You local?"

"St. Ignatius, Cal, and Boalt. You?"

"Mercy, State, and Hastings." She tugged at her denim work shirt, which seemed out-of-place in a button-down era where men still wore suits and ties and women wore dresses to the office. "When I was at Mercy, the sisters taught us to beware of boys from S.I."

"When I was at S.I., the brothers taught us to beware of girls from Mercy."

"Did you follow their advice?"

"Most of the time."

The Bay Area was transitioning from the chaos of the sixties and the malaise of the seventies into the early stages of the tech boom. Apple had recently gone public and was still being run by Steve Jobs and Steve Wozniak. George Lucas was making Star Wars movies in a new state-of-the-art facility in Marin County. Construction cranes dotted downtown as new office towers were changing the skyline. Union Square was beginning a makeover after Nieman-Marcus bought out the City of Paris and built a flashy new store at the corner of Geary and Stockton, across from I. Magnin. The upstart 49ers had won their first Super Bowl behind a charismatic quarterback named Joe Montana and an innovative coach named Bill Walsh.

Her straight black hair shimmered as she let out a throaty laugh. "What parish?"

"Originally St. Peter's. We moved to St. Anne's when I was a kid. You?"

"St. Peter's. My parents still live on Garfield Square."

"Mine grew up on the same block."

St. Peter's Catholic Church had been the anchor of the Mission District since 1867. In the fifties and sixties, the working-class Irish and Italian families had relocated to the outer reaches of the City and to the suburbs. When they moved out, the Latino community moved in. St. Peter's was still filled every Sunday morning, but four of the five masses were celebrated in Spanish.

"I was baptized at St. Peter's," I said. "My parents were married there."

"Small world."

"How long have you worked here?" I asked.

"Two years. I was just promoted to the Felony Division."

"Congratulations."

"Thank you. I need to transition about six dozen active misdemeanor cases to somebody else. I trust that you have time?"

"I do."

"Where do you sit?"

"In the corner of the library near the bathrooms."

"I'll find you."

Twenty minutes later, I was sitting in my metal cubicle when I was startled by the voice from the file room. "Ever tried a case?" Rosie asked.

"It's only my second day."

"I'm going to take that as a no. Ever been inside a courtroom?"

"Once or twice."

"To work?"

"To watch."

"You took Criminal Law at Boalt, right?"

"Right."

"And you've watched Perry Mason on TV?"

"Yes."

"Then you know the basics. The courtrooms are upstairs." She handed me a file. "Your first client is Terrence Love."

"The boxer?"

"The retired boxer."

Terrence "The Terminator" Love was a six-foot-six-inch, three-hundred-pound small-time prizefighter who had grown up in the projects near Candlestick Park. His lifetime record was two wins and nine losses. The highlight of his career was when he was hired to be a sparring partner for George Foreman, who was training to fight Muhammad Ali at the time. Foreman knocked out The Terminator with the first punch that he threw—effectively ending The Terminator's careers as a boxer and a sparring partner.

"What's he doing these days?" I asked.

"He takes stuff that doesn't belong to him."

"Last time I checked, stealing was against the law."

"Your Criminal Law professor would be proud."

"What does he do when he isn't stealing?"

"He drinks copious amounts of King Cobra."

It was cheap malt liquor.

She added, "He's one of our most reliable customers."

Got it. "How often does he get arrested?"

"At least once or twice a month."

"How often does he get convicted?"

"Usually once or twice a month." She flashed a knowing smile. "You and Terrence are going to get to know each other very well."

I got the impression that it was a rite of passage for baby P.D.'s to cut their teeth representing The Terminator. "What did he do this time?"

She held up a finger. "Rule number one: a client hasn't 'done' anything unless he admits it as part of a plea bargain, or he's convicted by a jury. Until then, all charges are 'alleged.'"

"What is the D.A. *alleging* that Terrence did?"

"He *allegedly* broke into a car that didn't belong to him."

"Did he *allegedly* take anything?"

"He didn't have time. A police officer was standing next to him when he *allegedly* broke into the car. The cop arrested him on the spot."

"Sounds like Terrence isn't the sharpest instrument in the operating room."

"We don't ask our clients to pass an intelligence test before we represent them. For a guy who used to make a living trying to beat the daylights out of his opponents, Terrence is reasonably intelligent and a nice person who has never hurt anybody. The D.A. charged him with auto burglary."

"Can we plead it out?"

"*We* aren't going to do anything. *You* are going to handle this case. And contrary to what you've seen on TV, our job is to try cases, not to cut quick deals. Understood?"

"Yes."

"I had a brief discussion about a plea bargain with Bill McNulty, who is the Deputy D.A. handling this case. No deal unless Terrence pleads guilty to a felony."

"Seems a bit harsh."

"It is. That's why McNulty's nickname is 'McNasty.' You'll be seeing a lot of him, too. He's a hardass who is trying to impress his boss. He's also very smart and tired of seeing Terrence every couple of weeks. In fairness, I can't blame him."

"So you want me to take this case to trial?"

"That's what we do. Trial starts Monday at nine a.m. before Judge Stumpf." She handed me a manila case file. "Rule number two: know the record. You need to memorize everything inside. Then you should go upstairs to the jail and introduce yourself to your new client."

I could feel my heart pounding. "Could I buy you a cup of coffee and pick your brain about how you think it's best for me to prepare?"

"I haven't decided whether you're coffee-worthy yet."

"Excuse me?"

"I'm dealing with six dozen active cases. By the end of the week, so will you. If you want to be successful, you need to figure stuff out on your own."

I liked her directness. "Any initial hints that you might be willing to pass along?"

"Yes. Watch me. Do exactly what I do."

"Sounds like good advice."

She grinned. "It is."

There's more to this story and it's yours for FREE!

Get the rest of **FIRST TRIAL** at:
www.sheldonsiegel.com/first-trial

Sheldon Siegel is the New York Times best-selling author of the critically acclaimed legal thrillers featuring San Francisco criminal defense attorneys Mike Daley and Rosie Fernandez, two of the most beloved characters in contemporary crime fiction. He is also the author of the thriller novel The Terrorist Next Door featuring Chicago homicide detectives David Gold and A.C. Battle. His books have been translated into a dozen languages and sold millions of copies. A native of Chicago, Sheldon earned his undergraduate degree from the University of Illinois in Champaign in 1980, and his law degree from Berkeley Law in 1983. He specialized in corporate law with several large San Francisco law firms for forty years.

Sheldon began writing his first book, Special Circumstances, on a laptop computer during his daily commute on the ferry from Marin County to San Francisco. Sheldon is a San Francisco Library Literary Laureate, a former member of the Board of Directors and former President of the Northern California chapter of the Mystery Writers of America, and an active member of the International Thriller Writers and Sisters in Crime. His work has been displayed at the Bancroft Library at the University of California at Berkeley, and he has been recognized as a Distinguished Alumnus of the University of Illinois and a Northern California Super Lawyer.

Sheldon lives in the San Francisco area with his wife, Linda. Sheldon and Linda are the proud parents of twin sons named Alan and Stephen. Sheldon is a lifelong fan of the Chicago Bears, White Sox, Bulls and Blackhawks. He is currently working on his next novel. His work is currently under development for a TV series.

Sheldon welcomes your comments and feedback. Please email him at sheldon@sheldonsiegel.com. For more information on Sheldon, book signings, the "making of" his books, and more, please visit his website at www.sheldonsiegel.com.

Connect with Sheldon
Email: sheldon@sheldonsiegel.com
Website: www.sheldonsiegel.com
Amazon: amazon.com/author/sheldonsiegel
Facebook: @sheldonsiegelauthor
Goodreads: www.goodreads.com/sheldonsiegel
Bookbub: bookbub.com/authors/sheldon-siegel
Instagram: @sheldonsiegelauthor

Also By Sheldon Siegel

Made in the USA
Las Vegas, NV
01 May 2025

21596927R00164